CODA

By Tom Topor

TIGHTROPE MINOR
BLOODSTAR

CODA

TOM TOPOR

CHARLES SCRIBNER'S SONS
NEW YORK

Copyright © 1984 Tom Topor

Library of Congress Cataloging in Publication Data

Topor, Tom, 1938–
  Coda.

  I. Title.
PS3570.065C6 1984   813'.54   84–10663
ISBN 0–684–18237–8

1 3 5 7 9 11 13 15 17 19 v/c *20 18 16 14 12 10 8 6 4 2*

Printed in the United States of America.

For my family

There are not ten people in the world whose deaths would spoil my dinner but there are one or two whose deaths would break my heart.

—*T. B. Macaulay*

CODA

1

The trouble began in bed.

I was propped up on the pillows, eyes shut, wondering whether I felt strong enough to walk to the living room for a drink and cigarette. Fiona Shaw was lying next to me, her head on my chest and her right hand on my crotch. Every few seconds she would scratch gently and giggle.

"Kevin . . ."

"Ummmmmmmm."

"Can you do me a favor?"

She was ten years younger than me and as tireless as a beaver building a dam, so I immediately got a picture of some acrobatic marathon, a decathlon of lust that would twist me into a pretzel and send me quivering to the coronary-care unit at New York Hospital. "Ummmmm," I said slowly.

She must have caught my hesitation, because she sat up, laughed, and said, "A professional favor, Kev. I need a detective."

"Oh, sure," I said. "Let me get a drink." I climbed off the bed and started toward the living room.

"Kev," she said, "it's safe to look at me; you're not that old." I turned my head. She giggled, pulled her mouth open with her two little fingers, crossed her eyes, and stuck out her tongue. At the same time, she arched her back and spread her legs. "Pretty, isn't it?"

"Ummmmmm."

"God, contain your enthusiasm," she said.

When I came back, she was wrapped in the sheet, and

when I reached out to touch her shoulder, she twitched away and said, "Uh, uh. Business now." I lit a cigarette and waited.

"Kev, did you ever hear about the orchestra at Auschwitz?" I shook my head, no. "The Nazis wanted to be entertained, so they set up an orchestra of prisoners." She pointed to the glass in my hand. "Can I have some of that?" I passed her the glass, she swallowed half of the liquor and made a face. "Ugh, bourbon. One of the prisoners in the orchestra was a pianist named Max Weill—did you ever hear of him?" Again, I shook my head. "He was very famous once. Anyway, just before the liberation of the camp, they shot him and buried him; at least that's what the records say." She sniffed the bourbon, took a small sip, and looked at me.

"Go on."

"His widow lives here, on the Upper West Side."

"Uhuh."

"She came over in 1949, after spending four years looking for him all over Europe."

She paused theatrically—it was an occupational habit; she'd been working as a journalist so long she couldn't tell a story without squeezing every last effect from it. "She's never remarried." She tilted her head and smiled. "I guess they were in love. Did you ever hear that expression, Kev—in love?"

"Once or twice," I said. "I never did figure out what it meant."

"What a shame. She's a waitress at a place on Seventy-second Street, and I met her when I went in there for lunch one day." She stopped to take a breath, and I knew she was getting to the point. "She thinks she saw her husband on the street."

"Uhuh."

"More than once. She thinks he's still alive."

"Uhuh."

"The last time was at the promenade at Rockefeller Plaza."

"Was he skating?"

"Kevin, don't be a smartass. Forty is too old to be a smart-ass." She reached for my hand. "She really believes he's alive."

"Uhuh."

"Could you look for him?"

"You know," I said, "it sounds like the story of an old woman with weak eyes and a lot of memories seeing some-body for an instant and wishing he was the husband she'd lost thirty-five years earlier." She pulled her hand away. "I'm sorry, but that's what it sounds like."

"She's only sixty-nine, and her eyes are pretty good." She pulled the sheet higher around her. "I like her, Kev. She's important to me."

"Yeah," I said, "I can see how she'd make a good story."

"Goddamit, Kev, she's not a story to me."

"You mean, if I found her husband, you wouldn't run to your typewriter and start banging away about the poor little immigrant waitress who found her long-lost soul mate after searching for thirty-five years across two continents? Are you telling me you *wouldn't* write that story?"

For a moment she tried to look indignant, but she couldn't keep it up, and she smiled. "Well . . . it is a great story . . ."

"So you want me to look for this pianist so you can write a story and win another prize—is that it?"

"No, that's not it! I told you, Kev, she's important to me."

"Why?"

"It doesn't matter why! She's important to me. Isn't that enough for you?"

Actually, it wasn't—I couldn't remember the last time I'd accepted something on faith, but it was the wrong moment to go into that. I looked at her for a second, trying to read her face and not getting very far. It's hard to read somebody through the filter of your own lust. "Could you look for him?" she said again.

"Okay, have your little old lady call me."

"Kev, she's never called a private detective. Why don't you go and see her?"

I was about to tell her all the reasons—that going to see a client put me at a disadvantage because they thought I was hustling for business and that made haggling over money very hard, that I liked being behind my desk because that put me in control, that I didn't like the Upper West Side, and that little old ladies gave me a pain in the ass—when she touched my palm and said, "Can you do that, Kev?"

Her tone was even enough, but her face was tight, and her eyes were pleading. Fiona Shaw wasn't a small woman—maybe five-seven, maybe 118 pounds—and pleading wasn't her style. She'd left one husband to come to New York, married another, and left him and scrambled to the upper reaches of the news business. One drunken night she told me that after she won the Pulitzer Prize, she wanted to go on to become the first woman managing editor of the *New York Times*. No, she wasn't small.

But that morning, wrapped in my sheet, she looked it. I'd said no to smaller, more vulnerable people, but never when they were in my bed. With the makeup gone from her face—I'd kissed it away—and her dark eyes wide open, and the sheet covering everything but her neck and head, she looked like a hungry teenage orphan. How could anyone say no to a hungry teenage orphan?

"Okay. I'll go talk to her."

She grinned and slowly pulled the sheet down her body until it rested just above her breasts; the sound of the sheet on her skin gave me goose bumps. She winked and pulled the sheet below her nipples; then up again, then down, then up, till her nipples began to tighten. "Look at that," she said, "and the color is changing too. Look how they go from pink to red." She glanced down. "They harden at different speeds," she said. "Touch."

I stretched out my right hand and, with my pinky, touched her left nipple. She took my left hand, licked my thumb and forefinger, and put them on her right nipple. "Squeeze," she said, "gently."

I started to squeeze, and we moved closer, to kiss. Her mouth was sweet—her mouth, no matter what she'd eaten or drunk, was always sweet; even after a night's sleep, her mouth was aways sweet. As I kissed her, she closed her eyes, which was unsual for her, and I wanted to ask her to open them. But I didn't ask her.

For the next hour or so, we made love—no, she made love to me. There were moments when I almost got lost in it, but most of the time I felt as if I were a radio and she was repairing me. I didn't want to feel like that, but I couldn't tell if the feeling was there because of her working so hard or my holding back because I believed she was working so hard. I should have stopped it and talked to her, but I wasn't good at that, not good at that at all, so I let it go on and tried to sink into it. But couldn't.

Just before she left for work, she wrote the waitress's name and number on a slip of paper and put it on the night table.

2

Her name was Lilli Weill, and when I called, hoping she'd be out, she answered on the second ring. "Mrs. Weill?" I asked.

"Fiona says you will call, so it must be you, the remarkable Mr. Fitzgerald," she said. "Do you understand me? Is my bad accent too bad?"

"I understand you fine—you've got almost no accent."

She laughed. "A genuine gentleman. When will you come to visit me?"

"Wednesday?" I said.

"Wednesday? But it is only Monday today. Tell me, do you eat dinner?"

"Do I eat dinner?"

"I will make you latkes—potato pancakes. The right way, not how they make it in the restaurants. It is two o'clock. Why do you not come here at six?"

"Tonight?"

"Of course, tonight. You must eat tonight, no? Or do you not eat on a Monday night? Come a little earlier if you like."

"But—" I made it a rule not to go to clients' homes. "Okay," I said, "I'll come at six."

"Good. Do you like apple sauce or sour cream? Never mind; I will buy both."

"Mrs. Weill, do you have a picture of your husband?" For a second she didn't answer. "Mrs. Weill—"

"Yes, I have a picture. But they are old, very old. Maybe they will not help you—I am sure they will not help." Her accent was thickening. "Mr. Fitzgerald, perhaps this is not so good an idea, perhaps I am asking you to run—what is the saying *auf Englisch*—to run after the wild goose chase. It is possible, no?"

"Yes," I said neutrally. "It is possible."

She was silent for a bit. "It is not always so pleasant, to run after the wild goose chase . . ."

"It won't be the first time," I said.

She laughed. "Ah, then you must come and look at the old pictures of my Max. You have the address, no? Good. I see you at six." She took a breath. "Mr. Fitzgerald, I, I am not a rich woman—is this bad for you?"

"I'll see you at six."

"Thank you."

*

Lilli Weill lived on the tenth floor of a 1920s apartment building at Broadway and Eighty-first Street. There was a doorman, but he didn't belong to the old school of West Side doormen—no neat uniform with epaulets, no smile, no hello, no leaping to his feet when people walked into the lobby. He stayed put in his chair and didn't glance up from his *Post*. Probably he figured the closed-circuit TV camera scanning the space would do his work for him. Probably he was right.

"Weill?" I asked, and he pointed lazily to the directory next to the mailboxes.

When I rang her bell, 10J, she opened the peephole, pulled the door apart a couple of inches, and peeked out. Her eyes were deep brown, round and as curious as a six-year-old's.

"Fitzgerald," I said. "The remarkable Mr. Fitzgerald."

"Of course," she said, and smiled. Her smile was like a six-year-old's too. She unchained the door and stepped back to swing it wide. As I walked in, she took my hand and said, "I am sorry. I should not be afraid, here in America, but—I am not a brave person." She tilted her head and looked up at me. "A hat. Oh I am pleased. A man is not properly dressed without a hat. Max never left the house without a hat. Here, let me have it."

After giving it a quick flick with her fingers, she carefully put it on shelf in a hallway closet. She had to stretch to do it because she was only around four-eleven. Her legs were round and strong, but ripe with varicose veins: waitress legs. She was wearing a dark crimson dress that looked as if it had been altered and realtered, plain low-heeled black shoes, and a plain black leather belt. Her hair was short, gray, and curly, and her face seemed to match it—a perfect dumpling of a face, oval and fleshy, the result of too many slices of bread and too many helpings of rice and potatoes. Her hands were stubby and liver spotted. Her only jewelry was the narrow gold band on her left ring finger.

The apartment—one large room and a kitchenette—was

filled with cheap sculptures and knick-knacks; there wasn't a surface that didn't support a carved dog, or cat, or elephant, or tortoise, or panda. Against one wall was a bookcase. Two shelves of it contained dozens of copies of old magazines— *Life, Colliers, Look,* the *Saturday Evening Post.* The other two shelves contained books, and I went nearer to read the titles. All of them were about the Holocaust.

She came up behind me. "It is stupid to be obsessed, but I am a stupid woman perhaps." She took a book from the shelf and handed it to me. "This one, it is good. She tells the whole story of how the Nazis kill the Jews, the whole story from the start to the finish." She took the book from my hand and returned it to its place. "Perhaps not the whole story. The whole story has a why, no? Or perhaps I am wrong. No matter."

She took my arm—her touch was tentative, as if she were afraid to hurt me—and led me across the room to what appeared to be a large piece of furniture covered in muslin. She pulled back the cover. It was an upright Steinway, polished to a shine. Leaning on the music rack were some framed photographs. She chose one and handed it to me.

In the picture, a slender man in evening dress sat smiling at a concert grand. "My husband Max," she said. "Before the war."

His face was large, with large laughing eyes and a large laughing mouth. He looked as if he owned the world, as if nothing bad could ever happen to him. As old and faded as the print was, it was still easy to see how beautiful his hands had been.

"This is taken in Amsterdam. He has a very big success with this recital—many, many encores. I am sitting in the fifth row, and I am wearing a dress with a neckline like so." She put her fingers on her sternum and smiled. "Then, I can wear such dresses. At the end, when he takes his last bow, he

8

holds his hand to his eyes like a sailor to look for me, and he blows me a kiss, like so."

She turned away from me for a second, and when she turned back, her face was still.

"I am not crying, Mr. Fitzgerald. When they put me on the train, I cry. And when I come to Maedenek, I cry. When they tell me Max is dead, I do not believe them, but I cry just the same. And after the war, when I look for him, I cry. When I come to the United States, for fifteen years, each time I have a shower, I look up and I think of Cyklon B; I hold the soap in my hand and I must throw it on the floor, and I cry." She laughed. "Now I take a bath—with a liquid soap, and I do not cry. Now, this is just a number."

She pulled up her left sleeve. The five small digits were tattooed about three inches above her wristbone.

"My friends, they say, Lilli, have it taken off; it is easy, and the Germans will pay for it. In and out of the hospital in one day. In one hour. All gone."

I wanted a drink but I wasn't certain she had any in the house. I glanced over her shoulder to look for a bottle among all the knick-knacks. "I am talking too much, perhaps?" she said.

"No, no," I said, "I just wondered whether . . ." I made a gesture.

"Ah, some schnapps. Forgive me. I am not used to being a host anymore." She fetched a bottle of Remy from a sideboard and poured a large shot for each of us. "It helps me sleep." She rolled down her sleeve. "It is so foolish, nearly forty years later, to keep the number. But—" She touched my hand. "You think I am a foolish old lady, no? A little immigrant who does nothing right, not even to remember to give a guest a drink. You think this, no?"

"No."

"But it is true. I am a foolish old lady. When I look for

him over there, I am walking through the towns in Austria—
we are both born in Vienna—I am walking through the towns
with a big sign on my front and on my back. Lilli Weill.
Wien. So if anyone sees him, they can say, Max, I see your
wife, Lilli, on the road to Salzburg. I go many times to Salzburg because there he plays Mozart. He plays so you will
laugh and weep at the same minute."

She took the picture from me and put it back on the piano.
"As I tell you, old pictures are not so good." She draped the
muslin back over the piano. "Perhaps they are right; he is
ashes." She refilled my glass. "Do you enjoy Mozart, Mr. Fitzgerald?"

"A little. The operas."

"Ah, *The Marriage of Figaro, The Magic Flute*—we go
when he isn't playing." For a long moment we sat in silence.
I hadn't eaten all day, and I was starting to feel the cognac.

I was scared to begin. I'm not sure why—maybe because
I guessed how stupid her search would be, maybe because I
wanted to run away from her pain, maybe because I was
afraid I'd fail her and bring her more pain. Finally, I said,
"How many times do you think you've seen him?"

"I beg your pardon, Mr. Fitzgerald?"

"How many—"

"I have seen him six times." She picked up her purse from
the coffee table and drew a folded piece of paper from it.
"Here."

On the paper were printed the dates, times, and places she
believed she'd seen her husband. The first date was Septem-
ber 1957; the last was May 1982, a week back. She watched
me as I read, her breath held. She didn't release it till I took
out my notebook and began to copy the figures.

"Did you tell anyone?" I asked.

She laughed. "But of course. I tell the Immigration Department; I tell the State Department; I tell the Red Cross; I

tell the Federation of Jewish Philanthropies. At the beginning, everyone is very kind. They listen to me, they write letters, they make telephone calls. Then, as the time goes by, they are more in a hurry, they have no time to write letters, it is too expensive to make phone calls. They ask me about my eyes. They ask me if I would like to talk to a counselor. They ask me if I dream about Max. They ask me to describe the man I see on the street, and they say to me—*they* say—this does not resemble your late husband. Your late husband."

"The times you saw him—how long was it for?"

She smiled wanly—obviously, she was good at hearing the unspoken. "Not so long, Mr. Fitzgerald. Short enough so that anyone, me, too, would doubt what I see. One of us is always moving—I am walking, or he is walking; I am on a bus, or he is in a taxi. Here"—she pointed to a date on her list—"here he is on First Avenue, near the United Nations, and I am on the First Avenue bus. I see him, I push aside this poor girl so I can put my eyes to the window, but he is gone." She shrugged. "It is a sunny day, and there are many people walking near the United Nations on a sunny day."

"How far away from him were you?"

"Not so far. Not so near—across the street. Once, I call, Max! Max!, but he does not turn. I run after him, but he is gone in a taxi. Another day, he walks by the restaurant where I am working, and I put down my tray and run outside, but he is not there."

"He never recognized you, or acknowledged you?"

She shook her head slowly. "I think about this, and I say to myself, he is not well; the Nazis do so many things to him he does not have his memory."

"Was he alone?"

"I am not sure, because I do not look for someone else—a woman I would notice, but a man not so easily. Last week he is not alone. He is getting up from a table at the skating rink, and the man with him is leaving the money. A big man, as big as you, bigger perhaps. His face I do not know; he is wearing sunglasses."

"Did you tell all this to the Immigration people?"

"They say to me that even if he is alive I would not know him." She smiled ironically. "He is changed, they say. This is true. I am changed." She reached into her purse and found a photograph. In it, she and Max were sitting in a rowboat. Max was shielding his eyes from the sun; she was staring at him adoringly, a delighted smile on her face. I looked at her, at the picture and back at her. "I was not so ugly then," she said.

"Beautiful," I said, meaning it.

"No," she said. "Never beautiful. Young, and very much in love, which makes everyone look better. Would you see the same person?"

"I don't know. If I saw your eyes, maybe . . ."

"Ah, yes. But when I see Max, I *do* see his eyes. And his hands. My hands"—she held them—"they are changed. But not his. His hands I would know from five hundred yards away." My face gave away my doubt. "He touches me with his hands for six years. I feel him touch me and I watch him touch me." She looked down at the carpet, as though she wanted to say something more but didn't quite have the nerve.

"Tell me," I said.

She turned away a few inches, so I couldn't see her eyes. "Do you believe in . . . ?"

"What?"

She turned back. Her eyes were anxious, like those of a child who's about to explain that he found a brand-new baseball bat lying in the street. "Max is psychic." She pronounced the P.

If I hadn't had so many cognacs, I would have tried to

leave—gracefully, for sure—but definitely. She knew I was tuning out, because she quickly put her hand on my arm.

"I don't mean with the crystal ball or the tea leaves," she said. "Not such nonsense. He reads my thoughts. Not exact. But like so: if I am going to a place, a shop, a hairdresser, he would, with no plans, arrive there. I take the bus to visit my mother, and he is on the bus. I lose something, a brooch, something he does not see, and he says, look in such and such a place, and it is there. We wake up in the morning and he says, tell me about your wonderful dream, and it is true, I have had a wonderful dream."

She tightened her fingers around my arm. "It is not only with me. It is not because he loves me and I love him. With others, too, he reads their thoughts. No. Perhaps not their thoughts. Their feelings. All the time he is able to do this. Sometimes it frightenes me—Max, I say to him, it is not fair to us that you can do this. And he kisses my lips to quiet me.

"At Immigration, they say to me, why do you believe he is here, in America? And I say, because I am here. They say, America is a big place, forty-eight states—at that time, only the forty-eight—why do you believe he is in New York? Because I am here."

She leaned forward and looked at my face. "You do not believe this, do you, Mr. Fitzgerald? You believe B must come after A."

If I'd been sober, I would have told her, right, I don't believe it. Sober, I would have told her that coincidence was coincidence, and she should forget about her husband and his beautiful hands and find a nice rich widower and go live in Fort Lauderdale.

But I wasn't sober, and I couldn't drive out of my head all the times in my life when things happened that didn't quite make sense: all the times when I'd been on a subway and somebody, against the odds, was there in the same car, all the times I'd put the pieces of a case together and come up empty, and then thrown away all the pieces, gone with a feeling and made the case. Sober, I would have told her, no, leave that to the burned-out children of the sixties, leave that to actors who'd given up on psychotherapy and found peace through vegetables, leave that to the millionaires of the supernatural in California who taught the faithful the value of nothing while buying up miles of beachfront, and I would have been right to tell her.

But I wasn't sober. I was tired and hungry and half blown on cognac, and even if I didn't believe in Max's ways, or understand a love that went on half a lifetime, I wanted to. Normally, when a wife wanted me to find a husband, or a husband a wife, it was because she needed some good wet evidence for the divorce, some sweet slice of ugliness that would raise—or lower—the price of the settlement. They, or their lawyers, came to me with hatred on their faces and Casio calculators in their hands.

I couldn't understand her feeling for Max Weill, just as I couldn't understand what the number on her arm meant to her. But I envied the feeling, and ached at her refusal to erase the number. She should have been worn down, beaten, and more cynical than me, but instead she had kept the faith. Keep the faith, Kev, they used to tell me, and none of them did.

I finished my drink, stood, and looked around.

She smiled. "The bathroom is there, Mr. Fitzgerald, past the curtain." I took a couple of steps before she stopped me by touching my sleeve. "Mr. Fitzgerald . . ."

She had risen, so when I turned I nearly knocked her over. The skin on her throat was taut, and her eyes blinked as though she'd suddenly been trapped by a harsh light. "Mr. Fitzgerald . . ."

For an instant, I wanted her to disappear, to vanish in a

puff of smoke or a shower of sparks. I wanted to tell her I was sorry for her pain, but that I was the wrong man for her, she needed somebody softer and more stupid; that everyone lived in pain and I had spent fifteen years becoming very selective about what pain I'd pay attention to; that I was committed to the idea of corruption, you were corrupt, I was corrupt, we were all corrupt, that goodness was something that belonged on television, and I couldn't be seduced by it any more, the same way I couldn't be seduced by the right cause or the right woman. I wanted her to die, because she didn't belong in my world, in *this* world. It was too late for her. But I liked her, and I liked Fiona.

"I'll start with Immigration," I said.

She slipped her hand in mine. "Let me show you the way to the bathroom; the light switch is not so easy to find."

3

The next morning, before going to the Immigration Department, I deposited Lilli Weill's $400 check and went to my office to begin the scut work. I didn't expect it to do much good, but I had a routine for finding lost people; the routine had paid off in the past, and it was as useful a way to begin as any.

It's hard to hide in the United States because every place a person goes he leaves a trail of paper behind him: social security forms and diplomas and draft cards and W-2 forms and voter-registration cards and insurance certificates and credit applications and God knows what else. Most records on anyone are available for a ten-dollar fee, so I took out my checkbook and a batch of printed request forms and got down to it.

Using Max Weill's name and birth date and Lilli's address, I asked the department of motor vehicles whether he owned a car or had a driver's license; asked the board of elections whether he voted, and where; asked the county clerk whether he'd ever served on a jury; asked the city register's office whether he'd ever applied for a loan; asked a credit-reporting bureau whether he had bank accounts or charge accounts anyplace; asked an information bank in Albany whether he'd ever been in an accident, or had surgery, or been arrested, or applied—anyplace—for any kind of license—marriage, dog, massage, liquor, pistol, mortician, hair stylist, hunting, peddler.

While I was checking ten years' worth of phone books to see whether he was listed (he wasn't), Fiona Shaw called. "Did you like her?" she said.

"She makes great potato pancakes," I said. "Not soggy."

She was quiet for a second. "Thank you, Kev."

"Don't be stupid. I'm getting paid."

"Will you please stop being so tough," she said. "Why won't you ever let people thank you?"

I must have have been in a twisted mood, because I said, "I thought you thanked me last night."

"Goddamn you," she said, "you are such a suspicious sonofabitch. You simply can't believe anybody will treat you well unless you're doing something for them. I think I understand why your wife left you."

"That's good. Anything else?"

"Yes. Can we have dinner, the three of us?"

"Sure."

"And will you let me know how it's going?"

"No. She's the client, not you."

She hung up, noisily, and I put down the receiver and

leaned back in my chair. A knot started to form in my stomach, not a large knot, just a tiny, tight little ball to let me know that someone had affected me more than I wanted her to.

When my wife left, she said she'd be gone for a few days, to think things over. She was a deliberate thinker, because that was the last I'd seen of her. After that, I only heard from lawyers. Except once. She sent me a long letter, telling me how she saw me and how much she didn't like what she saw. The letter was in the file cabinet, behind my right shoulder, and for a second I thought of reading it so I could once again learn the truth about myself, ha, ha.

Instead, I made a list of all the people I'd need to call on behalf of Max Weill. It was a long list, and looking at it gave me a slight but nasty buzz over my left eye. The sun was shining through the window, the other cases I was working weren't that urgent, and I was tempted to call Lilli Weill and tell her there would be a slight delay, emergency business, etcetera, etcetera. I was tempted to wander up to the park and sit near the duck pond and pretend that the trees and the water and the ducks were all there were in the world. I was tempted to call Lilli Weill and tell her that I didn't need her $400, that I couldn't help her; that her husband Max was at the bottom of some pit dug thirty-five years ago by the SS, and even if he wasn't, even if by some freak chance he'd escaped the pit, he'd put together a new life, with a new name; and, at bottom, there was no Max Weill anymore. I was tempted to call her and tell her that once people disappeared, once they left, whether they died or not, they might as well have died. They were gone, and they were gone because they wanted to go, because what they were going to was better than what they were coming from, and looking for them—and worse, finding them—was as dumb and as painful as strolling into a burning building.

But I didn't call her. I was too chicken. I called a few of the names on my list, called my answering service to say I'd be out, and headed downtown to the Immigration and Naturalization Service. I walked part of the way, thinking I'd enjoy the spring. It was one of those days in May when the sun shone, the breeze kissed, and all the people on the street looked goofy and happy. They couldn't have been, but they looked it. And since I wasn't, and couldn't bear to see them that way, I took a cab. The driver's name was Lee Chin, and he looked goofy and happy too.

The man they finally sent me to see at Immigration was named Julius Frances, and I had to guard myself from calling him Mister Julius. His office wasn't big enough or placed properly for him to be important—not that that stopped him from behaving as if he were. Since he was a middle-level bureaucrat in an agency notorious for ineptitude and dishonesty, I expected somebody small and fussy, with, say, rimless glasses. So much for cliché. He resembled an out-of-shape, decaying linebacker, big all over, especially in the belly and chest. He wore his hair early-fifties style, like a new-mown lawn. On the wall behind his desk was a framed sign that read, "Thank you for not smoking;" I hoped the talk would be short.

He stared at my business card and placed it delicately in the center of his green blotter. "Mr. Fitzgerald, I'm sorry you had so much trouble. They should have sent you directly to me." He wrinkled his forehead. "Was anyone rude to you? Here at Immigration, we pride ourselves on courtesy." He leaned forward and lowered his voice. "We try to close our eyes to the fact that technically we're a branch of the Department of Justice; we all know all too well that Justice has a poor reputation for courtesy. Extremely poor."

While he told me how polite he was, I pushed a metal

chair closer to his desk and sat down. "Not rude," I said. "Maybe confused."

He lowered his voice even further. "It's the people we get nowadays. When I first started, you had to have something on the ball—Immigration *counted*. Of course, that was a long time ago, when we thought of Immigration as almost a calling. It's a great country—" he waited for my nod, so I nodded —"and we want to keep it that way, don't we?" He grinned, one true American to another. "Enough of my commercial; you didn't come here for that."

"I don't mind," I said.

He reached behind him and picked up a folder from a stack on a file cabinet. "Right here," he said, rattling the folder. "We're not like Justice here. The second they told me what you were after, I found the file. Immigration isn't afraid of efficiency. I used the computer yesterday, and I expect to use it tomorrow." He opened the folder and lifted out a pale green form. "I can't show you this, you realize that, but I'm certain I can answer your questions—if you phrase them in such a manner so my answers won't break any laws."

He sat back and folded his hands across his belly. His nails were square cut and large, all-American nails, except for the chewed-up cuticles. I spoke carefully, since he was the kind of civil servant who expected a lot of deference. "An immigrant named Lilli Weill believes her husband is alive and here. His name is Max Weill and he was reported killed during the war. The Big War."

"Ah, yes, Mrs. Weill," he said mournfully. "Mrs. Weill . . ."

"Mrs. Weill asked me to look for her husband."

He shook his head sadly and made a noise that sounded like a dog scratching at a door. "I've met Mrs. Weill . . . a dear woman, very dear." He moved his hands so he could glance at the file. "How can I explain this, Mr. Fitzgerald . . . We here at Immigration feel enormous compassion for the

19

Mrs. Weills among us. Although I personally am not of the Jewish persuasion myself, many of my closest colleagues right here—" he waved to take in all of Federal Plaza—"follow that ancient and noble faith. We are not unmindful of the fact that our record—America's record—during the Second World War fell far short of our highest ideals. In utmost confidence, there are many of us here at Immigration who believe that President Roosevelt betrayed the tradition of the service by locking out victims of the Holocaust. Not our finest hour, I am the first to shamefully admit. The Mrs. Weills suffered, and my heart goes out to them."

He closed his eyes and sent his heart out to Lilli Weill. "We here at Immigration believe that the Mrs. Weills—and she's one of *us* now, a naturalized citizen, with all the rights and privileges thereof—have, for good and great reasons, shut their eyes to reality. Mrs. Weill has called on us many times. Many, many times. I understand. I *do* understand: a loved one lost, no trace of the remains, questionable documents—of course a relation searches. If I were one of the Mrs. Weills among us, and I'd lost a loved one, I would search. No stone would I leave unturned. I told her—many times—I told dear Mrs. Weill, I understand. And yet . . . and yet . . . we are talking about a lost cause." He tapped the folder in time with his words. "A lost cause."

"You think he's dead?"

"Mr. Fitzgerald, the Germans—no, not the Germans, the Germans are an exemplary people—the Nazis did something unprecedented. Do you know the expression, the only sure things are death and taxes? The Nazis made death unsure.

"I cannot swear to you that Max Weill is dead. Nobody can swear that. Across the Atlantic, in forgotten fields and swamps, thousands, hundreds of thousands of the Nazis' victims lie in unmarked graves.

"My experience tells me—and it is supported by the few skimpy records we have—that Max Weill is one of those invisible—but not unlamented—victims." He riffled through the papers in the file. "I have here a photostat of a Nazi instrument indicating that Max Weill, born Vienna, civilian occupation musician, was buried in January 1945." I stretched out my hand. He shook his head. "Mrs. Weill already has a copy of this document.

"Now this poor woman will tell you that the Nazis made mistakes, that the guards faked shootings, that the graves often lay empty, and that when she went to look for her husband's remains in the grave site—number two-six-three —the remains were not there.

"She *may* be right. But I doubt it. I deal with these cases day in, day out." He patted the stack of folders behind him. "There are many Mrs. Weills, by many names. I won't swear to you that Max Weill is dead. But he is."

I took my cigarettes from my pocket but before I could pull one from the pack, he pointed to the framed sign. "Sorry," I said, and put the pack on his desk. "If he'd survived and come here under another name—"

"Mr. Fitzgerald, we're not talking about a dishwasher or a shoemaker; we're talking about a concert pianist. Don't you think if a concert pianist suddenly surfaced, we wouldn't investigate?" He winked three times. "We've found immigrants who tried to hide under other names. We weren't born yesterday."

"So you believe I'm wasting my time?"

"Mr. Fitzgerald, I don't know you but I'm going to be blunt. Lilli Weill is a poor woman, a simple waitress. Now I know a little bit about your profession—you're an expert and you demand an expert's pay. Which is as it should be." He looked straight into my eyes, very blunt. "Now do you truly believe it's right to take what little money this poor woman has when you know—deep down, you must know—that you can't possibly help her?

"I ask you this as one compassionate human being to another. I do not speak as an official of the Immigration and Naturalization Service. Simply as one compassionate human being to another."

"You may have a point," I said. I smiled; it wasn't easy because I felt like kicking him in his fat belly. I stood and stretched out my hand. "You've been a lot of help." He half rose and gripped my hand. "Football?" I said.

He lowered his eyes modestly. "Fordham. Not the varsity. Why don't you simply tell Mrs. Weill you're too busy. Let the poor woman down gently."

"Maybe I'll do that," I said. "Make a few more calls so I don't have to return her money, and then tell her it's a dead end." I grinned. "I'd feel like a crook if I didn't make a *few* calls."

"Of course," he said, all man of the world. "Now if you'll excuse me . . ."

I nodded and went out. As I was going down the hall, and reaching for a cigarette, I remembered I'd left them on his desk. I turned around, tapped on his door, and walked in. He was on the phone. I pointed to the cigarettes; he glanced at them and waved me forward. When I reached his desk, he lowered his head slightly and said into the phone, "No, I'll hold."

As I picked up the cigarettes, I noticed he'd moved my card so it was near the base of the phone. On the card he'd written a number. The prefix was covered; the last four digits were 0029.

Whoever he was calling came on the line, and he said, "Just a second, someone's leaving my office." He nodded at me and didn't say anything while I crossed the room and went out. Nor did he say anything for the thirty seconds I stood in the hallway listening.

4

The phone number Julius Frances had written on my card nagged at me, but I marked it off to occupational suspiciousness. A normal person sees a man reach down and tug his pants cuff and he figures the man's sock has slipped; I figure he's adjusting the ankle holster on his boot. A normal person says, it doesn't mean a thing that a bureaucrat wrote a phone number on your business card—people write phone numbers on any handy slip of paper. A normal person says, it doesn't mean a thing that the bureaucrat didn't talk on the phone while you were hovering over him—people usually like to talk on the phone in private.

I thought about it while I dialed the answering service and decided—since I wasn't normal—I would spend a while trying to trace the number.

But there were a couple of calls to be returned first—Fiona Shaw and a man named Norman Azenberg, who ran an agency for concert performers.

"I'm right on deadline," Fiona told me. "Can you call me in a bit?"

"I'm going to be chasing around some."

"I want to talk to you, Kev—are you busy tonight?"

"Not so far. I'll call your machine, okay?"

"Fine. 'Bye."

She had sounded anxious, but she regularly sounded anxious. She worked for the Associated Press, and I noticed once at a party she took me to that all the people there who worked for the Associated Press sounded anxious. I hadn't been able to tell whether the Associated Press attracted anxious types or they became anxious once they started working there.

I called Norman Azenberg, got his secretary, and she and I began the New York telephone gavotte:

"Mr. Azenberg's office."

"Hello. Kevin Fitzgerald returning Mr. Azenberg's call."

"What was the name again?"

"Kevin Fitzgerald."

"And you say you're returning Mr. Azenberg's call?"

"That's right."

"What was it in reference to?"

"It's a confidential matter."

"Oh, a confidential matter. Well, I'm his confidential secretary."

"Confidential, personal, and private."

A silence. "When did he call you?"

I switched the phone to the other ear—it gave me something to do instead of yelling at her. "Within the last couple of hours."

"You don't know exactly when?"

"Is he in?"

"He's talking long distance—would you care to hold?"

"Fine," I said, "but I'm in a phone booth at Forty-second and Broadway, and there's a man outside with a gun."

"I'll buzz him. Please hold."

There was a click. I spread a row of nickels on the shelf under the phone; I had a feeling I was going to learn to love the inside of the booth. Right after I'd dropped in the second nickel, she came back on. "Mr. Fitzgerald, Mr. Azenberg is coming on the line. Please hold." Click.

A nickel later, Azenberg came on. "Mr. Fitzgerald, Norm Azenberg. Sorry to keep you waiting, but I've got a conductor in Dallas who can't find his contact lenses and he wants me to ship him a spare set. Before his concert tonight. Help. You want to talk about Max Weill?"

"Right."

"Fine, let's talk. You're lucky today. I was supposed to have lunch with Renata Tebaldi, but she's back on her diet. Where do you want to eat. Not the Russian Tea Room. Let's go to . . . I don't know. Listen, the sun is shining, we'll walk, we'll make up our minds. Pick me up at the office at twelve-thirty. I promise you I won't be more than fifteen minutes late. See you."

He was twenty-two minutes late, but when he bounced into the reception room and bounced over to me with a huge, gold-flecked smile, I couldn't stop myself from smiling back.

"Problems, problems, problems," he said, as if he were counting winnings at blackjack. "I've got a tenor at Tully tonight whose wife just ran away with the co-captain of the women's Davis Cup team; so he's too distraught to sing. The promoter doesn't want to cancel, and I don't want to lose the commission, so I have to give them another tenor. Do you know a tenor? A tenor without a wife. Let's walk."

We rode downstairs and began strolling along Fifty-seventh Street. He kept chattering: tenors and baritones and lyric sopranos and mezzos and violinists and pianists and conductors; how much they earned and how much they spent; who they divorced and who they slept with; where they wouldn't play and where they wouldn't get a chance to play; and how he, Norman Azenberg, spent every waking minute of his short life lending them money and holding their hands. It should have come out a long, nasty whine, but he rattled on so ebulliently it came out like a cheer.

He was wearing a beautifully tailored dark gray suit, a light pearl-gray shirt, a silk burgundy tie, antique cuff links, a Patek Phillipe watch, and a slender gold ID bracelet. If he had nothing in his pockets, he was still worth five thousand dollars, and I felt dowdy alongside him. We reached the park and he waved to a bench.

"We'll talk here and then we'll eat. I concentrate when I eat and I can't concentrate when I'm talking." He took a cigarette case from his pocket, opened it and held it out to me. I accepted one and reached for my lighter while he slipped his cigarette into an ivory holder. "Six a day. Last year, I had what my cardiologist calls a coronary event. Don't ask me why he calls it an event. So. Six a day." I lit both cigarettes, and he inhaled gradually. "A lovely way to kill yourself. Not so lovely as caviar or sex, but not so far behind." He glanced at me. His eyes were dark, nearly black, and they were laughing. I guessed they were usually laughing. "All right: Max Weill."

"His wife lives here and she thinks she saw him on the street. Six times."

A hansom cab stopped in front of us and the horse arched his tail to shit. Azenberg sniffed and smiled. "I like the smell of horseshit; I grew up on a farm." He frowned. "If Max Weill were alive, he'd be working for me. Not because we were friends—I never met the man—but because Norman Azenberg is the best. When Hurok was alive, Hurok was the best. But Hurok is dead." He pinched out his cigarette and slipped the unsmoked half back in the case.

"You're too young to know about Max Weill," he said. "I'll tell you: before the war, there were some very good pianists, Horowitz, Rubinstein—you've heard of them?" I nodded. "In the music business, we knew—not hoped, knew—that Max Weill would be like those two one day. He wasn't there yet, but he was coming. There are a few recordings—the Mozart seventeenth, the twenty-first, the twenty-third, some sonatas, a rondo—Weill played a lot of Mozart—the Goldberg Variations, a bit of the *Well-Tempered Clavier*, but you can't find them. Maybe for a year's pay somebody will slip you a recording. They used to say Toscanini had some. A tuner told me Bernstein has three.

"I heard him play the first time in Paris. I'd just come from Berlin. Somebody said to me, don't take your coat off, we're going to hear an Austrian Jew named Max Weill. In those days, if you said a musician was a Jew, you were saying he was a good musician—it's still true, but you can't say it out loud anymore. So I went along. Five encores. We didn't want to let him go."

A couple climbed into the hansom cab and Azenberg stopped to watch them. When he turned back to me, his eyes weren't laughing.

"Once in a while, a musician comes along and he can play the notes and he can make music. Not so often. Today, Max Weill would be like Horowitz: a few big concerts a year, a few recordings, fees so large you couldn't count them; and music. I love money, but I love music more." He held out his manicured fingers. "A lousy pianist. Occasionally, I could make music, but I could never play the notes right. Usually, it's the other way around. When I saw Weill, I wasn't a manager yet; I was still playing. By the time I went into the business—with Hurok, who else?—the Nazis had Weill."

He took the half cigarette from his case, slipped it in the holder, lit it, and grimaced. "Later, I'll smoke one of yours and not count it." He hesitated. "Auschwitz . . . the orchestra there, oh, boy—the men, I'm talking about, not the women. All professionals, a few better than that. And Max Weill. I don't know why they shot him. They could have traded him. The Americans would have given them chewing gum, and the Russians would have given them vodka. Others weren't shot. Second-rate musicians. I don't mean it's all right to shoot second-raters, even a second-rate musician is worth something, he can make a few dollars in Akron and Tucson. But why kill a Max Weill?"

27

"You don't believe he could be alive?"

"Who knows? Every day, people who died in the war turn up. Most of the time, they're Nazis, living in Fort Lee, New Jersey and running cleaning shops. But a musician? I never heard, and believe me, I would hear. Unless he stopped playing altogether, I would hear. And how could he stop? He wasn't just a musician, a Glenn Gould, who hides in the recording studio. Weill was a performer. A performer needs an audience, he lives for an audience. Max Weill couldn't disappear in America—I've got spies all over the country. If a great pianist played in a saloon in Nome, Alaska, one of my people would call me."

For a while we watched the traffic on Central Park South. Azenberg tapped his foot in time with a melody playing in his head. Finally, he asked, "How is his wife?"

"She works as a waitress," I said. "Cheerful."

He flicked his ash behind the bench. "He had a . . . reputation . . . an international-class musician attracts women . . ." He smiled gently. "The opportunities . . ." He let it hang in the warm, spring air, and, at that second, a rich-looking man of around forty walked by arm in arm with a T-shirted redhead of around nineteen.

"Do you know anybody who ever played with him in the Auschwitz orchestra—anybody who lives here?"

He thought for a second. "Most of them are in Europe, and most of them don't play; a few teach." He tapped his cigarette holder against his front teeth. "There was a violinist, a Russian, or maybe a Pole. He came over here in fifty. Alexander something. What, what, what? Alexander . . . Cherkhov, Sacha Cherkhov. I think he was at Juilliard, but that was years ago. Cherkhov played at Auschwitz."

"Anyone else?"

"Let me think about it." He stood up. "I'll go through all the names." He smiled, and the sun flashed on the gold in his mouth. "Come. I know a French place where they don't cheat you on the wine. You tell me about the detective business, and I'll tell you about the music business."

He took my arm, European fashion, and led us east along Central Park South. His eyes were happy again, and he seemed to float eight inches up with each step. Abruptly, he stopped.

"Sacha tried to work for a while, you know. But he couldn't play in front of an audience. He could play for me, in the office, but with other people watching, he would put the bow to the strings and—" Azenberg shuddered. "Nothing." We started walking again.

"Tell me, Mr. Fitzgerald, do you carry a pistol, or do you just hit the bad people with a lightning karate chop?"

5

Alexander Cherkhov didn't teach at Juilliard anymore, but the school gave me his address after I explained that he had mistakenly abandoned a savings account and I was looking for him to give him his money. The address was only a few blocks away, so I walked over there.

Azenberg had made me feel good, as I imagined he made most people feel good, and, for a change, I didn't want to growl at anyone or stop for a drink. Fifty-seventh was jammed with pedestrians, most of them women, and the weather was warm enough for some of them to be wearing sheer tops. Their tits jiggled as they flitted along the sidewalk in their high-heeled sandals. It took me a few blocks to realize that I was watching so keenly—I realized when a woman on the corner of Sixth Avenue grinned when she caught me turning to stare at her—and it took me another few blocks to remember that until Fiona Shaw had dropped into my life, it had been a long time since I'd paid any attention to tits, or asses, or thighs, or ankles, or mouths, or any of the other edible parts of women.

I wondered whether I was recovering my animal senses or whether I was starting a second adolescence; the question didn't seem to matter much, not with so many women to look at.

When I was fourteen, my father took us to the Bronx Zoo—it was a tough trip for him because he hated animals nearly as much as he hated criminals—and while we were standing outside the reptile house, a Puerto Rican girl of around seventeen walked by us. There was nothing underneath her peasant blouse, and I couldn't take my eyes off her. My mother, who loved animals and hated Puerto Ricans, grabbed my arm, twisted me around to face her, and began to shout that I was a filthy pig, not fit to attend Our Lady of St. Anne's and a rotten example of a policeman's son; when my father—who stopped smiling at me the day I learned to walk —smiled, patted my mother on the cheek, and said, "Let him be. It's a good set on her, and looking doesn't hurt him and it doesn't hurt her."

I'm not sure it didn't hurt me—I spent the next three weeks daydreaming about the girl (whom I named Maria Theresa Elena) and jerking off to my daydream; but it was the first time I understood that it was okay to look at tits, everybody did it, even your father the policeman who never smiled at you.

By the time I got to Sixty-seventh off Central Park, where Cherkhov lived, I was so busy recalling my boyhood delight in tits—and then later, thighs and crotches—that I almost walked past his building. It was a brownstone, not too clean, but nicely maintained; the garbage cans in front had the house number painted on them, and their lids were chained to the spikes of an iron fence.

Cherkhov lived in 3F. I rang his bell and put my mouth near the intercom. After fifteen seconds, an accented voice said, "Yes, who is it?"

"I'd like to talk to you about Max Weill," I said.

There was no sound, not even breathing, and I thought he'd broken the connection. Then: "I do not know a Max Weill."

"The pianist," I said. "You and he played at—"

"Yes, yes, yes. Please do not talk anymore to the machine. It is the third floor. Wait. I buzz the door."

Upstairs, the door to 3F was open but chained. He must have been standing behind it, because all I could see were walls and furniture. "Are you police?" he said. "Immigration?"

"I'm a friend of Lilli Weill."

"Ah, Lilli Weill," he said. He unhooked the chain and pulled the door open.

I'd expected him to be thin, but he was shaped like a melon, one continuous curve. Everything about him was pink, his cheeks, his forehead, his neck, his hands, as though he'd been dipped into a vat of cotton candy. He was dressed in loose brown corduroy slacks, a white shirt, bright red suspenders, and frayed leather slippers. The knot of his blue and white striped tie was a couple of inches below his Adam's apple, and when he saw me he hastily pushed it up. Then he took a white handkerchief from his pants pocket and wiped his right palm. We shook hands formally, like two diplomats about to negotiate a treaty.

"Alexander Cherkhov," he said. "I am called Sacha."

"Kevin Fitzgerald. I am called Kev."

He smiled a little and pointed to a beat-up leather armchair in front of a fireplace—the apartment was one of those huge, high-ceilinged studios that still exist on the West Side—and said, "Please."

I sat in the armchair, and he went to a worktable on which a violin rested. "You will kindly forgive me," he said. "I am restringing." He held up the violin. "A Guarneri." My ignorance must have shown. "A very great violin-maker." He held it closer to me. "A gift from Bruno Walter. You have heard of Bruno Walter?"

"The conductor?"

"Exactly." He tugged at a string till it was taut before looking at me again. His eyes were gray and unsteady, like rain clouds in a wind. "Mrs. Weill—she is well?"

"As well as can be expected."

"Of course." He tugged at the string some more. "You say you are her friend?"

"I'm a detective"—he stopped moving—"a private detective. She believes her husband is still alive, and she hired me to look for him."

For a second, I thought his eyes filled with tears, but his head was bent and I couldn't be sure. "I have not seen Lilli Weill in fifteen years. No eighteen. We had tea. No. I had tea. She had coffee. She asked me if I knew anything of Max." He tenderly put down the violin and sat opposite me on a straight-backed wooden chair.

"You told her he was dead."

He glanced across the room at a photo on the wall. "They came in the night to take him. When they came in the night, it means only one thing. He is dead. I tell her this." He went to the hall, took the photo down and brought it to me.

After looking for a minute, I spotted Weill. Even in the strange uniform, even with his eyes sunken and his bones pushing against his skin, he still looked on top of the world.

Cherkhov leaned over me. "It is grotesque to believe that

Max Weill is dead. He did not consider that death would arrive until he, Max, willed it." He straightened up but didn't leave my side. He smelled of talc. "We were the privileged ones, the musicians. Each day, in Block Eleven, they killed ten thousand, and we played. This was our privilege. Max was our most privileged. For the smokers, he obtained cigarettes; for the drinkers, schnapps. For himself—" He stopped.

"For himself?"

"It does not matter anymore."

"If he's alive, it might."

He hesitated, torn. "Lilli was in Maedenek; Max was in Auschwitz. In Auschwitz, women were available." He shrugged. "To him, they were like cigarettes are to you."

"How did he manage it?"

Cherkhov glanced at the picture and rubbed his nose. "He was—how can one put it—he was a man of great sensitivity. He knew when they would come to inspect—quick, hide that, he would tell us, they are coming. He knew when they were impatient—and he would be the perfect Jewish prisoner, yes, your excellency, certainly, your excellency. He knew when they wanted Wagner instead of Beethoven—he did not conduct, not often, but he prepared the program, always, always, because he—and he alone—knew what would please them. Just as he knew what would please us. It was a gift, like the gift of his playing."

"Lilli says he could read people's feelings."

"Of course. Every great performer does this. But Max . . . Back then, I believed he was a saint. Not because he does everyone favors, though it is not such a bad thing to do everyone favors. But because he is such a great friend; everything he understands. Big matters, petty matters, he understands. He listens—he listens more closely, more compassionately than God. A best friend." He sighed. "Everybody's best friend. We all love him. Our Max. Our saint. But he is not a saint. He is a . . ." He trailed off.

"Lilli says he was psychic."

"Psychic? Acchh, women!" He raised his hands, palms up. "Listen: one day, some musicians sit down to play, and during the moments they play, they talk to each other in music; and you hear, and you nod your head, and there comes a bar, and your heart begins to beat faster, and the hair on the back of your neck goes ping ping, and a mystery begins to unfold that makes you weep because it is so awesome. Can you explain this to me? No, you cannot explain it.

"One day, a Bavarian, a sweet-natured man with two daughters and a son, has a toothache. A little toothache. Another man, a Yugoslav, walks too slowly. The Bavarian orders the Yugoslav to lie down in the mud. He lies down. The Bavarian orders everyone else, hundreds of others, to walk on the Yugoslav. Walk on him back and forth, over and over." He tucked his feet under the chair. "After an hour, there is nothing but fragments of the Yugoslav left in the bleeding mud. Can you explain this to me? No, you cannot explain it.

"I cannot explain Max Weill to you; I cannot explain his gift for music, and I cannot explain his other gifts." He took the photo from me and cleaned it with his shirt-sleeved arm. "A very likeable man. Charming. I enjoyed playing with him —I was the concertmaster." He put the photo down next to the violin. "I do not play anymore. They ask me—Norman Azenberg is always asking me—but the touring is too hard on me, the traveling, the hotels, the airplanes, the hotels . . ."

I offered him a cigarette; he shook his head, no, but watched me light mine the way ex-smokers watch: enviously. "I'm sorry I never heard him play," I said.

He walked over to a shelf, took a cassette from a rack and loaded it onto a deck. He was laughing. "An astonishing people, the Germans. Not only do they make films of the burn-

34

ing of bodies, they make recordings of the music of those they intend to burn. My legacy of Auschwitz. A copy of the master."

"Which is where?"

"Burned." He pushed a button and music came from the two speakers mounted on the wall. "The Mozart seventeen, in G. Max Weill, pianist."

We sat and listened, he in his straight wooden chair, his legs crossed and his eyes closed; me in the leather armchair, first sitting forward and smoking, then leaning back and trying to hear the music without recalling when and where it was recorded. When the tape stopped, Cherkhov opened his eyes and smiled. "It is nice, no?"

I leaned forward again. "If he were alive, do you think he'd come here?"

"Without doubt. Max liked money and comfort. Here, in America, there is much money and comfort. And much music. They are all here, Horowitz, Rubinstein, Gould, Serkin, and the new ones, the Russians, the oriental girl, they are all here."

"If he were here, would you have heard about it?"

"If he played, of course. Everyone would have heard about it."

"And if he didn't play?"

"If he taught, possibly. He would teach here, or perhaps Los Angeles. For his vanity, he would take only the best students, and that is where they are."

"For his vanity?"

"A teacher leaves a mark on a student, sometimes a strong mark—such a person must struggle to free himself—sometimes a—" He stopped, closed his eyes and scrunched up his face.

"What is it?" I said.

"It is not possible but . . . when I was at Juilliard, there was a painist, a black girl. One day, she played for us, and she tried a Mozart piece. Not too good, but not humiliating. In the fingering there were a few bars, perhaps eight, perhaps twelve, and for those measures I said to myself, this sounds like Max. Is Max Weill giving lessons to little black girls?"

A vein in my neck twitched. "Did you ask her?" I said. He shook his head. "You didn't ask her."

"It was only a few bars, and he was dead, so . . ." He shrugged.

"Do you know her name?"

"No. It is years ago."

"Can you get it?" Without realizing it, I'd stood up.

"He looked up at me. "Mr. Fitzgerald, you must not excite yourself—a few bars played at—"

"Can you get her name?"

He stared at me. "If you must have it, I can try. I will look up my records. Somewhere in there will be the name." He waved at a cardboard carton in the corner. It was labeled Sunkist Oranges. "I will try."

I gave him a card. "Call anytime; they take messages." He nodded. "When will you have a chance to look?"

"Mr. Fitzgerald, we are discussing something of many years ago. I cannot find this in an hour." He touched me briefly on the forearm. "I will begin tomorrow."

"You'll call me?"

"Yes, yes. I have your card. Here, watch." He put my card under the neck of the violin. "I will not forget." He walked me to the door and opened it. "You will do me a favor?"

"What is it?"

"You will say hello to Lilli Weill for me? You will tell her I remember our cup of tea. Tea for me, coffee for her. You will tell her—" He stopped. "Hello, you will tell her."

"Sure."

He touched me again. "Mr. Fitzgerald, I will not forget."

6

I went back to the office to make another round of calls, and as I walked toward my door I heard somebody in the corridor whistling. I turned the corner and found the whistler pacing casually in front of my room. When he saw me, he halted and smiled. It was a pleasant smile, the kind that announced how harmless and civilized the smiler was.

"Mr. Fitzgerald?" he said.

"Yes," I said, and walked nearer to him.

"I'm Richard Kleinman—Julius Frances and I work together occasionally," he said, and put his hand out for me to shake. His handshake was like his smile. "Do you have a moment you can spare me?"

I unlocked the door, pushed it open, and waved him in. He gave the waiting room a swift glance and walked into my office, where he looked around more carefully before sitting in the armchair across from my desk. I hung up my hat, sat in my seat, and with my knee pushed a switch mounted on the leg of the desk. "What can I do for you?"

"Well, it's really what I can do for you," he said. He noticed a piece of lint on his pants, picked it off, and dropped it in the standing ashtray next to the chair. I could understand that—he was wearing a dark blue suit, and any fleck of lint on it would ruin the effect he wanted to create. He reminded me of the lawyers who used to work for the kind of criminals my father could never put away—no lint on them, either. He had a smooth voice, more like a TV announcer than a salesman; the sort of voice your mother would believe when it told her the war hadn't started yet. He didn't seem like the type of man who would hang out with Julius Frances, even occasionally. "I feel a trifle awkward dropping in this way," he said, "but your answering service said you'd be coming back, so I thought I'd take a chance."

"What is it you can do for me?"

"Well, to come right to the point, Mr. Fitzgerald, I had a little chat with Mr. Frances—he's sometimes a tad dense, our Mr. Frances, isn't he?" I grinned, and he continued, "And he told me of his conversation with you." He discovered another piece of lint and dropped that in the ashtray. "The conversation about . . . Mr. Max Weill . . ."

"Uhuh."

"Mr. Frances said that Mrs. Weill has hired you to look for him . . ."

"Uhuh."

"Mr. Frances said he had told you that Max Weill is dead . . ."

"Yes he told me."

"Did you doubt Mr. Frances, Mr. Fitzgerald?"

"It's not a question of doubting him—but I can't justify closing an investigation on the basis of one man's say-so."

"Didn't Mr. Frances show you a document that indicates Mr. Weill is dead?"

"Mr. Kleinman, there's a piece of paper that says Max Weill is dead, and there's a widow that says he's alive. Now, to be honest, I'm inclined to believe the piece of paper—the widow is old, the widow is imaginative, the widow is desperate." He smiled, and I held up my palm. "But. The widow is paying me, not Mr. Frances."

He nodded agreeably. "Mr. Fitzgerald, I understand your position perfectly. In your shoes, I'd take the same position." He looked at his shoes, and polished the tip of the right one against the back of his pants leg. "How would you feel about proceeding with your investigation . . . say, delicately?" He waved his fingers through the air as if he were stroking a girl's face.

"Delicately?"

"Yes."

"Are you asking me to stop?"

"Not precisely."

"Imprecisely?"

He laughed. "Well, I do understand that it would be difficult for you to stop your inquiry without somehow explaining that to your client."

"Yes it would."

"Unless you lied to her."

"Which I won't."

"Naturally not. So it would be difficult for you to stop."

"Just about impossible."

"So we can't ask you to—"

"Right."

He crossed his legs and looked around the office, as though something on the walls would help him out. His haircut was as neat as his suit, and I considered asking him for the name of his barber. "I'm not sure exactly what we can ask you," he said regretfully.

"Before you ask me anything," I said, "why don't you tell me why you're asking."

"Ahhhh," he said, and shook his head thoughtfully. "This is awkward, isn't it?"

"Not for me."

"It is such a delicate business . . ."

"Is Max Weill alive?"

"Oh, no, not at all. But looking for him might lead to—" He rolled his eyes in mock horror. "Lord knows where."

"You're not with Immigration, are you?" I said.

"State Department."

"So, if I've got this straight, the State Department doesn't want me to keep on this because keeping on this might lead me to places where the State Department doesn't want me to go. Right?"

He nodded. "More or less."

"Well, that's not something to be treated lightly," I said. "Do you have an ID?"

He drew a cardholder from his inside pocket and passed it to me. The State Department card looked genuine enough, but so did a half dozen of the cards I carried around, and they'd been printed in Brooklyn by a felon named Sol Tanen.

I gave him back his card, smiled, and said, "Who knows? Maybe we can do some business."

"Ahhh," he said, sounding like a dieter who's just swallowed a hot fudge sundae.

"Between you and me," I said, "she's a nagging old bitch and she can't pay worth a shit." I leaned toward him and winked. "Even if he could, Jews always cheat you anyway."

He laughed sympathetically. "They Jew you down."

"Right," I said. "Okay. Tell me first how you know Max Weill is dead."

"Mr. Fitzgerald, I assure you—"

"Don't assure me, that won't do me any good. Tell me how you know."

"I'm afraid that's a matter of—"

"National security?"

"Why, yes. How did you know?"

"You are with the State Department, aren't you?"

"So you see, Mr. Fitzgerald—"

I interrupted him by tapping my pencil on the desk. "Try and think of my position. I've got to know how he died, or I can't tell the old bitch anything."

He glanced up at the ceiling, at me, at the ceiling again.

"Can you promise me there'll be no record of this conversation?"

"Do you see a stenographer?" I said.

"All right. It's quite simple." He stopped. "No notes, nothing to go in your files?"

"Don't worry," I said.

"Max Weill was not killed by the Germans at Auschwitz." He waited for me to respond, so I grunted. "He escaped, and, with the help of some people in the Resistance, he found his way to a unit of the American military."

"What unit?"

"I'm not at liberty to say."

"An infantry unit? An armored unit? An intelligence unit? An artillery unit?"

"I'm not at liberty to say. Now, once he arrived at this unit, he was placed in a holding pen. Obviously, he was one of many prisoners in that holding pen."

"Obviously."

"A mistake was made. A grievous, tragic mistake: he was wrongly identified, and because of that mistaken identification, he was—"

"Executed?" I said.

Kleinman nodded slowly.

"By Americans?"

He nodded again. "Now you might wonder why the American government did not inform Mrs. Weill of this incident. Things like that did happen during the war, God knows, and you might legitimately wonder."

"Yes, I legitimately wonder."

"Ahhh. Well, unfortunately, the mistake was compounded. Shortly after the execution—"

"Where was it?"

"I can't tell you that."

"Who was the man they were meant to execute?"

"I can't tell you that."

"What was his crime?"

"Mr. Fitzgerald," he said, like a principal talking to a backward student. "Mr. Fitzgerald."

"Sorry," I said. "I can't help myself."

"Now shortly after the execution, when the military learned that Max Weill was *not* the proper person, there was—how can I put this—the authorities concerned, instead of submitting a truthful report, submitted a false one. Several documents were . . . adjusted . . . and many affidavits were . . . edited. Because of the elaborate chain of command in the military and because of the gravity of the incident, many persons signed these documents." He put his hands on my desk and looked at me.

"And several of these persons are still alive," I said. He nodded. "And some of them are still in the military." He nodded again. "In the Pentagon even." Another nod, a sad one this time. "And some might have even found their way into the State Department . . ."

"Mr. Fitzgerald, these are persons who have made illustrious careers for themselves since the war." He sighed. "We are discussing the potential ruination of several lives. Because of a single, understandable error—and deceit—of thirty-five years ago."

"So you *do* want me to stop?"

"I'm sorry, but yes, we do." Quickly, he added, "Of course we don't ask this for nothing. We fully expect to pay"—he glanced around the office, appraising the furniture—"say, five thousand dollars."

"Five thousand dollars?"

"Yes." I hummed a snatch of "Love for Sale," and he said smoothly, "I'm certain we could arrange things so that figure would be net."

"Fine," I said.

"Really, Mr. Fitzgerald?"

"Sure. Five thousand dollars"— I grinned—"and a sworn affidavit describing how Max Weill died."

"That's out of the question."

"I'll give you a sworn affidavit pledging that the only parties to see *your* affidavit will be myself and Lilli Weill."

"Impossible."

I put a whine in my voice. "Be reasonable. I can't go back to her with empty hands—I've got to have a piece of paper or she'll accuse me of lying to her. Keep in mind that the old bitch is obsessive. We can't fob her off with a story. But she'll believe a piece of paper, especially if it's on State Department stationery and has a pretty seal and an incomprehensible signature."

"I simply can't see my way clear to doing that," he said.

I shook my head disappointedly. "I guess I go on."

"I couldn't appeal to your sense of patriotism, I imagine—" he said.

"In 1984?" I said. "After Nixon? After Ford? After Kissinger? After Carter and Reagan?"

"Yes, I see your point." He drummed his fingers on the arm of the chair. "Ten thousand dollars . . . ?"

"And the affidavit."

He exhaled noisily. "I'd need to talk to my colleagues."

"Fine."

"It would take a little time."

"As long as you want."

He stopped drumming. "You'll hold off until you hear from me?"

"I'll hold off when you deliver. Till you deliver, I keep right on working." I smiled unkindly. "That'll give you a strong reason to move fast."

"You're not making things easy, Mr. Fitzgerald."

"Lilli Weill came to me in good faith and gave me good

money to find her husband. You come to me with an ID card and a story and an offer—not good money, but an offer—and ask me to double-cross my client. Now, maybe your story is true—it *sounds* okay—and maybe your money is real, but maybe your story is a crock of shit and your money is a fantasy.

"Let's say you're the genuine article. Okay, I'm sympathetic to your pitch—careers shouldn't go down the drain for a mistake made thirty-five years ago. But back your pitch up; show me as much faith as Lilli Weill. Don't expect me to fuck somebody over because you wave the flag and a promise at me."

He stood up and shook the creases out of his pants; it was the gesture of somebody who was trying very hard to show how calm he was. "I'll have an answer for you in seventy-two hours, perhaps forty-eight. I can't guarantee anything, obviously, but I expect I can persuade my colleagues to see things your way." He gave me a polite bow, but no handshake. "Thank you again for your time."

He turned and walked through the door. By the time he got to the hallway, I'd reached into the recorder mounted under the desk, pulled the cassette out, and dropped it into my pocket.

7

Fiona Shaw cooked dinner that night for Lilli Weill and me, and I guess one of us—probably Lilli—inspired her because it was the first decent meal I'd ever eaten there. She'd worked hard at it—candles and two kinds of wine and a cognac older than me, and a main veal dish that kept me reaching for more. It was the only time I'd seen Fiona *try* to please somebody—usually she acted as though whatever she did would automatically please—and at first the whole business made me wary and suspicious.

But as the three of us ate and drank and told each other funny stories, I noticed that she was treating Lilli Weill with a tenderness she'd never wasted on me. Not a forced tenderness, either: she didn't strain to be kind to her, she didn't make herself laugh at Lilli's stories, she didn't baby her because she was old; no, the sweetness simply flowed from her to Lilli, and by the time we'd had our third brandy, some of it was flowing in my direction, too.

I felt odd because I felt comfortable, which I guess is not a sign of terrific mental health; but I hadn't felt that kind of comfort in years. The room was dense with warmth; the three of us seemed to like each other with a lot more depth than should have been probable. Maybe it was the wine and the cognac, or maybe Lilli Weill brought out the best in Fiona and me. Whatever. Just before I took Lilli downstairs to put her in a taxi, Fiona put "Tales From the Vienna Woods" on the record player, and the three of us danced a tipsy waltz.

On the street, Lilli kissed me softly, hesitated, then said, "No, I will not ask. The evening is too good."

I wanted to tell her that anything I told her would upset her, but that seemed like a waste of breath. "You're right," I said, and helped her into the taxi.

When I got back upstairs, Fiona was in the bedroom watching the late news. I poured two more cognacs and sat next to her. As soon as the hard news ended, she turned off the set, swiveled around and smiled. She'd taken off her shoes and pantyhose and her thighs were pale against the green of her skirt. She wriggled closer and kissed me on the eyelid. "Hi there," she said.

"Hi."

"Did you like dinner?"

"Uhuh."

"Are you glad you're here?"

"Uhuh."

"Do you want to stay over?"

"Uhuh."

"Did you miss me today?"

"Sometimes. It was a busy day."

"When did you miss me?"

"Between noon and twelve-twenty."

"Did you think about making love with me?"

"Between noon and twelve-twenty."

"Are you thinking about it now?"

"Hmmmmmmm."

She pulled her skirt up around her waist. She was naked under the skirt. "Are you thinking about it now?"

I reached behind me for a cigarette and lit it. "You told me you needed to talk to me."

"It can wait, Kev."

"I have a feeling that if we let it wait, we won't get to it. Not tonight, anyhow."

"Don't you want me?"

"Uhuh. Is what we're going to talk about make me want you less?"

She stared at me, raised herself a few inches, and pulled down her skirt. "What do you want?" she asked.

"Is that what we need to talk about?"

"Yes."

"We've been over this," I said. "Over and over."

"I don't care," she said. "Let's go over it again."

"Okay," I said, without bothering to keep the edge from my tone, "you want to be important to me, and everything else that goes along with that. Right?" She nodded. "Okay." I drank some brandy. "That's not what I want."

"Why not?"

"Because I've done that already, and so have you, and we both know—"

"*I* don't know."

"Well, I do."

"Then goddamit, Kev, what do you want?"

"I don't want to be yelled at."

"Another *don't*. Mister Negativo. Shit." She punched the pillow. "Don't you like me at all?"

"Yes, I like you, and—"

"Thank you."

"I like you and I want you to like me. I want to enjoy you and I want you to enjoy me. If you need help, I want to help you, and I expect the same from you." I put my finger in her palm. "And I do want to make love to you."

She thought about what I'd said, then said, "But you don't want to love me, and you don't want me to love you."

My chest tightened and I took a breath. "Loving you is fine," I said, "but I don't want to make you the center of my life. I don't want to live and breathe Fiona Shaw."

"I don't expect you to. I ex—"

"Yes you do. You talk like a real sophisticate, Fiona, but you're straight out of the last century—you want to be *it*, the one, the sun, the moon, and the stars. You have to bite your lip a dozen times a day to keep from demanding more and more attention. You put up with me and my carelessness because you know I'm not fucking anybody else, and—"

"You swear?"

"And that makes me tolerable. You want it all—I don't mean marriage and that shit—but you want the Grand Passion."

"Well, what's wrong with that?"

"It's dumb. Look at Lilli Weill and her forty years of grief. There's nothing dumber than picking out one person and saying, this is *it*, this is where I deposit all the emotions. Nobody can give you that. Sooner or later, you stretch out your empty hand and nothing gets put in it. Sooner or later, you get your knees shattered and your neck broken. Not because she wants to hurt you, not because she's mean, but because you've been dumb enough to lay it all on her."

"Oh, bullshit, Kev."

"Listen. You've got one friend who's good to shoot pool with, another friend who's good to drink with, another who's good at getting tickets to the Knicks, and another who's good at rescuing you from the Tombs. But they're all different people. Nobody can be everything to somebody. No matter how much you want them to, no matter how hard you push them, nobody can do it all for you."

"Great," she said, "you made a big investment in someone, you lost, and now I have to pay for it. No more putting down the chips, strictly percentages. Very good. Rational. Logical. Bullshit."

I started to move off the bed, but she grabbed my arm. "Don't run away."

"I'm getting another drink."

"Jesus," she said. "Can you let go of the nickel-and-dime toughness. The hard jaw and the cold eyes, the intimations of endless bravery. Who gives a shit? You're terrific at walking through fire. You just can't sit on a bed and talk about loving somebody. Except by saying you won't love somebody."

"Fiona, I can say it—I can say it in eighteen different tones and four different languages, but I still don't know what the hell it means. I know that after a certain age you make a choice between intimacy and convenience. This year, I'm choosing convenience."

"Well, aren't you rational."

"Okay, have it your way: I'm not rational. I'm your typical middle-aged asshole, emotionally constipated and busy hiding it by reducing everything to reason. Is that better? Now that I've admitted what a chilly bastard I am, do you feel better?"

She wrenched a cigarette from my pack, lit it, and began to cough. She didn't really smoke, but she liked to use cigarettes as props. While she coughed, I went to the other room and filled our glasses. She didn't look at me when I came back, so I sat down and closed my eyes. There were things to be said, but there was too much anger in the air for either of us to say them aloud.

We sat silently for a few minutes, until I said, "I see now why you like Lilli so much."

She shifted slightly, so I couldn't see her eyes. "You know that my father killed himself?"

"Uhuh, you told me."

"You sound indifferent."

"I never met the man." I couldn't tell her that my father had blown his brains all over the bathroom wall with his off-duty Smith & Wesson. It would have been too neat, and too cheap.

"You would have liked him," she said. "He used to write for TV, for all the big comics. At night, he'd come into my bedroom with his first drafts and say, all right, baby, what do you think of this; and he'd try out his routines on me. I was the only child at my school who went to bed laughing. When he and my mother had parties, I would sit next to my door— it was open around two inches—and listen to him and the other writers swap stories about the people they worked for. My father was the only comedy writer who wasn't Jewish, but he knew more Yiddish than all of them. And he was funnier. My mother couldn't stand the parties, and she hated jokes. Her idea of a good time was to fly to Nieman-Marcus in Dallas and buy a gown." She pinched her nose till it turned white. "In 1956, he killed himself. I was at school. He closed

49

all the windows and turned on the gas. In those days, the gas was poisonous, not natural like it is now, so it worked pretty fast.

"My mother fell apart and wound up in the hospital. When she came out, she was sort of okay—I mean, she could cook and clean, all that stuff, but every once in a while she'd come home and say, 'I saw your father today—he was crossing the street against the light again; why must he always cross against the light—he's going to get run over one day.' Like that." She turned to face me. "Do you understand?"

"Not really."

"I don't care whether Max Weill is alive or not; I just care that Lilli finds out. I mean, I wasn't crazy about my mother— she shit all over my father and she shit all over me—but I hated seeing her go through that, and I don't want Lilli to go through it. Do you understand?"

"Uhuh."

She leaned a bit closer. "Are you getting anywhere?"

I held up my hand and crossed my fingers.

"Honest, Kev?"

"Honest."

She clapped her hands like a little girl. "Oh, Kev, oh, Kev!" She dipped her forefinger in her brandy and drew an X on my forehead. "When my father told a joke and I laughed, he did that. His thank you."

"You're welcome."

She scuttled closer. "I feel better now." She smiled. "I do like talking to you, even if you're such a hardass."

"Easy," I said. "Flattery kills."

She brought her mouth next to my ear. "Do you feel better now?" I nodded. "Well, Mr. Fitzgerald, in that case, will you make love to me?"

"Hmmmmmm."

"Will you undress me? Very slowly, and kiss me each time you take something off?"

"Hmmmmm."

"Or we could leave the foreplay till afterward. . . . Will you keep your eyes open the whole time, even when you're coming?"

"Hmmmmm."

"Will you bite my thighs and eat me till I scream and—" She stopped. "Damn, I've got my period."

"My father's side of the family is from Transylvania," I said, "so we're used to drinking blood."

"Gross, Kev, gross," she said, and put her arms around my neck. "Did you ever hear the story about the girl who was captured by a gorilla?"

I never heard it, and she spent the rest of the night trying to tell it to me.

8

The next morning, I called the State Department, in Washington, to find out whether Richard Kleinman worked there. He did, in the Office of Public Information in the Division of Educational and Cultural Affairs.

No, a receptionist told me, he wasn't at his desk, he was in New York, but he would be calling for messages, did I wish to leave one? No, I didn't.

I was surprised that Kleinman was a flack—he seemed too sure of himself and too educated to be in public relations— and I brooded on that while I slid the cassette into the recorder to play back my conversation with him. A friend of mine who worked for an outfit that transcribed radio and TV programs told me once that if he listened to people often enough, he could tell when they were lying.

By the time I'd played the cassette through five times, I was nowhere. Either I could no longer hear deception, or Kleinman never stopped lying. I pushed the rewind button to try again when Sacha Cherkhov called.

"Mr. Fitzgerald," he said gleefully, "I have found my papers, and soon I will have for you the name of the *schwartze*—the little black painist."

"How soon," I said.

"At twelve, I have a student. At one-thirty, I take Mrs. Silverman for her walk into the park—she is in her wheelchair, and her daughter comes only on Sunday; her son, the *mamseh*, does not come at all. So. I will be back at two-thirty and begin to search. Why do you not call me at three-thirty or four? Is this soon enough?"

"Perfect."

"Ah, perfect, he says to me, perfect." He coughed a couple of times. "Mr. Fitzgerald . . ."

"I'm listening."

"Er . . . do you enjoy violin music . . . recitals, concerts, such things . . . ?"

"Sure."

"I was thinking perhaps that some evening—Mr. Fitzgerald, I am not a bad man because I did not die with the others. I am not a bad man because I played for them." I said nothing; I knew there was more.

"Some people," he went on, "they think this. They are very angry that we did not all go to the gas chambers. I do not always tell everybody that I played the violin for them. Believe me, there were worse things than playing the violin. People did much worse to stay alive, believe me."

"I can imagine."

"Mr. Fitzgerald, it is good to be alive, is it not?"

"Some days," I said.

"Ah, yes. Some days. We will speak later."

*

On my twenty-first birthday, my father, who had just helped round up a bunch of neo-Nazis, took me drinking at a saloon over on Twelfth Avenue. We didn't talk much—we never had—but at least I matched him drink for drink, and that seemed to make him happy. When they finally threw us out, at five in the morning, it was drizzling, so to keep dry we stumbled over to a spot under the West Side Highway. To drown out the hissing of the cars above us, my father began to sing "Blue Moon." As usual, he forgot the words about half way through, and as usual he stopped singing and glared upward as though God had personally sabotaged his memory.

To break the silence, I asked him about the neo-Nazis. He misheard me, because he gripped my arm and snarled, "I told you, I'm not going to talk about that, the fighting yes, but not the camps, I told you; it makes me sick to talk about it, how many times do I have to tell you that?" And he stopped, turned away, and threw up all over my shoes and his.

The next day, in the kitchen, I tried to ask him about it, but he shut me off. I remember being confused, because I knew my father wasn't squeamish—he'd worked emergency service and homicide, and gore never disturbed him. So I went to the library and read the descriptions of the liberation of the camps. One book showed pictures of Allied soldiers using bulldozers to push bodies into huge open pits; other Allied soldiers were standing around with cloths over their noses. For a flash, I thought I recognized my father, sitting at the controls of a bulldozer, and I couldn't take a breath till I read the caption and found out the soldiers were English. But there were other pictures in which the soldiers were American, and I was scared I would come across his face.

I leaned back in my chair and wondered whether my father had ever run into Max Weill or Sacha Cherkhov; whether he had been one of the soldiers to spray them with disinfectant, or force food down their throats, or hand them a rifle to shoot a Nazi. I wondered if he had been one of their liberators, marching into the camp to say, Max, Sacha, it's all over. It was hard to think of my father as a liberator, but then it was hard to think of him as anything but my father.

I turned to the typewriter and made notes on what I had. It wasn't much: a wisp of a wisp from Cherkhov and a hint of a promise from Kleinman. It was enough to keep going—I'd pursued a lot less—but not enough to call Lilli Weill to tease her with it. Anybody else would have called to say hello, but I was terrible at calling people to say hello; it was the kind of impulse I throttled before it got too intense. So, naturally, she called me.

"Mr. Remarkable Fitzgerald, I do not hear from you and I think to myself, he does not like my latkes, he does not like how I waltz, so I ring to learn if your stomach and your toes are in pain. How is your stomach and your toes, Mr. Fitzgerald?"

"Fine," I said, "I was just thinking of calling you to say hello."

"Hello," she said, "this is all—to say hello?"

"It's a bit early to tell you anything definite."

"So tell me something not so definite," she said. "A piece of gossip, a rumor. I am not so hard to please."

"Can I call you later?" I said.

She was quiet for a few seconds. "There is nothing, is there, Mr. Fitzgerald?"

"That's not true," I said, "but it wouldn't be fair to either of us if I talked too soon—if I were wrong, you'd be disappointed, and I'd feel rotten, and then you'd feel rotten, and I'd feel even more rotten."

"Heaven forbid we should start such trouble. All right, I will wait. I am making Hungarian goulash with noodles this evening—are you hungry?"

"I'll let you know."

I felt crummy. I was doing the right thing, which was not to give the client dribs and drabs of ambiguous information, but I still felt crummy. Lilli Weill affected me in a way that I hated; her voice, her face, her bad jokes, all stuck in my mind. She, and Sacha Cherkhov, existed in a different place from the other people I knew, even the other people in trouble. Without meaning to, without announcing it, they carried something extra on them, at least for me. Their presence was like a stain of blood on a child's face. They were proof that nothing in the world was safe, and that people could do the worst things to one another for the smallest of reasons. I'd spent a lot of my life dealing with nasty, mean, murderous people, but I understood them because I could be nasty, mean, and murderous myself. So long as I felt strongly enough and could put my victim in my sights. But I didn't understand the people who tried to kill Lilli Weill and Sacha Cherkhov; I didn't understand that kind of mean and murderous, because Lilli Weill and Sacha Cherkhov weren't worth trying to kill. They weren't bad people, and they weren't even dangerously good.

I transcribed the cassette, listened to it twice more with my eyes shut, and by the time I got done, it was twenty to four. I called Cherkhov.

His phone rang six times before he picked up and said hello. His voice sounded strained, as though he'd been shouting.

"Hi, Sacha. Kev Fitzgerald."

"Yes," he said.

"I wondered whether you'd found that name for me yet."

"It is not always good to be alive," he said.

"What?"

"Only some days. Not every day."

"What are you talking about Sacha?" He was barely audible.

"It is difficult sometimes to cling to life," he said. "I cannot speak with you now."

"Sacha, do you have the—" There was a click. "Sacha? Sacha?" I pushed down the button and dialed his number. Busy.

I replaced the phone and stared at it. "Goddamn flaky old fart!" I said aloud, and dialed again. Still busy. "Get off the goddamn phone, you goddamn flake!" I yelled.

I tried to keep the anger alive, but the memory of the emptiness in his voice stopped me. I locked the office, went downstairs, found a taxi and told him to take me to Central Park West and Sixty-seventh.

The sun was very bright and for a change the sky was clear, not choked with haze and dirt. During the ride, I worked hard to think about how pretty Manhattan looked under the sharp yellow sunlight, how the buildings seemed cleaner and how the windows reflected the afternoon glow; but all that kept coming into my head were pictures of bodies being pushed into pits by bulldozers.

Sixty-seventh was quiet: no police cars, no ambulances, no meat wagon. A boy rode down the middle of the pavement on a skate board, a mother carried her infant up a stoop, an old man squatted behind a mongrel, waiting for it to shit on a paper towel. The parked cars looked empty, and there wasn't a single thing going on to indicate that it wasn't a placid spring afternoon on a pleasant West Side block.

I went into the vestibule and rang Cherkhov's bell. No

answer. I rang again. Nothing. I stepped outside to see whether he'd gone to buy a can of tuna fish or something, but he was nowhere in sight. I rang again. Still nothing. I stood there, waiting, looking for any sign that would make me feel it was worth it to risk an arrest for breaking and entering. No sign. Disco music came from one of the ground-floor apartments; on the second floor someone was using a vacuum cleaner. Simultaneously, I opened the door to look at the street, and I rang Cherkhov's bell. He didn't answer and he wasn't outside.

A car pulled out of a spot up the street; I waited till it passed me, turned back to the vestibule, and, covering myself with my body, opened the lock with a card that identified me as a regular blood donor, type O positive.

No new noises greeted me as I climbed the stairs—the same disco music and the same vacuum cleaner.

No sound came from Cherkhov's apartment; no violin, taped or live. I was so intent on listening that I didn't notice the smell until I was nearly flush up against his door. It wasn't a hard smell to recognize; it comes out of every kitchen range in the city. I snapped the lock with the card, took a deep breath, kicked the door wide, ran across the room and hoisted the two windows open as high as they would go.

I didn't see Cherkhov anywhere, but that's because he was in the kitchenette, where I went to turn off the gas.

He was on his knees in front of the range. His head rested peacefully on a pillow, and the pillow lay deep inside the oven.

It was a tight squeeze in the cramped kitchenette, so I sat on the floor to pull him out. When I tugged, his head bumped the top of the oven, and I said, "Sorry, Sacha."

He slumped down on my lap. In my head, I heard the long-ago voice of a first-aid instructor:

Clean the victim's mouth of any foreign matter, such as tobacco, gum, or false teeth; if mucus or vomitus is present in the mouth, wipe it away by passing the index and middle fingers through the mouth in a sweeping motion; place the victim's head in the sword swallower's position, the head as far back as possible, the tongue forward, the neck stretched, and the chin extended. Pinch the nostrils together to prevent air leakage through the nasal passage. Inhale deeply, place the mouth tightly over the victim's mouth and blow into the air passages. Repeat twelve to fifteen times a minute, rhythmically and uninterruptedly, until spontaneous breathing starts. Our nickname for this procedure, class, is the kiss of life.

He never explained why it was nicknamed the kiss of life, because it isn't at all like a kiss. And he never really explained that it only works if you get to the victim right away; and even if it does work, it usually doesn't prevent brain damage because of loss of oxygen.

He did say that it should show some results after twenty minutes, and by then it's handy to have somebody around who actually knows how to do it, like a fireman, say, and it helps even more if he's brought a respirator with him.

He never explained what to do, or how to feel, if you're too fucking late.

I eased Cherkhov down to the floor and stood up. My back ached from leaning over him, and my mouth was pinched and sore. He looked smaller than when we'd talked, but dead people always look smaller. On his left arm, his Auschwitz number showed clear and blue, and I remembered that the first time I'd seen him—the only time I'd seen him—his shirt-sleeves had been rolled down.

On top of the range was a small plastic prescription vial and an empty brandy glass. The label on the vial said that Dr. Morris Shuler had prescribed fifty ten-milligram Valium tablets for Alexander Cherkhov; one tablet was left in the vial. Next to the brandy glass was a half-filled fifth of Courvoisier.

Downstairs, the vacuum cleaner had stopped, and so had the music. The only sound was the swish of the drapes as a breeze from the park wafted down Sixty-seventh Street and blew into the room. I moved quietly to the door, pushed it nearly closed, then reached around to the jamb and ran my finger along till I found the lock. It was an old mortise type, the kind that has two buttons mounted below the bolt. If you push the lower button, which I did, a person outside can twist the doorknob and walk right in. I turned my back to the door and leaned on it till it closed.

The Sunkist Oranges box was on his worktable, next to his violin. The flaps of the box were bent open, and I peered in to try to make some sense of the jumble of papers and notebooks. There wasn't a chance. It would take hours to go through them, and I had no idea of what I'd be looking for.

I began to turn away when I noticed that the neck of the violin was resting on a sheet of music paper. I wrapped my handkerchief around my hand, shifted the neck of the violin, and picked up the paper. It was dated that day in the upper right-hand corner, and in the center, written carefully on a staff, were the words "It is enough." Cherkhov's signature filled the lower right-hand corner.

I lifted the violin so I could put the note back in place. Under the belly of the violin was a small, old, spring-binder notebook. As I reached for it, a stair creaked in the hallway. I froze, not breathing, staring at the door so intensely my eyes began to water. Heavy footfalls, the kind that might be made by a uniformed cop, came closer. Then they went farther, past the door and up the next flight of stairs; and I breathed again.

I had no notion of what page of the notebook might be useful, and I started to turn leaf by leaf. Each page contained a list of names and what appeared to be grades. No name was marked in a special way, no checks, no stars, no dots, and I was afraid I'd have to take the damn thing with me when I found my business card.

Dear God, I prayed, let Sacha Cherkhov be a careful man, and I ripped the page out, folded it till it was around three inches long, rolled it tight so it looked like a cigarette, and slipped it behind the cigarettes left in my pack. I jammed the pack in my pocket, put the notebook and sheet of music paper back under the violin, and did my duty as a citizen.

Things must have been slow at the police switchboard, because 911, the emergency number, answered on the third ring. For the next few minutes, the operator and I played a game. The rules were simple: no matter what I told her, she asked me to repeat it—the address, the apartment number, the telephone number, the name of the person in need of assistance, the spelling of that name. Some things I repeated four times, some things I repeated six times. Nine times I told her Cherkhov was dead. Nine times she refused to believe it.

After I hung up, I went back to the kitchenette. Cherkhov's tongue was drooping from the corner of his mouth and three flies were circling noisily over his face. I squatted and waved them away with my handkerchief, but they flew right back. I was still waving away when I heard the siren.

I went to the door so I could buzz them in when they rang the bell; they don't like to be kept waiting. Once they buzzed, I shifted my face so I looked open, shocked, and not too bright.

They came up the stairs slowly—policemen spend lots of time climbing stairs, and they hate it—and when they reached the landing, I stepped out and said, "Hi. It's this way."

Without a word, they pushed past me into the apartment. "In the kitchen," I said. "To the left."

"Stay with him," the older one said, pointing to me, and went into the kitchenette. After a second, he shouted, "Is this the way you found him?"

I walked toward the kitchen. The younger cop followed me. "His head was in the oven," I said. "On the pillow. I tried to give him resuscitation."

The older cop turned to look at me. He shook his head. "Wrong," he said. "Dead wrong."

"Sorry," I said.

To his younger partner, he said, "You got a ninety-five?" The partner nodded. "Put it on him." He turned to me. "When did you get here?"

"Fifteen, maybe twenty minutes."

"And you waited till *now* to call us?" He moved closer to me and I stepped back. "Till now?"

"I told you, officer, I was trying to revive him."

Again he shook his head. "Dead wrong." He looked at his watch, counted slowly to himself, and told his partner, "Make the time four-thirty P.M. approx."

The younger cop licked the tip of his ball-point pen and slowly began to fill out a ninety-five. A ninety-five looks like a parcel post tag, and it has a string on it so it can be tied to a corpse, usually around a finger or a toe. When the body arrives at the medical examiner's office, the M.E. reads the tag, which tells him the date, the time, and the probable cause of death. Most of the people at the M.E.'s office think of ninety-fives as the last surviving form of short fiction.

The older cop glared around the room, as though he wanted to attack it. "When you're done," he said to his partner, "go down and call it in. Make it a ten eighty-three." A ten eighty-three is a D.O.A. "How'd you get in here?" he said to me.

"The door was unlocked."

He snorted and said to the partner, "Call in a ten-eighty as well." A ten-eighty is a referral to a detective squad.

The younger one tagged Cherkhov and trudged downstairs to the patrol car. The older one stayed with me. He kept his hand on the butt of his pistol.

About fifteen minutes later, long before the ambulance from the M.E.'s office, two detectives walked in the door. When I saw who they were, I knew it was going to be a late dinner.

"Oh shit," the older detective said.

"Fitzgerald," the young detective said, "turn around, put your hands on your head, stare at your shoes, and keep your fuckin' Irish mouth fuckin' shut."

10

The older one's name was Paul Caruso and he was a detective first grade; his partner, who was younger by maybe fifteen years, was named Jed Davis and he was a detective third grade. When I'd first bumped heads with them, five years back, they'd started out treating me okay because Caruso had known my father. But the case had turned messy, and by the end of it, after I'd held out on them and lied to them, they made my life miserable. I would have done the same.

They were good at what they did, but they did it a certain way—A-B-C-D-E-F-G, and so on—and since that way worked most of the time, they couldn't allow any other way. I knew that the moment they'd stepped from their car Caruso had checked all the nearby windows to see whether anyone was sitting at one; neighbors who sit at windows watch who comes and goes. I knew that Davis had written down the name of all the tenants in the building, and when they left he would write down the names of all the tenants in the surrounding buildings. And if they believed they had a killing, I knew the two of them would visit all the people attached to all the names, visit them over and over until one of the people they visited would give them the one skinny fact they were after.

I knew that Caruso, who smoked cigars, and Davis, who smoked cigarettes, would not smoke while they were in Cherkhov's apartment because they wouldn't want to mix up their ashes with anyone else's. I knew that Caruso would drive the forensic team up the wall, forcing the fingerprint man to dust everything except the ceiling (and maybe that) and making the photographer take shot after shot, from every angle, with every kind of lens, in black and white and color.

And I knew that Caruso, who hated the people in the district attorney's office and didn't trust them to make the simplest case unless he led them by the hand, would make the uniformed cops tell him everything they'd touched, and he would make me do the same. He would do that to me long before he drifted around to asking me how I got in and what I was doing there and what I knew about Sacha Cherkhov. He would do that even before he smilingly asked to see my license and before Davis smilingly patted me down. A-B-C-D.

Afternoon became evening and evening became night. By the time they were ready to talk to me, Cherkhov had been stuffed in a bag and hauled away to the morgue, the room had been officially sealed, and Caruso and Davis had loosened their ties and hung their jackets on the hallway banister. Caruso turned to me and smiled wanly. "Warm," he said, as though we'd just bumped into each other on a subway platform. I nodded. He ran his forefinger across his brow and stared at the sweat that came off. "Do you know," he said conversationally, "that spring is the big time for suicides?"

"I would have thought Christmas," I said.

"Yeah, everybody thinks that—cold, and snowy, and the family isn't talking to you. No. Spring. The idea is that the poor schmuck drags himself through the holidays and the rest of winter 'cause he's waiting for the good weather when everything's gonna get better. Then the good weather comes along and everything don't get better, so . . ."

"It makes sense," I said.

Caruso took a half cigar from his shirt pocket and stuck it in his mouth. "I'm not allowed to say, I'm just a cop, only the M.E. can say, but this looks like suicide. Don't you figure?"

"Uhuh."

Davis, who as usual was clipping his fingernails, said, "You're calling it suicide, Fitzgerald?"

"I'm not allowed to call it anything, either," I said, "but from all the signs"—I waved around the room—"suicide is what it seems to be."

They looked disappointed, like small boys who'd just been told they couldn't go to the ball game because it had been rained out. Each took his notebook from his hip pocket. Both looked at me. Davis said, "Okay. Tell us."

I'd had some time to think so it flowed easily enough. I didn't lie—cops resent being lied to, and they're sharp at catching lies—I simply left a few things out. If you leave something out and they catch you later, you can always pretend you forgot. I'm not sure why I even bothered. At the time, I convinced myself that if I told them the truth they'd make it much harder for me to keep hunting Max Weill, and Lilli Weill was my client. I also figured it didn't matter all that much—it was a suicide, not a homicide, so a few missing facts didn't count. And then maybe it was a habit: I'd lied a lot to my father the cop, and I kept on lying to every other cop in the world. I didn't leave out much—the black painist, Richard Kleinman, the notebook.

I told them who I was looking for, I told them who hired me to look, and I told them about Sacha's asking me whether it was good to be alive. I even told them about the tape, and after I mentioned it, Davis rooted around the shelf and found it.

They went over it with me a couple of times but their hearts weren't in it. First, because a suicide didn't interest them, and second, because they knew I knew the routine, and using it on me would have been nothing but a finger exercise.

For a few minutes they ignored me and checked their notes with each other. Finally Caruso said, "How'd you get in here?" His pen was poised above his notebook, and he looked bored as hell.

"Somebody was leaving through the downstairs door, and this one was unlocked."

Caruso raised an eyebrow and Davis went to check the door. "Unlocked," Davis said.

Caruso made a big show of writing this stuff down. "Fuckin' convenient," he said to me, not warmly.

"Come on," I said, "you're pissed because you haven't got a case. Don't take it out on me."

"Eat shit," Davis said.

"Advice from an expert," I said.

Caruso moved closer to me. He was just overweight enough to sweat heavily, and his cheap dacron shirt stuck to his chest and back. He didn't smell wonderful, either. "Fitzgerald, your old man had a good rep, and you spend your goddamn life with your nose up people's drawers. Every rogue in the department, the day he loses his tin, he goes and gets his license. He finds a job as hired gun for the kind of people your old man put away for all his goddamn life. Don't shake your head at me, Fitzgerald, I know you're not a hired gun. Not you. You're better. You rip off the suckers and mess up a few lives and then get up on the stand and lie your goddamn balls off. How come you never joined the force, Fitzgerald?"

Davis answered for me. "It doesn't pay enough. Right, Fitzgerald?"

"I wouldn't know," I said. "Weren't you with Narcotics a long time ago? I heard that paid. What did they use to say about that squad—'poor at twenty, rich at thirty, in the slam at forty'—was that it?"

"Don't fuck around," Davis said.

"The last time you and I did business," I said, "you got two convictions. Good convictions."

"Yeah," Caruso said, "and if we hadn't pushed you to the fuckin' wall, you'd have let the both of them walk."

I could feel the blood rising to my face, so I took my cigarettes from my pocket and pulled one from the pack. Dumb. Davis reached out, saying, "Let me have one of those, will you?"

"Fuck you. There's a candy store on the corner," I said.

"Give him a goddamn cigarette," Caruso shouted.

I shook the pack to loosen one and got it out before Davis grabbed the pack from my hand. He lit it and nodded curtly. His way of being gracious.

"Fitzgerald," Caruso said, "take it easy." I looked at him to see whether he was heckling me. He wasn't; his face was sagging with fatigue, and his small eyes held no malice for a change.

"It's been a long day," I said. "Can you do me a favor?"

"Jesus," Caruso said, "give him one kind word, he asks for your wife and your daughter."

"When you've closed it—after the M.E. does his number—I'd like to copy that tape."

"For what?" Davis said.

"To give to the old lady, asshole," Caruso said to him. "Give me a call in a few days, Fitzgerald. I'll see what I can do. Jed, tag it as evidence."

"Thanks," I said.

"Who can say no to a prince like you, Fitzgerald," Caruso said.

11

I didn't realize the impact the day had on me till I got home. I collapsed on the bed and spent the night staring at the television, waiting for the pictures on the screen to wash away the picture of Sacha Cherkhov with his head in the oven.

My mind kept darting back to finding him, his cheek resting on the misshapen pillow, his arms resting on the bottom of the oven. I remembered how pink he'd looked, nearly as pink as when he'd stood near me and tightened the strings of his violin. I remembered how warm his skin was when I pulled him from the oven, as warm as if the blood were still moving in the veins and arteries beneath the pink skin. People don't die all at once. The heart stops, the brain shuts down, but there are parts of the body that stay alive for hours. Sacha was like that; my father was like that, too, when I opened the bathroom door and found him.

It's deceptive because the person looks as if all he needs is to sit up, get a quick slap in the face or a whiff of ammonia, and he'll be fine, good as new. The bacteria haven't gone to work yet, eating their way through the flesh and letting loose the gas, the gas that makes bodies swell. The blisters haven't arrived yet, growing larger and joining each other, attracting the hundreds of flies. The flies haven't dropped their eggs yet, the eggs that become millions of maggots, crawling over every square inch of surface, devouring everything in their way.

I thought about Sacha Cherkhov covered with maggots, and the thought made me take another drink. For the next five hours, every thought about him, about his funny accent, about his suspenders, about his goddamn fiddle, made me take another drink.

It is enough, he wrote, and that was easy to grasp. Everybody wakes up a few times a year and says, it is enough; and a fair number of people do something about it, with ropes, or pills, or razors, or shotguns, or gas. In the spring. It wasn't hard to grasp, and I grasped it: okay, fine, the only right left was the right not to live.

And who the hell was Sacha Cherkhov anyway?

I'd never bought him a cup of coffee, or shot a game of pool with him, or stood drunk with him under the old West Side Highway. He was just an old Jew I'd met, a survivor with a number on his arm who was willing to do me a small favor; a survivor who wanted to take me to concerts; a survivor who'd had enough of surviving.

Kevin my boy, my father used to say, everybody dies, and you can't mourn for all the people who pass through your life and die along the way. He said it at every wake we went to, and at every cop's funeral and on the day I caught him sneaking off to a mass for the priest who'd married him to my mother.

I jumped up from the bed, found a pad and pencil, and made a list of all the people I'd known who'd died. It wasn't a long list, about average for somebody forty years old: a few relations, a few friends, a few friends of friends, a few enemies, a few acquaintances, two clients, a lover, four dogs, three cats, a turtle, a chameleon, and eight goldfish. It wasn't a long list, but it was enough.

12

A paid death notice in the *Times* said that Alexander Cherkhov would be buried at noon in the United Hebrew Cemetery, on Staten Island. There was no reason for me to go, but I was still feeling morbid, so I put on a dark suit and drove out there. I parked outside the arched gate, asked the guard for directions, and walked along the narrow paths among the thousands of grave sites.

The sun was shining but there was a cooling breeze, so a decent number of visitors were on hand. Knots of them stood around graves or strolled slowly across the grass. Every few yards, I'd come across somebody alone, gazing at a tombstone or bending to lean a wreath on a carved name. I hadn't been to a cemetery for a while, and I'd forgotten how natural they always seemed. The patterned rows of stones should have looked out of place amidst the grass and trees, but they didn't. They belonged.

The spot where they were burying Cherkhov was only a few yards ahead, and without intending to, I started walking slower and putting my feet down more gently. Don't stomp, Kevin, my mother would say, you'll wake the dead.

I was surprised to see how many mourners were gathered around the grave, but then I recalled that Jews needed ten men present to hold a service, and if there weren't enough relatives and friends, they drafted the ten from anywhere.

At first, nobody looked familiar; then I noticed Julius Frances standing a few discreet feet away. He saw me, nodded, and offered a funeral-polite smile. As I touched my hand to the brim of my hat, gravel scuffled behind me and a second later Lilli Weill caught my jacket sleeve and stepped up next to me.

"Mr. Fitzgerald," she said, "what are you doing here?"

"Tell you later," I whispered.

In a few minutes it was done. The prayers were chanted, Cherkhov was in the ground, a few people threw handfuls of dirt on the box, and the professional gravediggers moved in to fill up the hole.

Lilli Weill went to speak to one of the mourners, and when she came back, Frances walked over to join us. Before she could say a word, he took her right hand in both of his and jiggled it as though it were a broken water pump. "Mrs. Weill," he said solemnly, "I'm mortified that we have to meet under such tragic circumstances. Mortified."

"Mr. Frances," she said, "each time we meet, the circumstances are not so—"

"What brings you here, Mr. Frances?" I cut in, before she could tell him how little she ever liked meeting him.

"Ah, Mr. Fitzgerald," he said, "out there . . ." He waved in the direction of the rest of the United States, "Out there, the citizens think their public servants have no heart. The citizens think we file our forms and don't comprehend that people—vital, living people—dwell under those forms. Mr. Fitzgerald, we do comprehend."

He stopped and turned to the grave before continuing: "I knew the late departed Mr. Cherkhov. Not well—it would be insincere to avow that I knew him well. But, in all modesty and humility, there were times, more than once but less than a hundred, as they say, when I was able to offer my assistance.

A telephone call here, a personal letter there. A little oiling of the squeaky bureaucratic machinery on behalf of a decent man—a gifted man—who had suffered more than his human share." He bowed his head. Lilli was watching him as though he'd just stepped from a spaceship. "We shall not see his like again," Frances intoned. He raised his head. "And you, Mr. Fitzgerald, what brings you to these sad and mournful precincts?"

"Cherkhov and Weill played together at Auschwitz—you knew that, of course," I said.

He snapped his fingers. "Yes, yes, yes, of course. How foolish of me not to put two and two together." He turned to Lilli. "Mrs. Weill, I am at a loss for words, knowing how difficult this day must be for you." He swung back to me. "Mr. Fitzgerald, did you perchance meet the late departed Mr. Cherkhov?"

"We talked a couple of times."

"And was he able to help you"—he glanced at Lilli—"in your quest?"

"He told me what you told me," I said.

He shook his head consolingly; he looked like a St. Bernard after a swim. "I'm sorry," he said.

"How long since you saw him?" I asked.

He looked at the sky, as though a calendar were printed along the cloud bank. "I would say . . . a year, possibly eighteen months. There was a certain problem with his landlord, and although naturally that is not my province, I was happy to lend a hand." He beamed. "An effective hand, I might add in all modesty."

"What kind of shape was he in then?" I asked.

"Can one man read another's heart?" he said, putting his hand on his. "Distressed about his problem, definitely. More, I cannot speculate."

"Usually, the signs are right there," I said.

He hung his head as though I'd accused him of molesting a

crippled child. "Perhaps I did not see them," he said. "May the Lord forgive me." He glanced up to look at the Lord. "Of course, that was some time ago. Perhaps some new and horrible sadness fell upon him since then. The police told me he was extremely depressed."

"Police?" Lilli said. "What means police?"

Her face was genuinely puzzled and I suddenly realized she didn't know. "You know that he killed himself?" I said.

"Sacha?" she said, "Sacha killed himself?" She shook her head and at the same time dug into her purse and drew out the death notice. "The paper, it does not say this. Look: it does not say this." Her eyes flicked from me to Frances and back to me. "Nowhere, does it say this."

"There's no doubt, dear lady," Frances said.

"How?" she said to me. "What does he do?"

"Let's talk about it on the way home," I said.

She grabbed my arm. "Tell me now, please."

"Gas," I said. "In the oven."

"In the oven," she said. "Sacha puts his head in the oven?"

"He took some tranquilizers and cognac first," I said, which seemed like a stupid thing to say.

"His note said—" Frances began, but she cut him off.

"Sacha Cherkhov puts his head in the oven and breathes gas?" She moved her head from side to side, and when I reached for her, she took a faltering step backward. She brushed her hand across her eyes, as though an insect were flying at her, and pivoted to look at the grave. Sweat dripped down her face and blotches of it soaked her dress under her arms and between her breasts. For the first time, she looked old.

Frances glanced at me, and I shrugged. He watched her for a second, stepped closer to her, and said, "Mrs. Weill, again, my condolences from the heart." He took her limp hand and shook it, but she paid no attention.

He stepped back to me. "Mr. Fitzgerald, Mr. Kleinman

wanted me to—" He looked at Lilli, winked theatrically at me, and said, "A pleasure to see you again, Mr. Fitzgerald. Let us hope that next time will be under happier circumstances." He bowed and backed away, like a headwaiter expecting an oversize tip.

I waited till he reached the footpath, then took Lilli by the elbow and steered her slowly toward the main gate. She didn't resist. Her face was white and because she was wearing a black dress and a black hat, it looked even whiter, almost leprous. For a hundred and fifty yards, the only sound was of our shoes scraping through the gravel. Once she stumbled, but she righted herself by gripping my arm.

Ahead of us were some of the other mourners. One, a tall, wiry man in a dark suit and dark homburg, glanced over his shoulder when he heard our footsteps. He nodded briefly and touched his fingertips to the brim of his hat. Lilli didn't notice.

As we came through the gate, a movement in the distance caught my eye. Down the road, behind a clump of trees, a man climbed hastily into a maroon car. Before he pulled the door completely closed, he turned the car on the road and stood on the gas pedal.

13

For the first ten minutes of the ride back to Manhattan, Lilli Weill stayed silent. She gazed out the window and once in a while ran her palm across her lap to smooth her dress. At last, she touched me gingerly on the arm. "May I speak?" she said.

"I wish you would."

"I do not believe Sacha Cherkhov puts his head in the oven and breathes gas. You do not understand this because you are an American, but it is not possible.

"From the camps, perhaps seventy-five thousand people survive. How much percent is this?" She closed her eyes to calculate. "This is one and one-half percent. This means that when the Nazis bring one hundred of us into the camps, ninety-eight die. One or two do not.

"I will tell you why I do not cry. Because to cry there is to be asking to die. I remember a girl, Greta; one morning she is crying, bitter tears, and another girl says to her, why do you cry, why are you so different that you weep? We are all here the same; nobody is suffering more."

She stretched out her arm and stroked the number with her thumb. "One day, at the restaurant where I am working, a gentleman—a generous gentleman, always he leaves a big tip—asks me with a happy smile, Lilli, why do you wear your phone number on your arm? Do you have a weak memory? I laugh and tell him it is not my phone number, it is the phone number of my new boyfriend. This is fifteen, perhaps seventeen, years ago. Today I do not do this; today, I am not so ashamed. Today, I say, this is what they put on me the first day.

"They bring me into a room with hundreds of other girls, and they make me undress—me, who wears a nightgown the first week of my marriage. A woman comes with a razor—only a razor, no water, no soap—and she shaves me; she shaves me all over; she does not watch how she moves this razor, she does not look, so I bleed from a hundred little cuts, and each time I bleed, she makes a little laugh. Then, when I have no more hair, they put on this number.

"You see, they are very smart, the SS. They understand that if they make you naked and take away your wedding ring and your hair, and put on you a number, then you are not any more a person. Now, you are a thing. It is not so hard to kill a thing. In my apartment, when I kill the roaches, I do not concern myself. To the roaches, I am the SS."

She lowered the window and took a breath. "Am I talking too much?" she asked. "It is, how do you say, old news, no?"

"Not to me," I said, half hoping she would go on, half hoping she would quit.

"On the television now, they show you the gas chambers; they show you the crematoria; they show you the piles of bones, and your stomach revolts, and you must turn away. This is nothing. This is only the result. The result.

"They have a secret, the SS. Their secret is to make you beg for death; beg. This is not so strange as it sounds, believe me. It begins in the railroad cars; we are hundreds, locked in for days, and in one corner is one bucket. So when we arrive, when they unlock the doors, those who are not already dead are like pigs, covered in their own dirt.

"In the camp, we lie in cages. All of us have the diarrhea, so the best happiness is to have a place in a cage above so one can shit on those in the cage below. Forgive me, Mr. Fitzgerald, there is no other word. That is their secret: *sheis*, shit, is their secret.

"There is one toilet for forty thousand—a plank over a ditch. We are put in a line, but this line is their funny joke, because we are all with dysentery, and we cannot wait in a line. But not to wait means to be whipped. Twenty-five strokes for not waiting. And if the guard is strong, or has eaten a big breakfast, twenty-five strokes is to die. Those who are able to wait reach the plank and try to sit, holding each other, unable to hold the plank because it is slippery with the shit of thousands, sometimes not holding, sometimes falling in. How the SS laugh when this happens; and if one is stupid enough to try to pull out those who have fallen in, one dies with them."

She laughed angrily. "A girl from Cracow, a prostitute, teaches me how to tie up my underwear, like a baby's diaper. I learn it is easier to live with full underwear than to be whipped. Her name is Grusha. Most of the days she stays to herself. In the beginning, we respectable ladies are not kind to the prostitutes. We are too good for them. We shit respectable shit. When she helps me, I thank her, in Yiddish—she speaks no German, and I speak no Polish—but her Yiddish is not so good, and she does not realize I am thanking her, and she walks away angry. She is gone.

"There is a woman, a Hollander, and she comes to the camp like so"—she spread her arms—"perhaps one hundred and eighty pounds—and she is very fast hungry. The cabbage soup gives dysentery, and this fat Hollander is going crazy for something to eat. One night, she steals from someone a piece of bread, a piece no bigger than a book of matches, and she is caught, by us. Beat her up, a girl says, to teach her not to steal. But someone else says, no, you do not waste strength beating a person who steals bread, she will be hungry again and steal again. So we kill her.

"Yes, I say, we. I am not so large and I am not so strong, but I am strong enough to help hold her down while others choke her with her dress. In the camp, to steal bread is to kill the person you steal from."

I glanced at her. There was nothing in her face that went with what she was saying; she looked like an elderly woman enjoying a ride in a car.

"One January, I meet a Communist. Never did I meet such a person, a real Communist. A German Jew: Leah. She is tall and thin, like a long piece of wire. My rags are falling to pieces, and I am walking around with my hands over the holes. Lilli, she says to me, if you will find me a fish bone, I will make you a needle. So I make an exchange and find a fishbone, and Leah takes it and comes back to me with it, and it has a hole, and it is a needle. Then I exchange a week's bread for a piece of cloth without holes, and I make myself a new dress.

"Why, you say, why must you have a new dress? You are living in shit; to live in shit, one does not need a new dress.

"Ah, it is just so. The SS wishes me to live in shit, therefore I will show them: I will *not* live in shit, I will be clean. This is stupid, no? Who will I please if I am clean? Am I going to a tea party? Am I going to a ball? Will the SS let me live five minutes longer? Is it good in God's eyes to walk to the gas chamber clean instead of dirty?

"But we can see something: the ones who do not wash, they die very soon. Not from the dirt, no. But from the saying, all right, you want me to live in shit, I will live in shit.

"You see, Mr. Fitzgerald, their secret is to make us a thing, and our secret is to stay a person. For this, anything. A person gives another person a little something, a person gives a spoonful of soup, a person gives six inches of black thread, a person talks—for months I talked with a French girl about how to iron shirts. Yes, how to iron shirts. How hot to make the iron, and starting with the sleeves or the yoke, and going around the buttons and folding over the collar. And sewing: the different stitches. And cleaning: the dusting, the sweeping, the mopping, the waxing the floors, the washing the windows, the beating the carpets, the polishing the knives and forks and spoons. God, such tiny details we talked.

"Leah the Communist says to me, Lilli, you must have a reason to live, otherwise, you will die; and staying alive is not reason enough. This is the kingdom of death, and unless you have a reason to live, they will make dying a blessing. So all the time, we look for reasons. My reason is Max. Every day, I say to myself, Lilli, get up, wash yourself, one day it will be over, and you and Max will come together. Leah the Communist has no Max, so she says to me, Lilli, one day, when it is over, I will go out and tell the world. I will bear witness. If I do not live to bear witness, nobody will know what happened here, and anything they hear they will not believe."

"Did she?" I said.

She didn't answer, and I glanced at her. Her eyes were clamped tight and her front teeth were starting to pierce her lower lip. I tugged her arm and she opened her mouth.

"Leah has two children, and they take them first. They do not bother to put them in the gas chamber, or to shoot them. It is late in the war, the SS are in a big hurry, so, alive, they throw the children into the crematorium. The smoke is so dark and so poison no birds can fly over Maedenek.

"In 1972, I go to the Braunmeister trial. Not to be a witness, only to listen. They argue, should she be allowed to stay here, should she be sent back to Germany. For hours, they argue. A young man with a little tape machine comes to me and says, madam, I see by the number on your arm that you were a prisoner of the Nazis—do you still feel hatred for Mrs. Ryan—this is who Fraülein Braunmeister is in America, Mrs. Ryan. Is enough time not passed, madam?

"I tell him a story: one morning, in front of the camp are three hundred women, many with children. The Vice Kommandant Braunmeister is telling them to let go of their children, the children are going to a summer camp. The mothers do not let go. Braunmeister tells them again, and still the mothers do not let go.

"So she begins to beat a woman who is holding a little child, a child of perhaps three years. She beats her, and the woman falls down, with the child, and she beats her, and she beats the child, and the woman and the child begin to break into pieces, and the pieces are scattering on the ground, and the blood is splashing on all of us who are nearby and on Braunmeister. Then the prisoners from the men's camp, they are waiting with the wagons, and they put the pieces of the

78

woman and the child on the wagons, and they take the pieces away.

"I tell the young man this story, and he looks at Vice Kommandant Braunmeister—she is sitting near the front of the room—he looks, and he sees a quiet woman in a gray suit, with nice hair and a nice husband; and he shakes his head and turns off his machine and says to me, 'I'm sorry, madam, I can't believe you.' "

We were in front of her building. She turned in the seat so she was facing me. "You have talked with Sacha Cherkhov, no?" I nodded. "Does he say to you he is ready to put his head in the oven?"

"No, but people usually don't."

"You are an intelligent man, Mr. Fitzgerald"—she actually smiled—"remarkable. Do you believe he is ready to do this?"

"I don't know," I said, and I didn't.

"Is he upset, is he miserable, are the tears falling from his eyes, is he not capable of speaking? Tell me."

"His note said, 'It is enough.' "

"Of course. But why now? Why, after all the years, why now? Was he so happy yesterday? Was his life such a paradise last week? No, it is not possible."

"Sometimes, Lilli, things catch up and—"

"You talk with him about Max, no?"

"Sure. That's why I went to see him."

"And, he says what?"

"He told me Max was dead." I hesitated, but I couldn't stop. "I don't think he was lying."

She lashed out. "Did he see him die? Did he see him walk to the gas chamber?"

"No, but—"

"Did he see them shoot him through the back of the head? Did he seem them beat his eyes out? Did he see him fall onto the electric fence?"

79

"No."

"He sees them come and take him away, no? This is what he sees."

"Yes," I said.

"And he tells you, when they come to take someone away, in the night, it means only one thing. He tells you this, yes?"

"Yes."

"Eighteen years ago, this is what he tells me; and to me, it is nothing. It is not proof." She touched my hand. "You must not be afraid of them, Mr. Fitzgerald. I am not afraid of them."

"Lilli," I said, "I think maybe you—"

"I tell you Sacha Cherkhov does not put his head in the oven. I am not wrong. Yes, his head is in the oven, but he does not put it there himself. I show you: I employ you to investigate this, I hire you. This is how sure I am."

"Lilli—"

"I will pay. I will work dinners on top of lunches, I will find the money."

"Lilli—"

She leaned over and kissed me on the cheek; her lips were rough but the kiss was tender, a mother's kiss. She opened the door, climbed out, shut the door, and stuck her head through the window. "So. Now you have double work, Mr. Fitzgerald."

I looked at her, not knowing what to say. Something glinted in her eyes, and I realized she was enjoying the spot she'd put me in.

"Lilli . . ."

"Mr. Fitzgerald, do not take this job for sentimental thoughts, for an old lady with a number. I do not cry, do not cry for me, not outside, not inside. Take the job because I pay you and I tell you the truth. Yes?"

"Yes."

She smiled and walked toward her door.

As I released the brake and edged into the street, a maroon car slipped past me and turned north on Broadway. By the time I reached the corner, the light had gone red and the car had vanished in the uptown traffic.

14

I sat at my desk with my notes and with the page of names from Sacha Cherkhov's book, and I thought about suicide and murder.

When I'd found Sacha, I'd played with the idea of murder for about ten seconds before sending it on its way. It's harder than it looks to make a murder imitate a suicide, and it's usually done with a gun, or a rope, or a razor, or a fall. I'd never come across anything like Sacha that wasn't what it seemed. There were no bruises on him, no sign of his being held in the oven. Which meant, if somebody killed him, they'd forced him to eat the pills, drink the cognac, and lie down in the oven. That's a roundabout way of killing somebody and carries lots of risks: if the victim puts up a fight, the killer has to use force, and that leaves signs. If Caruso and Davis had shown up at the funeral, I'd have thought about murder again, because they were the kinds of detectives who always went to funerals of anyone they suspected had been killed. When they didn't, I forgot about it.

I leaned back in my chair and looked at the photograph of my father on the desk. He was standing with the mayor on the steps of city hall; the mayor was about to give him a medal of some sort. My father was eyeing the mayor as though he were just another felon ready to offer him a bribe.

A headache started behind my right eye, and I got some aspirin from the wall cabinet. The bottle made me think of Cherkhov's Valium.

"Straight-out suicide," I said to my father's picture. "All the physical signs, a note in his handwriting, and his kind of expression—it is enough—very apt for a survivor who didn't want to survive anymore. All the emotional signs too—a burned-out case, couldn't play his fiddle, no family, no wife, no girlfriend, not sure whether life was worth the effort, what the hell, why not pack it in."

The picture looked skeptical.

"For Christ's sake, there's no real indication of anything going on that would lead to a killing. He wasn't doing a goddamn thing to anybody. The only thing he did was talk to me, and nobody in his right mind would kill him for talking to me, would they? That's pretty goddamn farfetched.

"You always told me, don't look for complications, most of the time, it's just what it looks like, don't play Sherlock. Okay, I'm following your estimable advice."

The picture still looked skeptical.

"Goddamnit, the only thing I've got is a flaky old lady who doesn't believe it. That's it. Nothing else."

Nothing, the picture seemed to say. Nothing?

"Don't tell me about Julius Frances being at the funeral, that's really off the wall; that's what he does, he takes care of the goddamn immigrants. And let's not put too much stock in the goddamn notebook. He told me he was going to look for it, he looked for it, he found it. There's not a scrap of hard evidence that he left it that way for me to spot. Anybody could have left like that. Right next to his goddamn suicide note. Right under his precious goddamn Guarneri!"

I slammed my fist down on the desk, and the picture

bounced. It was no use. As hard as I tried to keep it cozy, as much as I didn't want to mess with it, it was no use. I couldn't block the idea of murder any longer, and that was driving me crazy, because there wasn't a damn thing I could do about it. Whoever killed him had set it up perfectly. There wasn't a fact that didn't shout suicide, shout it so loud and clear even Caruso and Davis listened to it.

"Fuck all," I said to the walls. "Fuck all."

I swallowed two more aspirin and went over it again. The only person who knew I was going to visit Cherkhov was Norman Azenberg, and I didn't believe he'd tipped anyone. All he'd needed to do was either lie to me or keep his mouth shut, and I'd never have found Sacha.

That meant either I'd been followed, and I'd have noticed that, or Cherkhov's phone had been tapped. Which made no sense. Why would anybody tap the phone of an old Russian violinist?

Thick. Good old thick Fitzgerald.

I bent over and stared at my phone. It was the same old phone, black, with three lines and a hold button. I picked it up and turned it over, which was stupid, since nobody taps a phone by tampering with the instrument itself.

For a few minutes, I sat there, watching my phone as though it were a dozing python. I was waiting for a thought, a useful thought, and I figured if I concentrated on the phone, if I read the letters and numbers on the dial over and over, if I counted the scratch marks, if I pushed the buttons down one after the other and listened to the clicks, a thought would come.

A thought came, and I fished out the number Frances had written on my business card the day I'd been in his office.

There's a reference book for rent called the Cole Metropolitan Householders' Directory. It's like the phone book, except the listings are by street address and telephone number. If you have a phone number, you look it up and find the person it's attached to. I had part of a number—0029, and all I had to do was make a list of every 0029 in the city and see whether any of them meant anything.

There are 251 telephone exchanges in Manhattan, beginning with 221 and ending with 999. I got a clean pad and went to work; each time I hit 0029, I carefully printed the name and address of the subscriber. It was exciting work, something like counting the polka dots on a size fourteen dress. By the time I'd gone through fifty exchanges, I wasn't seeing what I was copying. The eye picked something out, the hand printed it, and the brain paid no attention. The brain was thinking about pastrami on rye, with Dijon mustard, and two beers. So, naturally, I missed it.

When I was done, I called out for the pastrami on rye and the two beers, walked down the hall to piss, emptied the ashtrays, made out checks for the rent and insurance, put the pad in the center of the blotter, and leaned back with my feet up. After the boy delivered my sandwich and beers, I ate and drank slowly, deliberately avoiding looking at the names on the pad.

Part of me was scared that I'd just wasted time, but another part of me, the experienced part, knew better. If I'd really been scared I would have gone through the list and let the sandwich grow cold. When I was in high school, I ran the mile, and in my senior year I won an all-city meet. At the end of the race, the coach and some of the other runners were waiting for me near the finish line to walk over and pick up my medal. Instead I trotted around for a few minutes and then sat on the grass and rubbed my calves. I knew they weren't going to give my prize to somebody else and the longer I made myself wait for it, the more valuable it got.

I swallowed the last of the sandwich, opened the second

beer, lit a cigarette, and put a ruler under the first name on the list. Moving the ruler down a line at a time, I read each name and address aloud to see whether it held a connection to Sacha Cherkhov, or Lilli and Max Weill.

When I did come to it, I laughed. It was too obvious, too corny, too storybook. I moved the ruler down another line, then another, all the way to the end. I wanted to find something less blatant, something indirect and subtle, the name, say, of an obscure association of East European refugees, or the address of the piano tuners' union. I wanted to come across something clever, so that I could feel clever. Nothing.

I moved the ruler back up to the line that had made me laugh.

The phone number was 755–0029. No address went with the number, simply a listing: Field Office, Central Intelligence Agency.

I'd never done any business with the Central Intelligence Agency and had no idea how it worked—there were days when I wasn't even sure it existed; it sometimes seemed to have been invented by movie writers and aging radicals. An FBI man I knew had spent his professional life trying to join the CIA, and when I asked him why he said it was because agency people could do anything they wanted—they could open mail, they could tap phones, they could lie, they could cheat, they could steal, they could fuck junior high school girls and not be charged. He had devoted ten years' worth of vacations to studying the CIA, hanging out at libraries, chasing down to Langley to watch the cars drive in and out, compiling a file room filled with articles. He believed that if he knew enough about the agency, it would hire him just to protect itself, but he got the cold shoulder every time he applied.

He finally decided that it was because he had gone to the wrong school—he'd read someplace that CIA men all were Ivy

League graduates—so he enrolled in Columbia at the age of thirty-nine and sent the agency a Xerox of his enrollment form. An anonymous personnel man in Langley wrote him a letter saying that he wished him well with his academic career and if he came across any others like him—but fifteen years younger—the agency would pay him a finder's fee. It broke his heart, and he quit school and left the FBI to run the security system at a chain of supermarkets in New Mexico. I never believed his version of the CIA, because he was the kind of FBI agent who spent his life going through doctored ledgers and always dreamed that the action was somewhere else. Dreamers make bad reporters.

I made a quick list of everyone I'd come across in the Weill case to figure out whether anyone made sense as a central intelligence agent. Three did: Richard Kleinman and the man in the maroon car.

Kleinman didn't look like a CIA type any more than he looked like a flack. But then again I'd never met a CIA type. I played his cassette again. The story still sounded perfectly plausible, and he still sounded like a liar. There was no way for me to know whether he sounded like a liar because State Department flacks sound like liars, or because he was lying about being with State and actually was with the CIA.

I turned the page of my pad and wrote: is RK with CIA? And next to it I wrote, maybe.

Then I wrote, Is the man in the maroon car with CIA? And next to it, I wrote, Maybe. Then I wrote, Are all three with CIA? And next to it, I wrote, Maybe.

I was starting to feel like a not very bright rat in a not very measurable maze, so I put aside who was who and wrote:

Would CIA kill Sacha Cherkhov because SC knew about the Max Weill story, the wrong man being executed, etc.? And next to that I wrote, maybe. Then: does this mean CIA would kill *anyone* who knows the MW story? And next to that, I wrote, doubtful. I studied that for a second, uncertain if maybe I hadn't been too impulsive. Maybe the CIA would kill *anyone* who knew the Max Weill story and threatened to blow the whistle on all those Important Persons in the Pentagon and the State Department.

I switched tacks and wrote, Would CIA kill SC because SC could somehow lead to the real real story about MW? And next to that I wrote, possibly. Does this mean, I wrote, that MW is maybe not dead? And next to that I wrote, possibly.

Then, after playing the cassette one more time, and recalling my conversations with Sacha, I stopped fucking around and wrote, would CIA kill SC because SC somehow could lead to MW? And next to it I wrote, Probably.

I ripped the sheet from the pad and held it at arm's length. My printing was very neat, and it gave my guesses a wonderful solidity, the way a nicely printed installment contract makes you believe you're not being robbed. Lilli Weill was a strong-minded woman and I could feel her certitude infecting me, the way my high school track coach used to infect me with the idea of being unbeatable. Of course he was wrong a fair amount of the time.

I glanced at my father's picture. He was frowning, which was his favorite expression. I put the pad back on the desk, crossed out probably and wrote, Very probably.

Then I crossed that out and wrote, Shit, yes.

"What can I tell you?" I said to my father. He went right on frowning.

15

If the phone was tapped, there was no point in staying in the office, so before I went to hunt for Cherkhov's black pianist, I walked down the hallway to my neighbor, Ben Begelman, the accountant, and borrowed his Xerox to copy all my notes.

One set of copies I put in an envelope addressed to myself at my post office box, another set to me care of a lawyer I worked with, and another set to me care of a bookmaker who owed me a favor. The originals I took with me.

Instead of using the phone booth on the corner—paranoia was rising in me like fever in a pneumonia case—I went east to Fifth Avenue and north to Fifty-seventh Street. I walked slowly, crossing the avenue every block to look in store windows at home computer games and X-rated video cassettes. I would have caught anybody tailing me on foot, and it was impossible to tail me in a car because Fifth runs south and I was walking north.

There was a vacant booth at Fifty-seventh, and I called the bookmaker. "Hello, Abe," I said.

"Something in the mail for me?"

"Right. And I need—"

"Got it. Safe as your baby sister's tush. I'll call when it—"

"Wait a second," I said. "I need something else."

"I hear ya."

"Do you have any friends in the real estate business?"

He let it penetrate. "You looking for a good buy on a condo, or what?"

"I need an office for a while, maybe a few days, maybe a few weeks."

"Where?"

"Doesn't matter so long as it's in Manhattan, and I don't care how small it is, but it's got to have a phone. I can't have one installed."

"You want the phone vetted?" he said.

"Yes."

"Okay. What else?"

"I want it in a building with at least two exits and a usable stairway—no locked stairway. No names, no checks, no receipts; cash and carry."

"When are we talking about?" he said.

"Right away. Today."

He ground his teeth. "Anything special you want in there? A couch? A copier? A piece—I got a friend with a bunch of very nice clean pieces."

"A typewriter, ashtrays, a couple of glasses, maybe a pencil. I'll bring the rest."

His teeth went to work again. "Give me a couple of hours and call me."

There was a saloon down the street, and I went in and ordered a cognac; since I'd met Lilli Weill, I'd switched from bourbon to cognac. For the next ninety minutes I watched the television set above the bar. I learned that the people on "One Life to Live" spent eighty percent of the time stumbling into trouble and the other twenty percent talking about the trouble they'd stumbled into. They never actually got around to getting out of trouble, which made their lives even messier than mine. I also learned that the bartender, whose name was Wally, had a cousin who pitched for the Mets' club in Tidewater; the cousin was a comer, Wally told me as he bought me a drink, and in three years would win the Cy Young Award. We toasted the cousin, and I promised to watch for him when he came up to the big leagues.

By the time I went back outside, the street was crowded with people going home from work, and I had to stand in line for a phone booth. Abe wasted no time.

"You got it," he said. "You got a pencil—one six three West four six, room five one five." Before I could ask, he said, "The door is open, the key is in the bottom right drawer of the desk. Two hundred a week, and you pay me after you move out." He chuckled. "I'm fronting the cash, so don't fall in love with the joint."

"Thanks, Abe."

"Self-service elevator, no starter, no guard. They got a dummy TV camera in the lobby. Front and back exits, fire escape, and an unlocked stairway." He paused. "What do you think?"

"Made to order."

For a few seconds he stayed quiet; not even his teeth made any noise. "You know, Kev, it wouldn't kill you to call me once in a while. It's still only a dime in New York."

"Why, Abe," I said, "I didn't know you cared. But what would your wife say?"

"Funny," he said. "You know, schmuck, just because you did me a favor once doesn't mean I don't like you. Why don't you grow the fuck up?" He hung up, leaving me holding the phone and wondering what it was about me that made him so angry because I didn't call him. I wouldn't have wanted to hear from me, not often, anyway, but Abe was strange.

Room 515 of 163 West Forty-sixth Street was about the size of a Volkswagen bus. The one window fronted on a wall, and the furniture made that in my office look as though it had just been delivered from a designer's showroom. There was a rickety wooden desk, a metal filing cabinet that looked as though it had been dropped from a tenth-floor roof, a swivel chair with one arm, and something that could have been a stool or a wine table. The typewriter, a black Royal, was old enough to have been built by hand.

In one drawer of the desk was a ream of white mimeo paper and six manila folders; in another was a box of no. 2 pencils, three Bic medium-point pens, and a handful of bent, rusted paper clips. The ashtrays were the aluminum-foil kind that caterers use, and the two glasses still wore their labels— one had started life holding apricot jam, the other holding creamed herring.

The page from Sacha's notebook listed six names, three of them men's. I put brackets around the male names and called my first number. The woman who answered spoke Spanish, and for a while we thrashed around trying to understand each other. My Spanish is city practical—which way is the men's room, give me another drink, turn left at the next corner, I don't carry cash at night—while hers was the real thing. She suffered through my forcing her to repeat everything slowly four times till I finally decided that who I was looking for wasn't there.

The next number I dialed was busy. A very busy woman answered the third number, and before I could tell her my name, she announced that she already had subscriptions to *Time* and *Newsweek*, that she didn't want to join the Book-of-the-Month Club or a fruit-and-vegetable co-op, and that she was sick and tired and disgusted of being hounded by telephone solicitors; she was up to her ears in work, she had no time to take trivial calls, her life was far too crammed with obligations to waste a second listening to anonymous salesmen. It took her ten minutes to explain all this before hanging up. I didn't bother calling back to ask any more questions; she was so white her blood could have been used for bleach.

I tried the second number again. "Hello?" a woman said.

"May I speak with Veronica Webster?" I said.

"She ain't here no more," the woman said flatly. "Ain't been here for close on to ten years."

"Can you tell me where I can reach her?"

"No, I can't."

"Do you have a forwarding address for her, or a place of business?"

"I don't know where she's at, and I don't give a care," she said.

I felt like a broken-legged man climbing up a glacier backward. "Is she still using the name Webster, or does she have a married name?"

"She don't use Webster."

"Is she married?"

"Hah!"

"Then why would she use another name?"

"Mister, when you find her, you ask her."

I didn't shout back. "Mrs. Webster, I'm calling you because I need help finding her."

"You keep her away from here."

I was lost. "What?"

"She ain't been here for ten years, and I don't want her here now. You hear that, mister? You keep her away from here!"

I felt as if I'd wandered into the middle of the taping of a soap opera, been assigned a role but not told the plot. I played it out. "Mrs. Webster, I promise you she won't bother you."

"Hah! Why should I believe you?"

"Mrs. Webster, I need to find your dauther so she can help me find an old man who's been missing forty years. I don't care about your daughter one little bit."

"That's two of us, mister."

"Do you happen to know the name she's using?"

"I don't remember it."

"You sure she's not married?"

"I'm sure, mister."

"Well, in ten years she might—"

She exploded, her voice leaping up in pitch. "She's got a married name, sure enough. Never married him, but she took his name. Good enough for her and the baby, she says. I tell her a thousand times if I tell her once, girl, where is your pride at? Give your child the name Webster; it's a good old name—Webster go back more'n one hundred and seventy-five years. And she says in my face, he's the father of my child, and I loved him, and she's goin' to have his name. I tell her a thousand times. She don't listen. Maybe if her father be in the house she listen, but she don't. Well, I say the hell with her—may the Lord forgive me—but I say it: the hell with her.

"I didn't rear her to go runnin' off and drop her little bastard; there ain't no bastards in the Webster family. Now when she uses her right name, when she call herself Webster and call my grandchild Webster, she can come home. Not a day before. Not an hour before. You hear what I'm sayin' to you, mister?"

As sympathetically as I could, I asked, "What was his name?"

"Gibson. Sonofabitch Gibson. I know from the first day I set eyes on him. Creases in his pants like folded paper. One of this big hats with a colored band and a feather stuck in it. I say to her, Ronni, he's gonna sweet-talk you and walk, and your whole life is gonna disappear like rain in a gutter. We got a life figured out for you, girl, don't let it disappear. And she say in my face, he loves me and I love him, and we're gonna be married. I go to the minister, Mister Johnson, and he say, this Gibson, be he a thief? A thief, I say, he's preparin' to steal my child's life, ain't that thievin' enough for you? Sonofabitch Gibson, thievin' Gibson." She went on for a while longer before hanging up. She didn't cry.

A V. Gibson was listed on West 122nd Street. A child answered. I asked to talk to her mother; after a half minute a woman with a soft, rich voice came on the line. "Veronica Gibson?" I said.

"Ronni Gibson," she said.

"My name is Kevin Fitzgerald, and I'm investigating a missing-persons matter, and I thought maybe you could help me."

She drew her breath in sharply. "Are you looking for my husband?"

"No," I said. "This is a bit complicated, so if you could bear with me for a moment, I'll—"

"I'm not that slow," she said.

"I wasn't implying you were," I said, thinking, Shit, this is some family. "Now, when you were at Juilliard—"

"How did you know I was at Juilliard?"

"Sacha—Alexander Cherkhov told me. He was—"

"The Russian. The one who taught harmony."

"Right. Now, he said you once played a Mozart piece at a recital and—"

"He remembered that? My word."

"You played the Mozart piece, and Sacha—Mr. Cherkhov—told me that a few bars of it sounded similar to the playing of a pianist he once knew. He thought—"

"What pianist?"

"Miss Webster—"

"Mrs. Gibson."

"Sorry. Mrs. Gibson, this will go a lot easier if you give me a chance to tell you what I need to tell you."

She was quiet, then laughed. "I do interrupt, don't I?"

"You sure do," I said.

"Well, excuse me!" she said, and laughed again. "Okay, go ahead. I'll bite my tongue."

"Mr. Cherkhov thought maybe you'd studied with this pianist friend of his and accidentally picked up part of his

94

style. He didn't teach at Juilliard; it would have been a private teacher."

"What was his name?"

"When Mr. Cherkhov knew him, his name was Max Weill."

She didn't hesitate. "Max Weill? Never heard of him."

"I doubt if he used Weill," I said, "because of the way he entered the United States. He would have been in his late fifties, small, slender, very long and beautiful fingers. When he was young, he had dark curly hair; good smile. A very fine pianist. Extraordinary."

"Doesn't ring a bell," she said. "In those days, though, I just bounced from teacher to teacher. I was kind of a pain-in-the-ass student."

"He would have had an accent," I said. "He might even have talked German once in a while. Maybe Yiddish."

"Oh, shit, so many of them came from the other side. One accent was just the same as another to me." There was a shout behind her. "Listen, I'm not helping you none, and my daughter's waiting dinner, so—"

"There's nobody that comes to mind?"

"It's so long ago, you know. It's a part of my life that's all gone. And I'll tell you the truth, my head isn't focused on it right now. Maybe if you called me another time, we could—"

"I'm in a kind of rush," I said.

She laughed. "Now who's interrupting?"

"Sorry," I said.

"Look, I'd like to help you, but like I say, this is a bad time. Tell me something more. I mean, did he have one leg, or smoke a pipe, or anything like that? Tell me something special I can get my mind on."

I cursed myself for not asking Lilli Weill about all her husband's idiosyncrasies. For a second, I drew a blank. Then I tried a wild card:

"Did you ever have an older teacher who came on to you?"

"From the time I was ten," she said, a grin in her voice.

I felt myself slump. "From the time you were ten?"

"Sure. That's why my daughter's piano teacher is a woman." She giggled. "Shit, I hope she's not a dyke. It's the kind of work that attracts a lot of dirty old men, you know. I remember when I started to fill out, I thought—" She stopped abruptly.

"Hold on, hold *on!*" she shouted. "Hold on! There was one old dude who came up to me after hearing me play one time and he said, miss, you are a good pianist, but there is a better way for the fingering.

"So I said, okay, dad, show me the better way, I'll try it, and he came over a few times. But it never worked out. I mean, maybe he could have taught me this better way, but he always sat next to me on the piano bench and rubbed his thigh against mine. So I figured he didn't really like my playing, he just wanted to get close so he could cop a few feels. He wasn't ugly about it, but boy he had shifty thighs. I sent him away."

I counted to five before saying, "What was his name, do you remember?"

"It's such a long time. Doctor somebody. I called him Doctor Grope. Let me think . . . Doctor . . . Doctor . . . shit, I can't remember."

"Where did he live?"

"I don't know," she said. "He always came over to the house. Mama never let me go to a teacher's house."

"He never mentioned where he lived—never mentioned something in his neighborhood, a street, a bridge, a store, a park."

"No. Wait. One time, he said something about liking to walk past the matzoh factory. He said he liked the smell."

"The matzoh factory?" I said.

"Sounds like the Lower East Side to me," she said, "or

maybe Brooklyn. How many matzoh factories can there be?"

"How did you reach him?"

"I called him."

"Do you have the number?" I said.

"Hey, baby, it's ten years ago, twelve. I don't save numbers for twelve years."

"Would it be anywhere around your mother's house?"

"My mother's house?" she said, her tone growing as distant as the moon.

"Yes."

"What did she say about me?"

"She didn't say anything about you," I lied. "Would the number be there anyplace?"

She said nothing. I heard her daughter asking about dinner in the background.

"I don't like you talking to my mother," she said. "What did she tell you about me?"

"All she did was tell me your name. Nothing else. Would the number be over there?"

"Shit, it might be. She never throws anything out."

"Could you find it?" I said.

"You want me to go over to my mother's house and root around for a twelve-year-old phone number that I don't even know is over there. Is that what you're asking me?"

"Right."

"Well, excuse me," she said. "Why don't you just ask me to stand in front of a runaway bus, or jump off the George Washington Bridge. Shit."

"Listen," I said, "the man I'm looking for, the old pianist, was in a concentration camp, and after the war he disappeared. His wife thinks he's alive and she's trying to find him."

Again, the only sound was of Gibson's daughter making noises about her dinner.

"Is that the truth—his wife is looking for him?"

"That's the truth," I said.

"You're not putting me on—that's the real truth?"

"Yes."

"Shit," she said. "Do you like the wife?"

"Uhuh."

"She's okay?"

"She's okay."

"All right," she said, sighing. "I'll do it." Quickly, she added, "But you have to go with me. I won't go to my mother's house by myself."

"Fine," I said. "When?"

"I've got to work later tonight . . . Why don't you come by for me in, say, forty-five minutes, an hour, we'll go over there —shit, is this a mistake?—and then you can take me down to work. Can you do that?"

"I'm on my way."

16

On the drive to her mother's home, Ronni Gibson hardly spoke. She sat straight in the seat next to me, chewed on her thumbnail, and nervously twisted the tuner knob of the radio, switching stations after a few bars of a song. When I'd arrived to pick her up, she hadn't said much either. She'd been waiting in the foyer and when she saw me push open the heavy glass door, she scrambled over and said, "Kevin Fitzgerald, right?" and took my elbow and pushed me out to the street. "Come on," she said. "I want to get this over with."

In the car, I tried to ask her a few questions—harmless stuff, was she still playing the piano, and how old was her daughter—but she shook me off.

She was a dark, tense woman, not big but giving an impression of bigness because of her strong shoulders and her full hips and breasts. Her hands were strong too, but more like those of a carpenter than a pianist; the fingers were long but square tipped, and the veins on the back stood out like strips of wire on a flat wall. Her face was wide at the brow, narrow at the chin, with a sharp, high nose and fierce oval eyes. Nothing was soft about her face, except her mouth, which looked like a child's drawing of a crescent moon, curved and sweetly swollen.

A few blocks from her mother's, she said, "You are coming in with me, aren't you?"

"I told you I am," I said.

"I don't want to do this by myself." She grabbed my arm. "Pull over for a minute." I stopped near a fireplug. She turned the radio off and looked at me. "Did your mother scare you?" she asked.

"My father," I said.

"I mean, really scare you. Scare you so bad you couldn't lie to her without being afraid you'd pee in your pants?"

"Uhuh," I said, trying to sound neutral, but not managing it, because I'd never talked about my father to a woman before.

"Shit," she said. "Families." She chewed on her nail again, finally saying quietly, "Okay."

I steered the car back into the street. "Listen," I said, "I'm not going to let anything happen to you."

She smiled, making her mouth even softer and sweeter. "Well, what do you know—a white knight. Thanks, Sir White Knight. In spades."

Her mother lived on the ground floor of the kind of tenement a landlord lets go to hell and the tenants help. The bell wasn't working, and Gibson gestured to me to knock. I did, hard, and footsteps clumped on the other side of the door.

"Who's there?" Gibson glanced at me, took a breath, and put her face within inches of the door. "Who's out there?"

"It's me, mama. Ronni."

"What's that?"

"It's Ronni, mama."

When the door didn't open right away, Gibson tried to prod me out toward the street. I blocked her. A lock unsnapped, then another. "Oh shit," Gibson whispered.

The door opened, and a woman who looked like Gibson— the same full body, the same triangular face, the same piercing eyes—centered herself in the doorway. Her mouth was clenched, and her arms were crossed over her chest. She stared at Gibson so hard that she stepped backward to get out of range of the heat from those burning eyes.

After what seemed like a day and half, she said, "What you want, girl?"

"Hello, mama," Gibson said, sounding about eleven.

"Don't you 'Hello, mama' me, girl. What you want?"

"Can we come in, mama?"

Webster glanced at me scornfully. "You tell me what you want, we see if you come in."

"Mama, this here is Mr. Fitzgerald. I've got a phone number of an old piano teacher, and he needs it, it's real important, mama, I wouldn't trouble you if it wasn't real important, but Mr. Fitzgerald drove me all the way here to get it, because it's so important; the number's on a piece of paper here someplace with my things." She ran out of breath and stopped.

Webster looked at me searchingly, looked at her daughter and back at me. She was a lot shorter than I, but I felt myself shrinking under her stare. "That's all you want?"

"Yes, mama," Gibson said, and I nodded emphatically in agreement.

Without saying anything, or shaking her head, she turned her back and strode down her hallway. "Come on, girl, I don't got all night to take care of you. Come on, and lock that door good behind you."

Gibson followd her mother down the hall; after locking the door, I joined them in the living room. "It's this way," Gibson said, but before I could move, Webster held up her hand, a cop stopping traffic.

"I don't allow no man goin' in a child's bedroom. You come to the kitchen with me."

"Mama—"

"Girl, mind your face, hear!" She looked at my head. "Where I come from, mister, a man removes his hat indoors, especially if a lady is present." I gave her my hat, which she flicked twice to rid it of dust before hanging it on an ancient wooden stand.

Gibson smiled briefly at me and went down another hallway to her room. Webster looked me up and down as though I were a plateful of slightly turned ground meat. She shrugged and beckoned me to follow her to the kitchen. There she pointed commandingly to a plastic-covered chair and waited, hand on hip, till I sat. Normally, I slump when I sit; not then.

Webster put her other hand on her other hip. "I got nothin' here to eat 'cept pecan pie, and nothin' here to drink 'cept coffee. *Just* coffee."

"I'm okay, thanks," I said.

"I'm makin' it anyhow," she said, and marched over to the sink to fill a percolator with water and coffee. After she'd lit the flame under it, she marched back to the table, glared at me, and sat opposite me.

"Thank you," I said.

"I ain't served it yet," she said. She rapped the table once, sharply. "I made the pie myself. Made the crust, too. It don't come in no package from no freezer in no store."

"I haven't eaten homemade pie since my mother died," I said, mentally apologizing to several pie makers, but not my mother, who never used the oven because she couldn't stand to clean it.

Webster stood up, opened the stove, pulled out a pecan pie, put it on the table, cut a huge wedge, slid the wedge onto a plate, and pushed the plate in front of me. "Forks is in that drawer right where your belly is."

I found a fork, worked loose the tip of the wedge, and dropped it in my mouth. "This is very good pie, Mrs. Webster," I said. "The best I've ever had."

"Hah!" she sneered. "Hah! You ain't had much if you believe that's the best. Of course you bein' from up here and all, you wouldn't truly know about pecan pie, now would you?"

I took another bite, and another; it wasn't hard to do. She watched me closely, probably to make sure I didn't spill any crumbs. I heard a noise. "The coffee's perking," I said, pointing to the pot.

"It's got time yet," she said.

"This is a great pie, Mrs. Webster, and it would be a crime to ruin it by serving it with burnt coffee—don't you think?"

She stared hard at me, and I stared hard back, neither one of us blinking or shifting our eyes. It was the kind of game I played in junior high school. She must have played it too. After a couple of minutes, my eyes began to water from the strain. She saw that and her eyes widened, and I thought she'd beaten me for sure. But I was saved by the percolator: the lid bounced, and her eyes flicked left to the range. I leaned back in the chair, about to tell her she lost, when I came up with something better.

"We can try it again when there's nothing cooking," I said. "It wasn't fair to you—good cooks are always too worried about what's on the fire."

She knew I was giving her a chance to save face, and she couldn't make up her mind whether to go with her pride, which resented that, or go with her grace, which appreciated it. "A man's got to have a heap of nerve to walk into my kitchen and tell me how to make a pot of coffee."

"Uhuh."

She lowered the flame under the pot. " 'Uhuh.' He say, 'Uhuh.' "

"Uhuh."

She came back to her chair and looked at me. After an instant, the left corner of her mouth started to curl; the rest followed, spreading into an embracing smile. She gestured in Gibson's direction. "How's she doin'?"

"We just met."

"Is the baby doin' all right? What am I sayin'? Melissa ain't no baby no more; she's got to be near eight years old. The last time I see her, she wasn't no bigger than—"

Gibson walked into the kitchen. Webster shut up.

"I smell coffee," Gibson said.

"It ain't ready yet," her mother said. "Any case, it's for him and me."

"You made enough for the three of us," I said.

"Mister," Webster said, "are you tellin' me how much coffee there is? Is that what you're doin', to my face?"

"Uhuh."

" 'Uhuh.' Where'd you find a man, all he know how to say is 'uhuh'?" She went to the range and hefted the coffeepot. "No. Ain't enough."

"You sure?" I said.

"I'm sure, mister."

"Fine," I said, smiling. "She can drink mine."

Oh, she glared at me then. Another heft of the pot. A wrinkling of the eyebrows. "Maybe there's enough for three, maybe not." She turned to Gibson. "I'll call you when it's ready. You go back to your searchin' and don't keep this man sittin' waitin'."

Webster watched her go down the hall and waited till she entered her room before saying:

"I kept her clean and I took her to school. I sew all her clothes; there wasn't no money to buy none from no store. One time I was workin' for this lady on Seventy-third Street, and she comes in when I'm sewin' Veronica's dress. What you doin', she say to me. I'm makin' my child somethin' fit to wear to school, I say. I don't pay you for that, she say, I pay you to clean. If you look around, I say, you can see it's clean. Are you talkin' back to me, she say, to *me*? Now who did she believe I was talkin' to—the Baby Jesus? Told me to leave her house and never come back."

She cut another wedge of pie and put it on my plate. "Eat it; you don't look none too good. Those days, there was lots of women like me around to do the cleanin'. Ain't like now when they loves you for just showin' your face at the door. Those days, I had me people, they'd say, girl, you be sure you wash your hands before you be startin'. Can you believe that, mister? I'm going to scrub their floors and dust their tables, and they're tellin' me to wash my hands first. No carfare in those days. No sandwiches left in the icebox. They used to put these scratch marks on their liquor bottles—somebody told 'em all us colored women had to have our little taste, mornin' and afternoon.

"Some days, when I was lucky, I'd be doin' the laundry for 'em, and I'd find me a nice little dress with a tear no bigger than your fingernail; and I'd quick make that tear a mite longer, like your whole finger, and I 'd say, real ignorant like, ma'am you want me to bother fixin' this? And if I'd prayed

104

that mornin', they'd say, no, girl, throw it out. And I'd make like I was throwin' it out, but I'd bring it home for her."

"Did you ever talk to her about it?" I said.

"Talk to *her* about it? No, sir."

"Don't you want her to know?" I asked.

Gibson appeared in the kitchen doorway. "Want me to know what?" she said.

"Nothin'," her mother snapped. "Turn off that coffee, girl, and bring it here with some cups."

"Want you to know what your mother's life was like when you were a girl," I said. "What it was like to work as a maid and—"

"Mister, will you keep your face still." Gibson was filling three cups with coffee. "Milk," Webster said. Gibson fetched milk from the refrigerator and sat down. "Girl, don't you get all comfortable—you go and finish up your business."

"I am finished," Gibson said, and passed me a dirty, tattered slip of paper.

On it was written the name Werner Mieskopf and a phone number, 226–9950. I couldn't help noticing that the initials of Werner Mieskopf were, backward, the initials of Max Weill, but I decided not to inflate that. "No address?" I said.

Gibson shook her head.

Webster took the slip of paper from me and read the name. "He was the little old Jewish man, wasn't he?" Webster nodded. "I recall him. One time he brought me a bunch of flowers. Yellow and white. He used to sit at this table and talk about Rome, Italy, and Paris, France, and places all over the world. Thought a lot of himself, I tell you; very important man, by his own lights."

"Did he ever mention where he lived?" I said.

"With all the Jews," Webster said. "Downtown someplace."

"The Lower East Side," Gibson said.

"I know it's the Lower East Side," Webster said. "I know where the Jews live." She looked at me and softened her voice. "Is there a Division Street down there? I recall him talkin' about Division Street, somethin' about the bus on Division Street was drivin' him crazy and he needed to move out of there."

"He didn't mention a house number, did he?" I said.

"He just talked about the bus," she said, and handed me the slip of paper.

For a moment, we all sipped our coffee.

"Mama," Gibson said, "will you tell me about that time?"

"Where's Melissa tonight?" Webster said.

"I asked you a question, mama."

"Where's Melissa tonight—or did you leave my grandchild at home alone."

"No, I didn't leave her at home alone. I left her with a friend."

"What friend?"

"Mama, will you please stop worrying about Melissa and answer me?"

"Somebody's got to worry about my grandchild!" Webster shouted, and banged her cup on the table.

Gibson jumped up and said to me, "Let's go. You got what you came for. Let's go."

Webster jumped up. "The man hasn't finished his pie and coffee."

Gibson grabbed my plate and cup, stepped on the pedal of the garbage can and dropped everything in. "Now, he's finished. Let's go."

They stood rigid, on opposite sides of the kitchen table, and looked at each other, neither moving, neither ready to give an inch. Except for their clothes and hair—Gibson's had no gray in it—they could have been copies of the same person. They planted their feet the same way, they squared their shoulders the same way, they pointed their chins the same way, and they both fired the same rage and the same pain out of their matching dark eyes.

I stood up and got between them.

"An old woman I know told me a story a few days ago that proves everything is funny. You want to hear it?"

"Yes," Webster said.

"No," Gibson said.

"I'm going to tell it anyhow. This little old Jewish lady was dying—"

"That's funny?" Gibson said.

"Wait," I said. "This little old Jewish lady was dying, and her family was gathered all around her, and they said, 'Mama, is there anything you want, do you have a last wish?' And the little old Jewish lady pulled herself up on the pillows and whispered, 'Yes, there's one thing.' And the family said, 'What is it, mama, tell us; anything you want, we'll do.' And she whispered, 'I want to be cremated,' and they all got very upset because cremation is against Jewish law, but she went right on talking. 'I want to be cremated, and I want my ashes scattered through Bloomingdale's.' The family was terribly confused. 'Mama, why in God's name do you want to be cremated and have your ashes scattered through Bloomingdale's?' And just before she sank back on the pillows and breathed her last breath, she whispered, 'Because that way I know my children will come and visit me.' "

They both stared at me as though I'd wandered in from Manhattan State Mental Hospital.

Gibson looked over my shoulder at her mother. "Did you hear that, mama? Did you hear that?"

"I heard it," Webster said, shaking her head dramatically, "but I surely don't believe it."

She began to laugh softly and, after a second or two, Gibson began to laugh with her. Simultaneously, they stepped forward, and I stepped back, giving them room. They didn't use it; they were still separated by the corner of the table, but the tension had left their bodies, and the rage had left their eyes.

"If you like," I said, "I can wait outside."

"No," Gibson said quickly, "no, I'm late for work. Mama, I'm late for work."

Webster nodded, and the three of us walked along the hallway to the door, where Webster gave me back my hat.

"Thank you for letting us in, mama," Gibson said.

"Next time," Webster said, "you call. Then I can fix somethin' good. You got to call in advance, child—it ain't right to shame me in front of your friends."

Hurriedly, Gibson reached out and squeezed her mother's shoulder. "I will, mama. I promise."

Webster cleared her throat loudly. "You know, child, it ain't no hardship at all for me to watch over Melissa while you're off workin'."

Gibson bit her lip, nodded, and bolted out the door. By the time I'd thanked her mother for the pie and coffee, Gibson was at the bottom of the stoop.

Gibson worked as a night engineer at a radio station on Fifty-seventh Street, and on the drive there she talked about running her board. I didn't ask how she started out a pianist and ended up a night radio engineer. I had a feeling the answer would depress me, since the answer to the question—how did you come to do this if you wanted to do that?—is usually depressing. I'd wanted to fly, and here I was, not only on the ground but spending most of my time burrowing under it.

Before Gibson left the car, she said, "Did you ever wake up in the middle of the night and realize you'd pissed it all away? No, that's not right. Not pissed it away. Missed it, somehow. You know, like the prize is right there, where you can see it and reach it, but every time you make a pass at it, you miss it? I don't think there was a day in my life when someone wasn't telling me all I had to do was put my mind to it and I'd win the prize.

"Ronni, you can do it, you've got the stuff, go get it. They all believed that, and I believed it, too. So why haven't I done it?"

Her eyes were dry, but there were tears in her voice. "I'm down, and I want to be held," she said. I took my hands from the wheel and started to move along the seat toward her. "Not now," she said. I stopped moving. She looked at me closely. "Can I come over after work?" My eyebrow rose. "I want to be held, that's all. Didn't you ever want to be held?"

"Never that I admitted it," I said, which was another admission I'd never made.

"Poor baby," she said. "Well?"

"About what time?"

"Three," she said.

"Three?"

"Oh, forget it," she said. "Forget it. You're not the man to ask."

"It's okay," I said. "It's not the kind of thing I'm usually asked, so I'm surprised. Most people don't see me as the sympathetic type."

"Neither do I," she said dryly. "You don't have a date or anything?"

"No."

She smiled. "Who told you the story about the little old Jewish lady?"

"The woman who's looking for her husband."

"Yeah, that's what I figured. See you later," she said, and climbed out of the car.

17

I went home, poured a drink, and looked up Werner Mieskopf in the Manhattan phone book. No listing. I was about to call information to check the other boroughs when it occurred to me that anybody who would take the trouble to tap the office would take the trouble to tap the apartment.

I played with the notion of going to my temporary office and doing some more work on Mieskopf, but I was too tired. Everywhere I touched in this case exposed more and more emotional depth charges. There were no simple phone calls; nothing was cool and dry; even the bit players were bloated with feelings. I didn't mind feelings—occasionally, I even enjoyed them—but they got in the way of the work; they were like oil on the street—they caused skids and bad accidents.

I poured another cognac and called my service: a message from Fiona Shaw and two messages from Richard Kleinman. Kleinman didn't answer; Shaw's line was busy. An hour later, Kleinman still didn't answer, and Shaw was still busy. It didn't bother me a bit. I switched on the television and lost myself in the fake feelings of fake people.

18

Ronni Gibson arrived at ten after three. I offered her a drink, but she refused, instead rolling a joint from a plastic bag full of grass she dug from the bottom of her purse. After she'd taken a few pulls, she asked me if she could take a bath.

I led her to the bathroom, showed her the clean towels, gave her my old blue terry-cloth robe, and left her alone. Not what she wanted: once the water had stopped running, she called out, "Why don't you come in here and talk to me?"

She was stretched out, the water nearly up to her chin. Her left hand was under her thigh; her right was dangling the joint over the ashtray. Her eyes were closed.

I lowered the toilet cover and sat. Naked, she was as firm as a nineteen-year-old. I tried to keep my eyes from her breasts and crotch, but I had no luck. She was the flame, and I was the moth.

"Feel better?" I asked, simply to break the silence.

Without opening her eyes, she grinned and said, "Warm water and dope—God, what a combination." She wriggled, pulled herself up a few inches, opened her eyes, and looked at her body. "What do you think?"

"Ummmmmmm."

"It's okay for a thirty-four-year-old mother, isn't it?"

"Uhuh."

"Listen, I need to see who I'm talking to—I'm not trying to turn you on."

"That's good," I said. "I can't imagine what would happen if you tried."

She laughed and lifted herself still higher. "What parts do you like best?"

"I thought you weren't trying to turn me on," I said.

She laughed again; it was a great laugh, contagious, like her mother's. "I'm sorry. I'm warm and I'm stoned, and you look so funny sitting there all uptight—I couldn't help heckling you some." She waved the joint. "You want a hit?" I shook my head and rattled the ice cubes in my glass. "I hate booze," she said, "even wine. Melissa's father drank a lot of wine. Coke and wine, wine and coke. Once in a while, 'ludes." She drew on the joint, held her breath, and then blew the smoke at me in little puffs. "How long has this old lady been looking for her old man?"

"A long time."

"Shit," she said. "Poor old bitch."

For the next two hours she talked about Melissa's father; how she'd met him and loved him and lived with him and come home one night to find him gone. She talked about playing the piano from the time she was five, and about fighting the other girls at school because they laughed at her hand-me-down dresses. She talked about calling her mother every day at four o'clock, and about scrubbing her skin with Ivory —because it was white—about brushing her hair eight times a day, one hundred strokes each session, because she believed that would straighten it. She talked about dousing herself with deodorant, her armpits and her crotch, because her high school gym teacher told her black girls smelled so strong you knew they were coming a mile off. She talked about carrying Melissa, and bearing her, and nursing her, and singing to her, and sometimes wanting to drown her or give her away.

She talked while she was soaping herself, while she was

shaving her legs with my razor, while she was brushing her teeth with my toothbrush, and while she was lying in my bed. Every once in a while, when an ugly memory came up, she wept for a bit. But then, a minute later, a funny memory would push its way forward, and she would laugh.

By six-thirty, she was drifting off. I was sitting in the armchair at the side of the bed, too tired and too drunk to really listen to her. "Aren't you going to sleep?" she said.

Before I could tell her that I was going to sleep on the couch, that I couldn't get in bed with her dressed, because that was absurd, and I couldn't get in bed with her undressed, because—well, there were so many reasons, I didn't even know them all myself—before I could explain, she fell asleep.

I turned out the bedside light, went into the living room, memorized Mieskopf's phone number, poured a last drink, and set fire to the slip of paper.

As it curled into ash, it started a sequence of random thoughts, and some of my own ugly and funny memories swam to the surface of my mind. But drunk as I was, I wasn't drunk enough to weep or laugh.

19

Later that morning, after driving Ronni Gibson home and before going to my Forty-sixth Street annex, I stopped at the office to try and trace Werner Mieskopf's number. He wasn't listed in any of the outer-borough phone books or in my back-year Manhattan books. My Cole showed that 226–9950 now belonged to an Antoine Mathilde, at 129 Ludlow Street. A call confirmed my guess—Antoine Mathilde was Haitian and had lived on Ludlow for fifteen months.

Fiona Shaw walked in as I was packing up to leave. She was wearing a cream-colored linen pants suit, a pale blue shirt, and dark blue leather sandals. It was a perfect getup for late May, and she should have looked like the nymph of spring. But she was frowning so hard she looked more like the crone of winter.

"Hi," I said, "this is a pleasant surprise."

She sat down and crossed her legs.

"Hello," I tried again. She simply stared at me, not affectionately. "Anything the matter?" No answer. "Bad cabdriver? Appointment with the dentist? Blown deadline?"

She crashed her purse down on my desk and said, "I passed your house a little while ago."

"And it did *this* to you?" I said.

"I thought I'd stop on the way to work and have a coffee with you," she said.

"Yes?"

"Who was that woman?" she said.

"Which woman?"

"Kevin, don't fuck around with me. Who was that woman you were putting in your car—that black woman with the hips?"

"She's connected to a case," I said, which was true. Narrowly.

"Did she come over in the morning or spend the night?"

"Spent the night," I said.

"Why?"

"Fiona, you know I don't talk about—"

"What case?"

"Fiona—"

She jumped up and leaned over the desk. "Goddamit, Kevin—"

114

"Why don't you sit down?"

"I don't want to sit down!" she yelled.

"Please. Sit."

"Don't talk to me as if you were training a goddamn dog."

"If you don't sit down, Fiona, I won't talk to you at all."

I began counting to myself. On twenty-nine, she backed up and dropped into the chair. "I'm sitting now," she said, challengingly.

"That woman is connected to a case. For professional reasons, I put her up. She slept in the bed, I slept on the couch. I tell you that strictly as a courtesy. As I recall, you said to me a long time ago that you were only concerned about what I did when I was with you, not when I was away from you. Remember?"

"That was a long time ago, Kevin. Things are different now."

"Nobody told me."

"I'm telling you now." She put her hand near mine on the desk. "Asking you, not telling you." She touched me with her pinky. "You didn't make love to her?"

"No."

She smiled in triumph. "I thought so. She doesn't look like your type."

"Hmmmmmm."

"Bastard," she said, but not meanly. "You look tired."

"I was up most of the night," I said.

"That's more than you do for me," she said. "Maybe I should get connected to a case."

"You are already," I said.

"Right," she said, "So I am. Does that mean I can spend the night?"

"I don't want to sleep on the couch again," I said.

She lowered her eyes in mock modesty. "Well, suh, I don't know what to say to you. How is my case coming?"

115

"What do the Chinese say? A journey of a thousand miles begins with one step."

"What does that mean?"

"I don't know. I'm not Chinese."

"Kev."

"I can't help it. Spring is in the air, and here you are, diverting me, looking beautiful, smelling wonderful—how can you expect me to take life seriously?"

She fluttered her eyelids and smiled. "Lilli is very impressed with you. Every time I try to warn her that the odds are against her, she says, yes, yes, yes, but Mr. Fitzgerald can do it; he can do anything. Kev, do you think there's a chance? Do you think Max is alive?"

"I can't say," I said.

"Do you believe in miracles?" she asked. I shook my head strenuously. "Neither do I. But Lilli does." She smiled. "Did you ever think how nice it would have been to have a mother like Lilli?"

"Don't be too sure," I said. "Lilli's a perfect mother because she's never been one."

"God, you're cynical, Kev. But diligent. Can I help you at all?"

"Not at the moment," I said.

"I really can help, Kev—all my friends are newspaper people, and they're useful."

"I'm sure they are, but I wouldn't know what to ask them."

"Well, when you think of something," she said, and came around to my side of the desk. She smelled of Givenchy and sweat. "I've thought it over," she said, "and I think I'll have to stop by for an overnight stay. You can stay on the couch—unless I feel a nightmare coming on, and then you'll have to join me in bed."

"Hmmmmmm."

"Bastard." She bent down to kiss me; as usual, her mouth

tasted sweet. "Any time you want to talk to my friends, Kev, let me know." She walked lightly to the door, turned, opened her blouse one more button, and put her forefinger on her lower lip. "I miss you," she said, and blew me a kiss before walking out.

20

When I reached the Forty-sixth Street office, I put Fiona Shaw out of my head—which was harder that day than normally—and got down to looking for Werner Mieskopf.

I started with the credit department at Con Ed. "Hi, this is Barry Stein. I'm doing a skip-tracing job for Consolidated Collections. Our guy's name is Mieskopf, first name Werner. The last address I have for him is on Division Street. No house number."

"Account number?"

"No, I don't have that, either," I said.

"Hold on," he said, "let me punch up the name." I waited a cigarette's worth. "No dice," he said.

"Listen," I said, a trace of supplication in my tone, "Division is only five–six blocks long—could you punch up the whole street?"

He sighed before saying, "Hang on." I waited again, longer that time. "Nothing," he said. "No Mieskopf. No Werner. Nothing like it."

"Okay," I said, "sorry to put you through so much crap. Can I buy you a drink sometime?"

"Sure," he said. "Ralph Crosswell. I'm at the main office on Irving Place."

I hung up and switched to tactic number two.

The Manhattan Yellow Pages listed four pages of piano dealers, about fifty piano tuners, and twenty piano movers. So I began with the movers. The eleventh on the list was named Milton Shuler. Very friendly, Mr. Shuler.

"Werner Mieskopf . . . Werner Mieskopf . . . Werner Mieskopf," he repeated. "It doesn't ring a bell. But why should it? I'm terrible with names. Can you describe the instrument? I always remember the instrument, not the customer. Forty-two years of moving pianos, and I remember most every instrument I've ever moved. How about that?"

"I don't know the instrument," I said.

"A grand? An upright? A spinet? A Baldwin? A Steinway? A Knabe? A Yamaha? Give me a clue."

"The only thing I know is that ten years ago he lived on Division Street and he would have moved from there."

"Well, that's a start. Not much of one, but a start. Now, where did he move to?"

"I don't know," I said.

"Oy," Shuler groaned. "Mister, it's like pulling teeth with you. Uptown? West Side? Brooklyn? The Bronx? The suburbs? Listen, you sound like a smart fella; make a smart guess."

I made a smart guess. "I'd say he stayed on the Lower East Side. In fact, I'd say he moved more than once, and always around the Lower East Side."

"Aha!" Shuler cried. "Why didn't you say that in the first place. That's a big, big clue." I heard him riffling cards. "You got the name wrong, mister. It wasn't Mieskopf. That was Holt."

"Holt?"

"Andrew Holt. Good customer. To me, he didn't look like a pianist, but he sure as hell was fussy about the moving. Let's see. You got a pencil?"

"Uhuh."

"One-oh-nine Division; we moved him to seventy-one Rivington, five A; then to four B at one-three-three Stanton; six B at one-four-seven Eldridge; five F at one-one-two Orchard; and then to six R at one-five-nine Norfolk."

"Is that where it is now?" I said.

"No, that was a couple of years ago. From one-five-nine Norfolk, we moved it to Premier Storage, Long Island City. Mr. Holt said he was leaving town."

"How do you mean, he didn't look like a pianist?"

"Big guy. I mean, not small. Like a lineman, you know. Big hands. Maybe he had a kid who played. Or a wife or girlfriend. He cared about that piano, though. I'll tell you the truth, I don't know what he was doing in that neighborhood—it must have been the girlfriend or the wife. They must have been Jewish. Good customer. Paid on time, and no complaints. So he wasn't Jewish—I never held it against him. It's a big world; it's bound to have goyim in it."

I thanked him, pushed the button, and called Premier Storage. A woman there told me that Andrew Holt's piano had been sold for nonpayment of storage fees.

I cradled the phone gently, stood, and kicked the desk as hard as I could. The shock ran through my foot, past my ankle, and into my knee. It hurt, but not enough to take my mind off how shitty I felt.

I paced in a circle, trying to crack the mood, because I knew if I went down to Norfolk Street feeling the way I was feeling, I would get no place. I would be so ridden with frustration and hopelessness I would let it taint everything I did. I would go down there believing I would come up empty, and I would come up empty.

After thirty minutes of pacing, I went down to 159 Norfolk.

Patiently and quietly, I asked everybody I could find all

the proper questions. I asked them in English, and with the help of an old Puerto Rican drunk, I asked them in Spanish. I described Max Weill and I spelled out the name Werner Mieskopf. I told them the dates he'd lived in the building and the floor he'd lived on. I told them he played piano and must have made noise when he played.

I asked the grocer on the corner if he'd bought his bread and eggs there, and the laundromat across the street whether they'd ever washed his socks and underwear. I did what a tireless detective is supposed to do: I checked the liquor store, the cigar store, the newspaper stand, the check-cashing place, the dry cleaner, the Getty station, the Mobil station, the parking lot, the firehouse, the two luncheonettes; I checked the crummy little record shop in case he'd gone there to buy the latest Horowitz. I did the whole routine, including going to the post office to ask whether Max Weill or Werner Mieskopf or Andrew Holt had filed change of address forms (they hadn't) and badgering the route man to see if he remembered anything (he didn't).

What I was scared of happened: I came up empty. And when I dragged my ass back uptown, all I wanted to do was climb my stairs, fall onto my bed with a fifth of Daniels, and put myself where nobody could reach me. It didn't seem like a lot to ask.

But as I walked toward my building, the door of a parked car swung open and Richard Kleinman stepped out.

In his hand was an eight-and-a-half-by-eleven manila envelope. On his face was an eight-by-ten glossy smile. As he walked over to me, a car rolled by. I watched it as it reached the end of the block, hesitated, and turned left. It was maroon, with only one person in it. I didn't recognize him, and I couldn't make out the plate number because it was caked with mud—maybe the oldest dodge in the world and maybe the most effective.

I turned back to Kleinman. His smile was locked in place. He patted me on the shoulder. "Mr. Fitzgerald, do you have a minute to chat?" He flapped the manila envelope. "Over a drink? Upstairs?"

21

Since it was after six, Kleinman was dressed in dark blue. When he sat in the good armchair, he undid his jacket button, hitched up his pants so they wouldn't bunch at the knees, and crossed his legs. His dark blue socks were held up by dark blue suspenders. He lay the manila envelope across his lap and watched me fix him a scotch and water.

Once he'd taken a sip and nodded approvingly, he tapped the envelope with the nail of his middle finger. "As promised," Mr. Fitzgerald.

Instead of putting my hand out for it, I backed away and sat on the couch. He raised an eyebrow. "You could have given it to me downstairs," I said, "so I assume you have things to say first."

"Correct," he said, opening the clasp and drawing three sheets of paper from the envelope. From his inside jacket pocket he took a pair of tortoise-shell glasses and put them on. "For reading." He tilted the top sheet of paper so the light fell on it, and gazed at it for a reasonable time; for all I knew, he actually was reading. "I think," he said, "you'll find the wording satisfactory; and I imagine if you will, so will Mrs. Weill."

He fluttered the papers, and this time I stretched out my hand.

He smiled bravely, like an oncologist about to tell a patient the grim news. "Mr. Fitzgerald, there is one little thing . . ."

"Isn't there always?"

He took off his glasses and dangled them by one leg of the frame. "Who are you working for?"

I was so surprised by the question all I could say was "What?"

"Who are you working for?"

"I don't get it," I said. And I didn't.

Very slowly, isolating each word as though he were talking to a slightly deaf and slightly retarded child, he again said, "Mr. Fitzgerald, who are you working for?"

"You know I'm working for Lilli Weill."

"No," he said. "No." He slid the three sheets back in the envelope, fastened the clasp, and again flicked the envelope. "No."

"Yes," I said.

He sighed and drained his glass. I took it from him and made him a fresh drink. When I brought it to him, he said, "You can tell me, Mr. Fitzgerald. Frankly, I'm afraid you must."

"There's nothing to tell you."

"Mr. Fitzgerald, you are not working for Lilli Weill." He held up his free hand to prevent me from interrupting. "Perhaps she hired you—"

"She hired me."

"But she is not your principal. Who is your principal?"

"I don't know what you're talking about."

He smiled again. I was learning to detest his smile. "As you wish, Mr. Fitzgerald. Until you tell me who you are working for, I can't possibly deliver this document to you. This document is meant for Lilli Weill, not for somebody else." He leaned back in the chair and crossed his legs the other way.

I was tired and cranky—the day on Norfolk Street had

stripped me down to the raw nerves—and so I figured he was just trying to run another number by me, either because that's what he enjoyed, or because he wanted to whittle down my price. The smart thing to do would have been to ask him to leave. But I was too edgy to be smart. "Kleinman, I don't know what you want, and I don't give a shit. You've been jerking me off since you walked into my office and you're still jerking me off. You want to hold out, fuck it, hold out. The longer you hold out, the longer I keep looking."

"Mr. Fitzgerald, I assure you this is not in any way a negotiating ploy. We made an agreement in good faith, and I'm prepared to keep that agreement—but it was predicated on the premise that you were working for Mrs. Weill—"

"And that you were working for the State Department."

One of Kleinman's trainers must have once told him that the best way to hide his feeling was to smile, but the trainer never taught him how to do anything else. His smile had disappeared, and his feelings were right there, as vivid as ketchup on a white linen tablecloth. He took a sip of his drink and then deliberately placed the glass on the side table. "I'm afraid I don't follow you," he said.

"Oh, for Chrissake, Kleinman! Do you believe everybody in the whole goddamn world except you is a moron? You're as transparent as fucking Glad wrap. You're so busy being smooth and smart you don't realize we all see through it."

He leaped from the chair, bumping into the side table and sending his drink flying. The scotch splashed on the carpet, and the glass bounced along the floor to the base of the bookshelf. He turned his back, walked to the glass, picked it up, and set it on the coffee table. "Will you tell me who you are working for?"

"I told you: Lilli Weill."

He snatched the envelope from the armchair, folded it twice, and forced it into an inside pocket.

"Fitzgerald, you are not playing with stupid, little people,

123

as I suppose you customarily do. I am not stupid and little—and whoever hired you is not stupid and little. Whoever he is, I promise you, you are no match for him. Moreover, you cannot trust him."

"But naturally I can trust you?" I said.

He let it pass. "Your principal will use you and then toss you in an incinerator as if you were so much trash."

"Won't you?" I said.

"Fitzgerald, my position is that we had an understanding, and you have broken it."

"That's my position too," I said. "The other way around."

He patted his pocket. "When you're ready to tell me."

He buttoned his jacket and walked to the door. "Forgive me," he said, "for spilling my drink." He opened the door, left, and pulled it closed behind him.

I went to the phone and dialed Lilli Weill's number. I let it ring fourteen times, disconnected, dialed again, and let it ring sixteen times. Then I asked the operator to get it for me, and let it ring sixteen more times.

I moved to the couch and picked up my glass—I needed something in my hands to keep them from shaking.

Any time a detective takes on a client, he runs the risk of being lied to. Anyone who goes to a detective, like anyone who goes to a lawyer, has something to hide. Most times, with a detective, the lie isn't so important that it really affects the case. But once in a while, it is. Once in a while, the lie the client tells is very important, especially if the detective has been too careless or stupid to see it.

Most times, when a detective catches a client in a lie, it stings, but not much and not for long, because the detective has expected a lie. A client is human, and humans lie.

So there was no reason for me to sit around clutching my glass till my hands turned white, or to dial Lilli Weill's number every ten minutes, or to feel like somebody who had

124

just bought the Brooklyn Bridge. Either way, it didn't matter to me—if Kleinman was jerking me off, everything was the same. And if he wasn't, well, Lilli Weill was human; therefore, she lied. And it was dumb to feel angry or betrayed. Dumb. As dumb as dumb could get.

22

I reached Lilli Weill at seven-thirty the next morning. "I need to talk to you."

"What is the matter, Mr. Fitzgerald?"

"I'm coming over."

"Are you all right, Mr. Fitzgerald?"

"No," I said. "I'll be there in an hour."

When I arrived, she was dressed and had a basket of rolls and a pot of coffee on the table. "I am sorry I have no croissants," she said, "but the bakery sells them all before I come." She poured me a cup of coffee. "Now, tell me, what is troubling you so much today? See how bright the sun is shining and how dark your face is. It is not right for your face to be so dark on such a nice day."

"Who told you to hire me?"

"What?" she said. "What is it you say?"

"Who told you to hire me?"

"I do not understand, Mr. Fitzgerald. What means this?"

I stood up and bent over her. "Who told you to hire me, Lilli?"

"Mr. Fitzgerald, what are you—?"

"When did they approach you? What did they tell you?

How much money did they give you? Did they send you to anybody else? How often do you report to them? Do they pay you each time you report? Who are they? Who, Lilli, who?"

With each question, she pushed herself farther back in her chair. Behind her glasses, her eyes began to roll upward. Her mouth began to make sucking noises.

"Herr Fitzgerald, *Ich bitte*—please, what are you doing—*warum haben Sie*—I am not—"

I picked up the nearly full coffeepot and held it near her face.

"Who told you to hire me, Lilli? I'm asking for the last time. Who told you to hire me?"

I lifted the lid of the pot and tipped the spout in the direction of her eyes.

She slid off the chair onto her knees and bent her forehead to touch my shoes.

"*Bitte*—please," she said, "do not hurt me anymore. Please. I will not do it again. I will not break the rules again, I swear to you. Please do not beat me anymore. It was not my fault; I was not seeing where I was going, I swear to you. Please, may I go back to work now? I will work very quietly. I will not speak. I know it is forbidden to speak. Please." She was banging her head against my shoes in rhythm to her words.

I put the coffeepot on the table and crouched to help her up. When she felt my hands touch her shoulders, she gasped and ducked her head between her legs. I sat on the floor and gently forced her head and body upright. Her eyes were closed. From deep in her throat came the word *"Bitte, bitte, bitte, bitte, bitte, bitte . . ."*

I stayed on the floor and stroked her temples and made soothing noises till she opened her eyes. She stared at my face, not recognizing it.

"I'm sorry," I said. "I had to know."

She nodded automatically, but I doubted if she knew what

I was saying. I helped her to her chair, where she sat quietly, her hands folded in her lap, her eyes cast down, the perfect picture of somebody waiting for the executioner.

I smoked a cigarette and explained. Then I smoked another and explained all over again. She nodded, but said nothing.

She had nothing to say until we rode down in the elevator together. "Mr. Fitzgerald, you frightened me."

"I'm sorry," I said. I didn't add that I wasn't bright enough to have thought of another way of getting the truth from her. Probably I didn't need to add it.

"For a moment," she said, "I am believing you are the SS. The enemy." The elevator stopped at the ground floor, and she tucked her arm in mine as we walked out of the lobby. "But somewhere inside of me I know you are not the SS." She laughed. "The smell is not the same."

"Lilli—"

"When Fiona tells me about you, I say, is he an honorable man? And she laughs and says, I do not know if he is honorable, but I trust him." She squeezed my arm. "So you see, Mr. Fitzgerald, we trust you. Therefore, you must trust us, yes?"

"Yes," I managed to say.

She squeezed my arm again and ran across Broadway to catch her bus. I stood on the corner and tried not to think of her tears dripping on my shoes. I felt like a sheet of cracked glass, not broken yet, but filigreed by a million hairline splits, with all the shards ready to shatter and fly in every direction and draw blood wherever they hit.

Two boys walked by, one of them carrying a large portable stereo, which was playing disco so loud it smothered the noise of the traffic. People on the sidewalk glared at the boys, which had no effect at all, and for an instant I thought of going over to them, taking away the radio, throwing it on the pavement, and then doing the same to the boys. I stopped myself. Boys like them had become part of the landscape, as unavoidable as unfilled potholes or overflowing trash cans.

To the other people on the sidewalk that morning the boys were the enemy, the disturbers of the peace. But it didn't mean anything; it was arbitrary. On any given day anyone could be the enemy.

On Monday, it might be the boys with the radio. On Tuesday, it might be parents who set fire to their children. On Wednesday, it might be the teachers going on strike. On Thursday, it might be the judges closing their courtrooms to the press. On Friday, it might be the reporters pouring slime all over somebody's reputation. And on Sunday, it might be the cancer researchers condemning chocolate cream pie.

There were enemies for every day of the week, every hour of the week, and the good old days—the days my father loved, when it was easy to point a finger and say, "There's the enemy"—those days were gone.

Of course, maybe they never were. Our parents always lie about the good old days. Maybe, in the good old days, there were enemies for every day of the week, too. But back then, in the good old days, the person you pointed a finger at usually was too weak or too stupid to point a finger back at you. So people like my father could get away with choosing the enemies they wanted and going after them.

Lilli Weill was my client, not my enemy. But an hour earlier, I'd made her my enemy. I'd pointed my finger at her and gone after her, the same way people on the sidewalk would have gone after the boys with the radio, or the way the Jews went after the PLO.

Oh, I'd had my reasons for going after her, just as my father had his reasons for going after his enemies. Never let it be said that we went after somebody without having all our reasons.

23

At the Forty-sixth Street office, I calmed myself down by typing my conversations with Kleinman and Weill. I read them through, fished out my notes, and read those through. I played Kleinman's tape. Then I went through the whole routine all over again. I was pushing, trying to feel busy, organized, and productive, but I knew I was treading water. No matter how often I dragged myself along the course, I always wound up in the same place: facing a blank wall.

Something was going on; no doubt about that. Shit, plenty was going on. Kleinman believed I was working for somebody who wasn't Lilli Weill. Another somebody was following me around in a maroon car, or maybe that somebody was the same somebody I was supposedly working for. Yet another somebody—or the same somebody—had killed Sacha Cherkhov. All very true, all very fascinating. But none of it told me where to look for Max Weill, and none of it told me he was alive.

I started to make a list of everyone I'd talked to and what each might have lied about and why. I was around halfway through it when I snapped.

"Fuck all!" I shouted, and crumpled the paper and threw it on the floor. I wanted to throw the ashtray after it, and the typewriter and the desk. But I told myself that I wasn't an infant in a highchair spilling his dish, I was a forty-year-old adult who happened to be momentarily stuck. Everyone got stuck, it was part of the cosmic scheme of life, and all a forty-year-old adult had to do was . . . pick himself up, dust himself off, and start all over again. I hummed a few bars of that song, and pictured Fred Astaire dusting himself off and starting all over again. Of course, when Fred fell down the wrong way, he could always ask for a retake. "Fitzgerald," I said, "in real life, there are no retakes." It sounded so pompous that I laughed.

Obviously, it was a good time to go have a cup of coffee. I threw the crumpled paper in the basket and called the service. One call from Shaw, one from Azenberg. I called him first, figuring I wouldn't get through and wouldn't waste much time. Wrong again.

As usual, he sounded on top of the world. "Fitzgerald! How are you? Did you hear about Sacha? I was in Delhi, so I couldn't make the funeral. I talked the board of directors into setting up a scholarship in his name at Juilliard. What the hell, it's deductible. Listen, I found another place for lunch. Nobody knows about it yet, not even one of my violinists, and he can find a new restaurant faster than an unhappy wife can find a lawyer."

He yelled something at his secretary, then said, "I nearly forgot—you have a pencil? I found another one for you." I squeezed the phone so hard all the blood left my fingertips. "I asked around the office. We got some people here older than God, and somebody remembered him—I didn't because he was a lousy musician. Leo Hirsch, with a C. Woodwinds. Fitzgerald, are you there? I don't even hear breathing."

"I'm here."

"He's a German. Not even Jewish; a Communist. After the war, he went East, to the Peoples' Democratic Republic, as they like to call it."

I tried not to sound disappointed. "Is he there now?"

"What!" Azenberg cried. "Would I call you to send you to the Peoples' Democratic Republic? Am I a buffoon? He's with the East German Mission to the UN. Trade, commerce, something dull and heavy. Sundays he plays with a bunch of other diplomats. Very cultural, these people, a genteel musicale before they hit the massage parlors. Fitzgerald, are you there?"

"I'm here," I said. "Flat with gratitude."

"Excellent. The lunch is on you."

24

The mission of the Peoples Democratic Republic was at 58 Park Avenue, but Leo Hirsch wasn't there. He was over at the UN, they told me, but they weren't sure where. Maybe in the lounge, maybe having lunch, maybe in conference with somebody about something. Did I want to speak to Mr. Hirsch's assistant? Did I want to leave a card? No, and no. I walked out to the street and looked for a cab. Also, no. So I strode up to the UN and stood in front of the General Assembly building while I figured out what would be the least futile thing to do. In my wallet was a forged press card, and I was calculating whether it would get me into the delegates' lounge when Leo Hirsch came through the doors and strolled toward First Avenue.

Oh, I knew it was Hirsch, all right. Life is too short for a coincidence like that: he wasn't wearing the dark suit, but he was wearing the homburg he'd worn at the funeral.

I moved alongside him. "Mr. Hirsch . . . ?"

He stopped and turned to me, puzzled. "Yes?"

"We don't know each other, but I saw you the other day at Mr. Cherkov's funeral." I put out my hand. "Kevin Fitzgerald."

"Of course, of course," he said. His German accent was very light, much lighter than Lilli's. He shook my hand. "You were helping that poor woman—a relative of Sacha?"

"No," I said. "Lilli Weill. Her husband was—" Before I could finish, he waved his hand abruptly to stop me. His face had gone white. "You know who he was?" I said softly.

He nodded and brought his hand to his eyes. They were glistening. "Forgive me, Mr.—"

"Fitzgerald."

"Forgive me, Mr. Fitzgerald. I had forgotten that Max had a widow."

"She thinks she's still a wife," I said.

He lowered his hand and stared at me. "I do not understand."

"She believes he's still alive. She believes she's seen him."

He shook his head slowly, like a whiplash victim testing a neck brace. Then, without a word, he took my arm, led me to the corner, and steered me on to a side street. "Is this some sort of perverted joke?"

I showed him my license. "She asked me to find him."

He sat down heavily on a low wall in front of an apartment building. "Is she senile? Mad? What?" I shrugged. "They came for him in the night. He is dead."

"You're sure?"

He looked up at me. His eyes were still wet, and he was having a hard time keeping his lip from trembling. "Yes, I am sure." He shut his eyes for a second. "I understand her. For a few years, after the war, I saw him, too. A face behind a window, a shadow across the street, a pair of beautiful hands around a demitasse. I wanted him alive, so I saw him. But it was never him. Never." He looked up at me again. "Never."

"If he were alive, would he get in touch with you?"

He laughed grimly. "Of course. He was my friend. He saved my life—and I saved his. Without him—well, now I am without him. Max Weill is dead. My fellow Germans killed him"—the same deadly laugh—"and they killed me along with him. Me, they forgot to bury."

He stood up and brushed the seat of his pants. "Tell Mrs. Weill that I wish I could bring back her husband. But I cannot."

He shook my hand and walked toward First Avenue. I almost followed him, because I had more questions, but I didn't bother. I was too drained to stagger down one more dead end.

25

The most I'd gotten had been from Milton Shuler, the piano mover, so I went to see him. I knew I was down to scraping dregs, but scraping dregs is a better way to spend time than brooding over futility.

Shuler remembered my call, sure enough, and he lifted his arms in helplessness. "What more can I tell you?" he said. "I already told you everything."

I asked him to go over it again. With a wheezing moan, he pulled out his records and deliberately went through them. There was nothing there that he hadn't told me. He saw my shoulders droop.

"You want a coffee? I always have coffee this time of day."

I didn't, but I didn't want to leave, either.

He poured us each a cup from a flask behind the counter. "It's funny that he put it in storage and then didn't get it back. Normally, a pianist, he likes his instrument, he hangs on to it."

I nodded, not really paying attention.

"They like the same instrument, they like the same stool, they like the same tuner—say, did you talk to his tuner?"

"I don't know who he is."

He shook his head in sympathy. "That's right, he never kept any of them, this fellow Holt."

"What?"

"Never kept any of them. I sent him some. One guy—the best: he does all the big shots. Expensive, but the best. Holt, he says no good. So I send him another. Also no good. Then another. No good."

"How long ago was that?"

"The last one—it's a few years now. I guess he found somebody." He laughed. "Or that piano sounds like shit. Wait. He never got the piano back, so maybe he don't need a tuner. I never thought of that."

I had, and it depressed me. But I asked him for the names and addresses of the tuners he'd sent, finished my coffee, and went to scrape more dregs.

All three tuners Shuler had sent had only worked for Holt once. The first didn't remember him at all. The second remembered that he seemed very big for a pianist. The third remembered a bit more.

"He wanted somebody blind."

"Blind?"

"Yeah, he had this idea in his head that a blind tuner is better. He's blind, so he hears good. It's a crock. A blind tuner with a tin ear is still a tuner with a tin ear." He paused. "Is this guy a friend of yours?"

"No."

"Yeah, well, he's kind of a prick. I walk up all these flights of stairs—it's July, you know—and I say, can I have a glass of water? And he says, when you're done. I mean, we're talking ninety-five degrees." He smiled unpleasantly. "I took care of him."

"Did you do something to the piano?"

"Nah. I sent him a blind tuner." He laughed. "Philly Feldbaum. Philly Feldbaum's ear is so tin it would make a great beer can."

Philly Feldbaum wasn't in his storefront on St. Mark's Place, and neither was his wife, who had gone with him on a call. His brother-in-law, who had a six-pack on the floor next to the chair he sat in, was watching the store. His brother-in-law didn't want to move. I promised him another six-pack. He looked more lively. I promised him two six-packs, and he pulled open a drawer stuffed with index cards.

"Holt, H-O-L-T," I said, "First name Andrew, or initial A."

"Let's see . . . Division street, Rivington, Stanton, Eldridge, Orchard—moves a lot, don't he—Norfolk, Hester—that's it." He bent to look at the card. "One-two-six Hester Street."

"How long ago is that?" I said.

He bent again. "Last November." He made a disapproving sound and put a red question mark on the card. "He's due."

"Last November?"

"Eleven-six. Paid cash."

26

My pulse was drumming so fast I thought my veins would pop. Every cab was either occupied, off duty, or on a radio call. I started trotting downtown, then forced myself to cut back to a walk. After I'd gone five blocks, a bus appeared and

I lunged aboard. Ten minutes later, I jumped off at Grand Street, a block north of Hester, and strolled slowly down the Bowery.

It had been a long time since I'd visited the neighborhood, and although the buildings all looked about the same, everything else had changed. The Lower East Side had always been the first home for new immigrants, but when I used to do down there the immigrants had been Italians and Jews. No more. The Italians and the Jews had, except for a few diehards, moved on. They'd been replaced by Puerto Ricans or Cubans or Haitians or Chinese.

One thing hadn't changed: it was still the busiest, most confusing section of town. Flophouses and cheap saloons alternated with commercial kitchen suppliers and wholesale lamp dealers. Grand Street was filled with Italian restaurants and bakeries. A couple of blocks south was Canal Street, the old border of Chinatown. On Canal and Bowery was the downtown diamond market, which, like the uptown market on Forty-seventh Street, was run by Orthodox Jews. So the avenue was packed with Chinese carrying vegetables and Jews carrying gems. Everyone moved fast, paying no attention to the teenagers dancing on corners or the drunks sleeping in their piss in doorways. On one corner of Bowery and Hester was a Chinese movie house; in front of it, a bunch of grade-school kids were practicing kung fu. The quickest and most agile was a tiny girl of about twelve.

One twenty-six Hester was a six-story old-law tenement a few feet in from the Bowery. I stood across Hester and stared at it for a while, but there was nothing special about it. A typical Lower East Side tenement: old and dirty, with chipped brick and the usual graffiti decorations done in Day-Glo on the ground-floor wall. A fire escape went down the front of the building, and most of the windows that led to it were crisscrossed with burglar gates.

After ten minutes, I crossed Hester and walked toward the entrance of the building. On the way, I took out a notebook and pen and made myself look official and harried.

The vestibule was as small and as dark as an outhouse and smelled like one. The tiny bulb in the ceiling fixture was covered with dust, and the only way I could read the names on the mailboxes was by propping the door open with my foot. I was carefully moving my finger from box to box—there were twelve of them—when the inside door opened and a man stepped out into the vestibule.

I smiled and pushed myself into the corner so he could pass. He didn't move, so I smiled again and waved toward the street.

He still didn't move. "What do you want?" he said.

He was a large man, maybe six feet and two hundred pounds; and, like me, he looked out of place in the building. Like me, he was white, and wearing a suit; and, like me, he looked like a plainclothesman. He was wearing sunglasses so I couldn't read his eyes.

Placatingly, I said, "Maybe you can help me . . . ?

"What do you want?"

"Do you live here, sir?" I said.

"What do you want?"

I pointed to the mailboxes. "I'm looking for a Julio Gomez." I flapped my notebook. "A little matter of some unpaid installments on a color TV."

"What was the name?" he asked.

"Gomez. Julio Gomez."

"No," he said, "never heard of him."

"It might be Juan Gomez," I said.

"No Gomez here," he said.

"How about Julio Lopez?" I said. "Or Juan Lopez." I laughed, very buddy-buddy. "I'll tell you the truth, all these spic names sound the same to me."

"There's no Gomez, and there's no Lopez," he said. "There's a Vasquez. Angelo Vasquez."

I looked at my notebook, shook my head, and put on my finest confused face. "This is one-two-six Hester, isn't it? This is the address they gave me." I pretended to read. "One twenty-six Hester. Of course you can never trust department stores. They sell 'em the merchandise, but when it comes to collecting the money, they're out to lunch."

I turned my head to look at the mailboxes again, and he put his hand on my arm. "Who you collecting for?" he said.

I made a clucking noise. "That's confidential," I said.

His touch on my arm became a grip. "Okay, Jack, off we go. The landlord doesn't want strangers hanging around the building."

"Do you represent the landlord?" I asked.

He sneered. "That's confidential." He moved his hand up my arm so that his fingers were close to the armpit. "On your horse, Jack."

"Can I try this Vasquez?" I asked. "Maybe he—"

"Forget it," he said, and pushed me toward the door. I let the shove carry me, stumbled, and clutched at the wall so I'd be facing the mailboxes.

"Shit," I said, with a hint of a whine. "I think I twisted my ankle."

"Put the weight on the other foot," he said.

"Give me a second, will you?" He eased his grip a bit, and while I groaned and pawed the floor, I read all the names I hadn't read.

Andrew Holt was in 6R.

"Okay," I said, fighting to keep the exhilaration from my voice. I limped through the doorway. He followed, his hand still near my armpit.

He let go once he'd walked me to the Bowery. "Listen," he said, "figure out where you're going first, Jack. How long you been doing this?"

"Not long," I said.

"Get it right before you barge in. People like their privacy —they don't want bill collectors coming around; it gives the building a bad name."

"I guess I'll try next door," I said.

"Jack," he said wearily, "go back and get the right fucking address."

"Well, as long as I'm down here, I can save myself a trip by—"

He shook his head sadly, like a veterinarian confronted with a horse he needs to shoot. "Jack, don't make everyone's life hard. Go get the right fucking address."

"Maybe I'll take the bus uptown and get the right address," I said.

"Now you're catching on," he said. He pointed to the bus stop. "Right over there."

I nodded, limped to the corner, and waited. In a minute a bus arrived and I climbed aboard, acting like a man for whom the step was the most serious obstacle in existence. I didn't look out the window to see whether he was still standing there, but he struck me as the type who would be.

I reached under my jacket and kneaded my armpit. The pain was sharp and mean, and, I guessed, would last a while. It was nearly four o'clock. I hoped the pain would be gone by dark, because once night came, I was going back to 126 Hester Street. The right fucking address.

27

Only a handful of people were on the Bowery when I went back downtown, and most of those weren't sober enough to see beyond the pints of wine in their hands. The sky was thick with clouds, which meant it would be hard to spot me once I reached the roof of 126 Hester; and the traffic was heavy, which meant the noise of the cars would cover me if I got clumsy.

I'd changed to old jeans, a hooded sweatshirt, a dark blue windbreaker, and a pair of sneakers I hadn't worn since I'd played handball at City College. In my pockets I had a small pad, a felt-tip pen, a Swiss army knife, a can of liquid wrench, a penlight, and a chamois rag. Around my waist I had five feet of nylon cord, and around my neck, under the sweatshirt, I had a loaded Minox C camera.

Instead of walking down the Bowery, I went a block east on Grand to Chrystie, and then south. I was looking for an alleyway that would bring me to the back of 126 Hester. There was no alleyway, which forced me to go through a building on Chrystie. I picked the oldest, dirtiest, smelliest one I could find—the poorer the building, the less likely I was to be challenged—walked into the vestibule and without pausing twisted the handle of the inside door. Praise heaven for cheap landlords: the lock was broken, and I passed smoothly into a long reeking hallway.

In a dozen strides, I reached the back door. It was fastened with a solid padlock, but the lock was mounted on the door with three puny screws. I squirted each screw with liquid wrench, counted to twenty, and removed the screws with my knife. To make sure the hinges didn't squeal, I squirted them with liquid wrench too; when I opened the door, it didn't make a sound.

In the courtyard, I closed my eyes for another count of twenty. When I opened them, I could see the silhouettes of five buildings around me. On the ground were a half-burned mattress, a cracked toilet bowl, a stack of old tires, and thousands of old newspapers. I couldn't see the rats, but I could hear their high-pitched squeaks and the scratching of their claws on the papers.

Moving a couple of steps at a time, I made my way around the court, checking the back door of each building for its number; 126 Hester was the fourth building I hit. The door was locked, and the fire escape was too high for me to reach.

I sidled back to the Chrystie Street building, let myself in, prayed everyone was either glued to his television set or making love and started up the stairs, two at a clip. Right after I passed the fourth floor, a door opened just below me. I stopped in mid-step and held the banister.

"Hey, come, on baby," a man's voice said. "Don't send me out there. A man ain't safe on the streets at night."

A woman giggled.

"I come all the way over here, I bring wine, I bring smoke, and here you is puttin' me out like I was a wet dog. What's the matter with you, woman?"

"It's late," the woman said, and giggled again.

"Late? What you talkin' about, woman?" His voice changed. "Have you got somebody you're expectin'? Is that the story? Somebody with better wine and better smoke? You can tell me, baby, I don't mind, I don't get jealous."

She giggled. There was the sound of a slap, a short cry.

"We got things to get straight," he said, and his voice

141

dropped to a murmur. My hand started to ache from holding the banister. Her voice murmured in return. Then silence. Then the sound of a door closing, the click of a lock sliding into its seat. When I heard no footsteps, I ran up the rest of the stairs.

On the roof I bent low, scurried along till I reached the first gap between buildings, and hauled myself to the adjacent roof. One-twenty-six Hester was the next building along but the space between roofs was too wide to be climbed; it had to be jumped. I cleared the space easily enough, but I landed with so heavy a thump I was sure everyone in the neighborhood had heard me.

I stayed crouched for a minute, listening for the sound of curious tenants. But the only sound was from a pigeon coop on the roof—a lulling combination of feathers brushing against the sides of the coop and the muted coos of the birds.

I crawled to the rear fire escape and lowered myself one rung at a time until my eyes were level with the top of the window. The room in front of me was nearly dark—only a glimmer of light shone through it—and I could barely make out shapes of furniture. Before scrunching myself against the rail of the fire escape to wait, I used my chamois to wipe clean a patch of the window and pulled the Minox from under my sweatshirt. Then I waited.

After a long, long time, my legs and back began to cramp. I shifted my weight and tried to tense and relax each muscle in turn. I wasn't any good at it—the cramps got so bad I was ready to scream. Forty is not the best age to do a stakeout on a fire escape.

A light blinked on in the room. After a beat, a man came into my line of sight. It was the one who'd thrown me out of the building.

He sat down in a large wicker chair, leaned back, and laughed. His jacket was off, and his tie had been loosened.

Under his right armpit was a shoulder holster; in it was what looked like a nine-millimeter Browning. He laughed again and said something I couldn't hear.

Into the room walked a slender man with carefully combed gray hair. His face was small but somehow very visible, like the face of a raccoon. There were lines around his mouth and eyes, but he looked more quizzical than sad, though I guessed he could look sad enough if the mood came upon him. In his hand was a half-filled glass of wine. He was wearing a forest-green smoking jacket. So I couldn't see whether there was a number tattooed on his arm.

I cocked the Minox and raised it, but he turned around to say something to somebody behind him. Whatever he said made the man with the Browning laugh, this time loudly enough for me to hear him through the closed window.

The gray-haired man had disappeared, so I pushed my face up against the glass to get a better angle. I still couldn't see him.

What I could see, flush against a wall, was a black spinet, a Winter, its wood polished like a mirror and its keys exposed, waiting to be touched.

I focused the Minox and took two pictures of the piano. The gray-haired man returned to the room, leaned over the *pistolero*, whispered in his ear, and clapped him on the shoulder. As they both laughed, I took a picture, then another; then, as the gray-haired man straightened up, another; then, as he turned toward the door, another; and as the man with the Browning rose and stood next to him, yet another.

I cocked, ready to shoot again, when what they were watching walked through the door.

She appeared no more than twenty, though it's hard to tell about Chinese women. She might have been forty, she might have been thirteen. Her shiny black hair fell almost to her thighs. Her mouth was wet with cardinal-red lip gloss, and her eyes were framed in a shade of blue-green I'd never come across. Around her neck was a long gold chain, and hanging at its lowest point was a green jade Buddha. Her hands, their nails the same overheated red as her lips, were cupped over her breasts. Around her hips and thighs she wore a fringed silk scarf, the same green as the Buddha.

She stood dead still in front of them. Her brown eyes looked past them, as if she were watching for a ship on the horizon. Her mouth was open perhaps a half inch, just enough to take shallow breaths. Nothing about her said that two men, less than five feet away, were staring at her the way a hungry tiger stares at a tethered lamb.

The man with the pistol leaned over and said something into the gray-haired man's ear. The gray-haired man nodded, smiled, and moved closer to the girl. I took a picture of the three of them; then, of him and the girl.

With his left hand, the gray-haired man uncupped the girl's right hand from her breast, and with his right hand he untied the fringed scarf and drew it from her thighs. She glanced down and dropped her other hand to her side. The gray-haired man stepped backward to see her better, and as he did, she opened her mouth another quarter inch and ran her tongue along her lower lip, first to the left, then to the right. She shook her hair and bent slightly at the knees so that her legs drifted apart.

The gray-haired man dropped to the floor, crawled to the girl, and buried his face in her crotch. The black of her hair formed a sharp border to the gray of his.

The man with the Browning gestured. The girl stretched her arms over her head, arched her back, and swung over gradually until her body formed a bridge, feet and palms on the floor. The man with the pistol waited till she was steady, strolled around to her head, unzipped his fly, and dropped to his knees.

I ran off six more pictures, put the Minox back under my sweatshirt, and started up the fire escape. My hands were wet with sweat and I was panting.

As I slithered along the roof, I noticed that the pigeons were quieter, and I wondered whether they grew quieter as it grew later.

Suddenly a light flashed in my eyes, and a young voice said, "Hey, man, what are you doing here?" I waved at the light, to have it turn away. But it didn't turn away, it came closer. "What are you doing here, man?" the voice said again.

"Turn it off," I said.

"Shit, no, man. I'm not gonna turn it off. What you doing on the roof, man? You tell me that."

The light was only three feet away, so I leaped from my crouch and grabbed for it. Instead I got hold of an arm, and the person attached to the arm wriggled and yelled. I tried to get my palm around his mouth but he was wriggling too hard, and by the time I dragged him down flat, I heard the roof door being opened.

"Who's there?" a voice said. I knew the voice.

The boy under me twisted and I pushed my forearm farther into his mouth.

"Who the fuck is up here?" the voice said. His shoes scraped along the tarred roof, then stopped. "Get the fuck out where I can see you, or I'll come find you and kick ass."

Again his footsteps scraped; again they stopped, and the only sound was the cooing of the pigeons.

Under me I could feel the boy's heart throbbing against my chest. I raised my body an inch to give him more room to breathe, and he sank his teeth into my arm. I stifled my cry but I couldn't stop my foot from jerking, and when it came down it thudded against the roof.

The footsteps started again, and I rolled off the boy and sprang behind the pigeon coop. The birds began to flutter their wings nervously and their cries become faster and shriller.

Through the mesh of the coop I could see the man with the Browning; he was leaning forward, turning his head slowly from left to right, like a pointer searching for a stray scent in a busy field. He took something from his pocket. An instant later, there was a snap, then a flame.

The flame cast enough light for me to see that his fly was still open. And enough light for him to see me behind the coop.

"Come out of there," he said. "Now."

I didn't move. He shut the lighter, took his pistol from its holster, jacked a shell into the chamber and pointed the barrel at the coop and me behind it.

"Hey, man," the boy said, and the man snapped his head around. Before I could move, he snapped it back. "Those are my birds," the boy said. "Don't point your goddam gun at my birds."

Without turning his head, the man said, "Kid, get the fuck out of here."

The boy's voice rose an octave, half fear, half rage. "Man, those are my birds."

"I don't give a shit what they are," the man said. "Get the fuck out of here."

The boy, torn, hesitated. Then he shoved his hand in his pants pocket and stepped toward the man. The man waited, twisted easily on the balls of his feet, and casually, almost peacefully, hit the boy across the face with the barrel of the Browning.

The boy screamed. I came from behind the coop and ran toward them. I was nearly there when the man brought the pistol back around, catching the boy on the other side of his face. Blood sprayed out of the boy's nose and mouth, splashing on the man's white shirt. The boy lifted his hands to his face; in the overcast night, the blood streaming through his fingers looked black, like motor oil.

The man raised the Browning to hit the boy a third time, and I slammed into him. As he tumbled down, I kicked at his kidney and tried to throw myself on top of him. He rolled sideways, as fast as an animal, and bumped into the boy.

The boy raised his leg so he could stomp the man, but before he could bring his foot down, the man jackknifed and—with both feet—kicked the boy in the belly. Careening backward, the boy crashed into the pigeon coop. His weight was too much for it, and the light wooden frame splintered, coming loose from the mesh.

Cooing frantically, the birds pushed their way through the torn coop, scattering in a dozen directions. Helplessly, the boy reached out and clutched at the flapping birds. But they were too scared to hold still, and he was too blinded by blood, and they eluded his clawing fingers.

The last pigeon forced its way through the tear and poised on top of the broken coop. The boy snatched at it, and it rose a foot in the air. He snatched at it again, and it rose again, moving a few feet away. He snatched again, this time catching one of the bird's feet between his thumb and fingers.

The bird pecked at the boy's hand, but the boy held on. The bird pecked again and pulled itself free. The boy, blood gushing from his ravaged face, jumped after it, his hands high in the air. The bird dodged; the boy jumped. Again he trapped a foot. Again the bird pecked and pulled free. Again the bird dodged, again the boy jumped.

But by then the pigeon was out over the courtyard, and the boy's jump carried him past the edge of the roof.

He didn't scream as he fell, and the crunch when he landed six floors below, could have been made by a large sack of garbage.

The pigeon hovered over the court. When it realized no

hand was reaching for it, it glided silently back to the coop, perched on it, and cooed quietly.

The man with the Browning was gone.

Below me I heard windows being pulled open. In English and Spanish, people asked each other what the noise had been. One person wanted to call the police. Another wanted no part of the police. One person wanted to go look. Another wanted to go back to sleep.

I jumped to the next roof, climbed to the next, and let myself into the hallway of the Chrystie Street building. There was blood on the sleeve of my windbreaker, so I took it off, rolled it into a ball and tucked it under my arm. The stairway was clear and I took the steps two at a time, not slowing down till I reached the street door.

On the way uptown, a sector car passed me going south. No roof lights, no siren, no hurry.

28

Cesar Concepcion—that was the boy's name—made page 48 of the *Daily News*. HS FRESHMAN KILLED IN FALL, the headline said.

Cesar Concepcion had been fourteen years old, lived with his mother and brother and three sisters, gone to Seward Park High School, worked Saturdays and Sundays at Pioneer Foods, and according to a neighbor, spent most of his spare time up on the roof with his pigeons. The article, which was maybe four inches long, said the police were investigating. It didn't say anything about an intruder, or about the smashed coop, or about Cesar Concepcion's blood all over the roof, or about Andrew Holt and his nine-millimeter Browning.

Carefully, I ripped the page from the *News*, folded it, and put it in my pocket. There'd been no photo with the article, so I still didn't know what Cesar Concepcion looked like—the light on the roof had been too dim for me to make out his features. That was appropriate enough since he'd been just an extra in the melodrama. He hadn't been a true character, like Sacha Cherkhov; he'd had no connection to Max Weill or Auschwitz or psychic phenomena. A disposable extra, that's all, who'd wandered into a scene and been disposed of.

I paid for my coffee, left the *News* on the luncheonette counter, and walked to the lab to see whether the pictures I'd taken had been printed. It was one of those abnormally clear days that grace the city about eight times a year, and the faces on the street came at me in sharp focus.

As I was coming to the corner of Sixth and Thirty-ninth, I saw ahead of me a large, rangy man in a lightweight tan suit. He was about to cross the avenue. I ran forward, yelling, "Holt!" and grabbed him by the shoulder with my left hand. My right hand was cocked, ready to drive his Adam's apple straight through to the back of his neck.

But it wasn't Holt. It was only a large stranger, dumbfounded because some New York crazy had grabbed him on Fifth Avenue in the middle of a clear May morning.

"Sorry," I mumbled. "Thought you were someone else."

I lowered my hands; he hugged his briefcase to his chest. He was struggling to control the fear in his eyes, but he wasn't having much luck. He was around thirty-seven, thirty-eight, and sinking into flab; he wore that look of borderline terror white middle-class men wear when an oddball confronts them in the street. To him, I was a menace—a beggar who wanted money, or a deranged disciple of a fringe Asian religion, or, worst of all, a mugger. These days, the newspapers and the TV announcers warned him, all the muggers were homicidal sadists—they robbed first and killed afterward, just for fun.

Once he caught on that I was white, and didn't have a knife or a gun in my hands, he stroked up his righteous indignation. "Watch what you're doing, asshole," he said loudly. "Keep your goddamn hands to yourself." Maybe he'd concluded I was a lust-maddened homosexual. He snarled, straightened his back, and marched across the street.

I walked the rest of the way with my eyes lowered. I didn't want to start another fight, and I suspected I was tense and angry enough to mistake any large man for Andrew Holt.

The pictures were ready. As I was paying the clerk, he leaned over the counter and said, "Far out. I mean, shit, that is some detail." He smirked. "I never knew you could get that kind of detail with a Minox."

For a second, I was puzzled; then I understood he was talking about the pictures of the Chinese girl. I winked. "Wait till tomorrow," I said. "That's when I bring in the ones with her mother and sister."

"I'll be here," he said.

In the Forty-sixth Street office, I locked the door and forced a chair under the knob. Slowly, I drew the prints from the envelope. The lab clerk was right: the detail was remarkable. Just as I had with my notes, I put sets of prints in separate envelopes and addressed them to all my safe drops. The negatives I addressed to Abe.

From the last set of prints I removed the pictures showing the girl and taped those to the underside of the top desk drawer. The others I replaced in the lab envelope.

There was a terrible stillness in the room, and I tried to banish it by smoking a cigarette, and then three more. But I couldn't banish it, because I knew the stillness wasn't in the room but in me. And I knew where it came from, and I knew I couldn't drive it away. I called Lilli Weill to tell her I would be over in twenty minutes.

29

The first picture I gave Lilli Weill was of Andrew Holt. She closed her eyes for a second, opened them, looked at the photo a second time, and said, "He is with Max when I see him." I gave her another picture of Holt. "He is a big man, no?" I nodded and passed her one more of him. "Yes, this is he."

We were sitting together on her couch. She'd made a pot of coffee, and this time had managed to buy croissants. She'd also bought a jar of black currant jam; how she knew I liked black currant jam was her secret.

I slipped out a picture of the gray-haired man and passed it to her.

She took it in both hands and held it a few inches above her lap. For a long time she stared at it. She said nothing and kept her head still. Then I heard an odd noise, a slow but steady plip, plip, plip, plip, and I couldn't figure out what it was till I glanced down and realized it was the sound of her tears falling one by one onto the photograph.

I passed her another picture, then the rest. When she finished looking at them, she squared them off and went through them again. She did that seven times.

Finally, she said, "He is well?"

"I guess," I said.

"He looks well," she said. "Age is not so bad on him. A fine-looking man, no?"

Her hands jerked up, the pictures slid from her lap on to the carpet, and before I could stoop to pick them up, she threw her arms around my neck and buried her head in my chest.

In a few seconds, her tears soaked my jacket and shirt and seeped through to my skin. She cried for a long time, at first quietly, matter-of-factly, then loudly, until she was no longer sobbing or weeping but instead keening and wailing.

The sound was something I'd never heard, and it came from a place I'd never been. It wasn't grief—I'd heard grief; and it wasn't relief—I'd heard relief. There was a lifetime of longing in the sound, a lament for all the meals not eaten together, all the nights not huddled together, all the shared ecstasies and shared miseries that had been stolen from her.

As the sound spewed out of her, I found myself holding her as tightly as she was holding me.

One night, near the end of my marriage, during one of our more lacerating fights, she'd said, Don't smear it all with mud, Kevin; just because it's bad now, don't poison the whole thing, don't steal our past from us. And I tried not to, but I didn't really know what she was talking about—at that moment, that night, to me it was all mud, a scum that covered us both—and I didn't think there was anything in our past, our roller-coaster conjugal past, that was worth protecting.

To me, as I'd once shouted at my walls, the enemy was memory. But as Lilli Weill wept on my chest, I wasn't so sure. I began to think that if having memories of life with somebody could drive you crazy, having them stolen from you could leave you so empty that going crazy might be a blessing.

When she stopped, she pulled her head back and wiped her

face with a paper napkin. Her eyes were so swollen they were nearly shut. "I must see him," she said. "It is possible, no?"

I had no idea whether it was possible.

"You'll see him," I said, and helped her to the bathroom so she could dab cool water on her face.

30

From Lilli's apartment, I went to 126 Hester Street.

I expected nothing, and that's what I got.

A storekeeper told me that a truck had arrived at seven in the morning and three moving men had cleaned out apartment 6R in less than an hour. The truck had no company name, no phone number stenciled on it. The men, the storekeeper told me, looked like moving men: big, stupid, and sweaty. The tenants of 6R hadn't been around for the move.

I got nothing at the post office, either. Nobody from 126 Hester had left a forwarding address. I tried the phone company and Con Edison. Mr. Holt had closed his account and not begun a new one. Thank you.

I stepped out of the phone booth and started walking north on the Bowery. I wanted badly to do something, but I didn't know what. I had found him, I had lost him, and I had to find him again because of a flash promise I'd made to a wailing old lady. I tried to think of something, anything, but my mind wouldn't go along; it went on strike, and no amount of goading or coaxing or begging would make it go back to work.

So I went home; everyone's entitled to a day off. A few minutes after I got in, the doorbell rang. A delivery boy climbed the stairs and handed me a wrapped bouquet and a receipt. I signed the receipt, gave him a dollar, and tore the flimsy pink paper from the flowers.

A half-dozen white roses and a half-dozen yellow. The card read, "I thank the remarkable Mr. Fitzgerald. Love, Lilli."

31

In the evening Fiona Shaw came over.

By the time she arrived, I wasn't sober, and when I tried to tell her what happened I kept garbling the events of the story. She listened eagerly for a while, then put her fingertips on my mouth and shook her head. "Tell me later," she said.

Very slowly, and very tentatively, as if we were crawling across a minefield, we kissed and undressed. Then, like two children exploring each other for the first time, we sat on the carpet and looked at one another's bodies, counting freckles and discovering birthmarks and noticing the way hairs grew. She leaned toward me and touched my chest with her nose; sniffing delicately, she moved her head across my chest, up to my neck, along my shoulder, to my armpit, and down the inside of my arm to my palm. When she began another circuit, I started to do the same to her, and by the time I had made it past her thigh to the bend of her knee, I was able to isolate each private smell of each part of her body. We resembled two puppies in a meadow, burying our noses in each other's flesh and, like dogs, learning each other's biographies from the scents.

We didn't speak and, once we started to kiss, our mouths were too full to speak. There seemed to be no other sounds—

no cars droning by, no neighbors' radios, no parakeets chirping, no footfalls in the hallway. We were as alone as two people could get in New York, and it should have been wonderful.

But it wasn't. Partly it wasn't because of what had happened to me earlier in the day. And partly it wasn't because we *were* two people in New York, in 1984; two people of a certain age and living in a certain age. Both of us knew too much, had been through too many other people, and tried too many positions and flirted with too many perversions, so that all our attempts to play at being fresh and unspoiled were tainted with so much savvy that we could barely remember how to play. We were prisoners of our dexterity and practice, and, like the pianists Norman Azenberg told me about, we could play the notes, but we couldn't make music.

I pulled away.

"What's the matter?" she said.

"I don't know," said. "Maybe I'm too drunk. Maybe I'm too upset."

"Don't you want me?"

"That's not it," I said, and it wasn't.

I lit a cigarette and watched her. She looked afraid. "I don't want to leave," she said.

"I don't want you to."

"I was really glad you asked me to come over," she said. "You don't ask often."

"I'll mend my ways," I said, meaning it. I reached out and stroked her neck. "Have you ever loved anyone, Fiona?"

She stared at me. "Have I ever loved anyone? What is that supposed to mean?"

"I'm not sure," I said. "When I showed Lilli the pictures of her husband, she—"

"What?" Her face had turned white.

"When I showed Lilli—"

Her arm moved like a snake, and her fingers seized my tricep. "He's alive?" She shook my arm, hard. "Max Weill is alive?"

"I told you before—"

"You did *not* tell me before. I couldn't understand a goddamn word you said before." She took a deep breath. "You're sure he's alive?"

"Yes, I'm sure."

"Oh, Kev." She wrapped herself around me and began to kiss my face over and over. "Oh, Kev." She tilted her head back. "Tell me everything. Where is he?"

"I don't know. The last—"

"I don't understand. If he's alive and you showed Lilli his pictures, how can you not know where he is?"

"The last time I saw him—listen, the details don't matter. Right now, he's gone."

"Gone!" She bounced to her feet. "Gone! Gone where?"

"I don't know, but—"

"Well, did you look? How can you find him and take his picture and then let him get away like that? What's the matter with you?"

She was standing over me with her legs apart, so each time I glanced up I looked straight into her crotch.

"Kev, will you please stop staring at my pussy and tell me about Max Weill."

I caught her by the hand, pulled her back on the carpet, and held her. "I don't know where he is, but I'm going to find out. Now will you calm down?"

She let herself go limp and rested on me. "I'm sorry for shouting," she said. "What's he like?"

"I don't know," I said. "I didn't meet him."

"How did you find him?"

"Most of it's pretty dull," I said, "and the rest of it doesn't make much sense."

"I don't care," she said. "I want to know."

I gave her a condensed version and tireless reporter that she was, she began asking questions. "But what has the CIA got to do with it?"

"I don't know."

"Who's Holt?"

"I don't know."

"Do you think he's with the CIA?"

"I don't know."

"Well, if he's with the CIA, maybe Max is with the CIA, too. What do you think?"

"I don't know."

"Oh, Kev!" She pouted. But it wasn't serious; her eyes were bright with excitement and delight, like a child who's just found out where her mother hides her change.

"I thought Lilli wasn't a story to you," I said.

She grinned crookedly. "I never said that. I said she's important to me. I also said it could be a great story. It *is* a great story, Kev—love and death and the present reaching back to the past, and the past reaching forward to the present. Shit, it's got everything."

Sarcastically, I said, "Don't forget the music."

She was too giddy to hear my tone. "Right, right, the music. Kev, let me work with you; let me talk to some people."

"No."

"Kev, I know people who cover this kind of stuff. Let me—"

"No."

"All right," she snapped. "You talk to them."

"No. Fiona, it's her life. It's not material."

She flared up. "Don't condescend to me, Kev. That's what I do, and it's sure as shit no worse than what you do. I wouldn't be hurting Lilli Weill if I told her story."

"And you wouldn't be helping her, either."

157

"Kev," she said, "I don't understand this whole attitude. We do exactly the same thing: we snoop around peoples' lives for our benefit, or for the benefit of the customers who pay us, and we use what we know. You use it your way; I use it mine. Are you trying to tell me that you don't do as much damage as me? When you go after somebody and dig up all the dirt about them so your client can come out ahead, are you trying to say you don't do damage? I know some of the cases you've worked; don't kid me."

"Lilli Weill—" I began.

"Lilli Weill is just as important to me as she is to you, Kev. You don't need to protect her from me." She touched my chest. "But I'm glad you care enough about her to protect her." She gently traced an F on my chest with her thumbnail. "Let's not talk about the story now; I don't want to fight with you tonight."

"Doubled."

"I'm pleased you found him, and I'm sure Lilli is, and I'm pleased you think you can find him again. Case closed." She kissed me on the earlobe. "You were talking about love."

I didn't say anything.

She pulled away to look at my face. "Don't close up on me, Kev. Talk to me." She kissed me on the earlobe again. "Come on, Kev, talk to me."

"Another time."

"Kev, don't be afraid of a little intimacy. It won't kill you." She laughed. "Or if it will, it's a grand way to go. Talk to me."

"I've never seen anything like what I saw today," I said. "She's waited all her life for him, and I don't get that. To me—" I stopped.

"Go on," she demanded.

"To me, it was always a contract. I love you, and I behave a certain way. You love me, and you behave a certain way.

Because I love you, I give you a little more rope than I might give somebody else, and you do the same for me. But there are always limits."

"What kind of limits?" she said.

"I had a dog once. Great dog. I loved him, but whenever I left the house, even for ten minutes, he chewed things up. Every day. One day, he chewed up five thousand dollars' worth of cameras and lenses, so I gave him to some friends of mine in Putnam County. That was his limit."

"You loved the cameras more than you loved him," she said.

"Fine, put it like that," I said. "I know what you're thinking. I should have just put up with it. I should let people be the way they are and not expect them to behave a certain way. It was the dog's way to chew things up, that's what lonesome dogs do, and I should have accepted that. Okay, I didn't love him enough to accept him as he was. I guess I'm one of those people who can only love other people so long as they're behaving a certain way. And maybe that's not love. Maybe that's something else, a business arrangement, a deal, I don't know."

"But you don't like it anymore?"

"No, I don't like it anymore," I said. "How the fuck do you think I felt when I sat in her apartment and held her while she cried for Max Weill? How the fuck do you think I felt when I looked at her, hanging on to a goddamn phantom for forty years, forty goddamn years of loving a phantom, while I ditch dogs I love and wives I love and friends I love and wind up with one safe contract after the other. No, I don't like it anymore."

"Well, well, well, well," she said.

"What the fuck is . . . well, well, well, well . . . ?"

"Are you turning into a romantic at age forty?" she said.

"I'm turning into a schmuck. Listen, I don't know what

I'm talking about. Nothing seems to work. Her way is crazy. My way is deadly. The other way, the way of my parents, where they spent their whole lives trying to reform each other, is the worst of all. Why do we bother? It's all goddamn crap; we learn it from bad movies and worse books. We sing about love, and we dream about love, and we argue about love, but we spend most of our time *doing* something else. Take any week of your life, from the time you can remember, and tell me how many hours of it were devoted to love. Any kind of love. Seven hours. Fourteen. Twenty-one. You've got more than a hundred waking hours in a week, even if you're a big sleeper."

She reached out and gently pulled my earlobe. "My father did that when he wanted me to listen closely." She smiled innocently; it took around twenty years off her age. "When I was little, I believed that if somebody loved you, really and truly loved you, cross your heart and hope to die loved you, you would never do anything bad. You wouldn't lie, you wouldn't cheat, you wouldn't ever hide your eyes. Did you ever believe that?"

"No. I don't think so."

"Kev, do you trust anyone?"

"Not really."

"Do you ever wish you trusted anyone—me?"

For a long time I didn't answer, maybe because I didn't know the answer, or maybe because I didn't trust her enough to tell her. I cheated, by asking her, "Do you ever wish that?"

"Christ, yes, Kev. I wish I trusted you—God, I wish I trusted *me*." She tugged my earlobe again. "I trust what I feel for you." She grinned, but I could see the fear behind it. "Do you trust what you feel for me?" Before I could open my mouth, she put her finger on my lips. "Truth, Kev. Do you trust what you feel for me?"

"Truth?" I said. She nodded. "I don't know. Truth."

She put her arms around my neck and pulled me closer. "Well," she whispered, "here I am, and there you are, two naked people connected by distrust. Okay. You give what you can and let me give what I can."

"And what can you give?"

She hesitated. "The usual."

"And what's the usual?"

She chuckled obscenely. "A little lust. A little warmth. A little terror, leading to a little dishonesty, leading to the usual little betrayal."

I licked her fingertips. "Can we start with the lust?"

She leaned forward, opening her mouth. Abruptly, she pulled back. "No," she said.

"No?"

"Don't fuck me, Kev. Make love to me."

I did. And later, again. And when I got tired, she made love to me. And again. Then I to her.

And finally, after going back and forth and using all the tricks each of us had learned, we found a tiny crevice in the wall of our distrust, and we crawled through it and made love to each other.

Not gracefully, not tenderly, and, until the last few minutes, not even passionately. We were too tired for grace and tenderness, so tired that the only thing left was nakedness. And so we made love nakedly, which meant, maybe, that we made love truthfully, not lying with our words or our bodies or even our eyes. And when the passion came, just before daybreak, it was so naked and so truthful that for a moment, before we passed out in fear of it, we melted and fused.

32

They had done a good and thorough job on my office, going through the desk, the filing cabinets, the closet, the undersides of the chairs, and the backs of the old framed prints on the walls. Pros that they must have been, they had put everything back in place just carelessly enough so I would know that they'd been there.

It occurred to me that they might hit my apartment next, but there was nothing there for them, either, so I stopped worrying about it.

Somebody knocked at the outer door. I pushed the buzzer, waited till I heard the door close, started the tape recorder and stood up. "This way," I yelled.

A short, stubby man—he looked like a knockwurst—bounced into the office on the balls of his feet. As he approached the desk, he waved with his left hand and held out his right, the sort of double greeting I associate with politicians at subway stops.

"Hi, there," he said, as though he'd been waiting all his life to meet me. "I'm Jeff Rydell."

I shook his hand. "This is a bad time for me, Mr. Rydell. I'm just on my way out."

"Sorry, sorry, sorry," he said. "I'm a friend of Fiona Shaw—she said you could use some help with a case." He caught my frown. "I got the impression from her that it was okay with you—isn't it?"

"Well . . ."

He laughed pleasantly. "When Fiona wants to do a favor, nothing stops her. Listen, you can say no. I won't be hurt."

I thought about it for a second, and practicality won. "How much has she told you?"

"Not much. An old woman is looking for her husband, and somehow the CIA is mixed up in it."

"Why does she think you can help me?"

He took a card from a brass case and slid it across the desk. It read: *Trans-Globe Report,* Jefferson Rydell, Publisher. "I put out a sort of international tip sheet—business, politics, economics. Inside information for big-time traders. I get to chat it up with spooks once in a while. They're good sources, some of them."

I nodded, and we went to a luncheonette on Sixth Avenue and settled into a booth. Rydell had an open, friendly face, with bright pink cheeks and round blue eyes that gleamed constantly behind contact lenses. He had a way of tilting his head that made him resemble a curious terrier. He didn't look like somebody who published a tip sheet for big-time traders. In his lumpy seersucker suit, his black Oxfords, his white cotton socks, his multifunction digital watch, he looked like a sales manager for a fertilizer company. The only discordant note was his body, which instead of being flaccid was agile and hard.

He stirred his tea and watched me, waiting. Not pressing, simply waiting. After I'd lit a cigarette, he said easily, "Maybe you better begin at the beginning . . ."

I told him enough so he would get the drift. He listened attentively, nodding every so often but not making a big thing of it. "What do you think?" I asked.

He waited till the waitress brought him more boiling water, refilled his cup, leaned back, and smiled in contentment. "The only thing that sounds wrong is that Weill was a prisoner. At the end of the war, all the Western intelligence services—especially the Americans—hired Nazis to work for them. Why let all that talent go to waste? I've never heard of them hiring a prisoner."

"Why not?"

"Two reasons. First, the Nazis they hired were professionals. Second, the spook trade is about access. A man like Weill—who would he have access to?"

"Who did the Nazis have access to?" I said.

"All sorts of people. Politicians, judges, generals, you name it. You have to remember, all those people grew up together. No matter what direction they took politically after the war, there were very old bonds. So—"

"Wait, wait, wait!" I said. "Can I try something on you?"

"Sure, Mr. Fitzgerald. But sit down first."

"In Auschwitz, Max Weill makes friends with a bunch of people. From what I hear, everybody loves him. After the war, some of these people go home—to Poland, to Russia, to the East. Some of these people go to work for their Communist governments.

"Now you said the Americans hired people. Okay, imagine this: at the end of the war, an American intelligence officer is interrogating Max Weill, and he finds out that this skinny little pianist is the bosom buddy of all kinds of people who have gone back East. Now if you're that intelligence officer, wouldn't you gamble and put Max Weill to work?"

Rydell thought it over. "Perhaps. Sounds like a pretty low yield potential."

"Ah, ah," I said. "It's a long shot, but what happens if one day one of those bosom buddies becomes a big shot? Even if it takes years, who cares, with a payoff that high."

"Mr. Fitzgerald, friendship isn't access."

I almost yelled. "You're dead wrong. You know why this bosom buddy will spill his guts to Max Weill? Because they went through hell together, because they love each other, because their connection in Auschwitz is more important than anything in their lives."

Rydell patted my arm sympathetically; he reminded me of my math teacher explaining that I'd just gotten a 58 on the midterm exam. "Mr. Fitzgerald, you've got a perfect thirteenth-century mind. Everything about your argument is correct except its premise. I don't know why the CIA is interested in Max Weill, but—"

I interrupted. "Listen, don't you see how beautiful it is? You know what cops do when they want to cultivate a snitch? They make friends with him. The snitch calls one cop, and only one cop. Now if that cop retires, he can sometimes turn the snitch over to another cop. But not always. Think of Max Weill as a cop with a great snitch, or a couple of great snitches. And these snitches will *only* talk to him. They can't be turned over to anybody else, because it's too late to make friends with them. Their connection with Weill is more than forty goddamn years old!" By then I was so excited I was pounding the table. I pulled myself down. "Sorry," I said. "Without him, zip." I turned my palms up.

Indulgently, he said, "Assuming any of this is true, why here—why not over there?"

"I don't know. But . . . but . . . look, maybe after all this time, there's only a couple of useful buddies; maybe he follows them from town to town—Paris, Warsaw, London, Budapest, Washington. I mean, Max can't just sit around while they move on. Whither they goest, he goes, or something like that."

"All right, Mr. Fitzgerald, grant that. But New York makes no sense at all."

"That's not true," I argued. "Every Eastern European country has a mission at the UN. Weill could have buddies all over the place." I felt a rush and said, "Did you ever come across a guy named Leo Hirsch?"

"Leo Hirsch?" he said, sounding astonished. "Leo Hirsch—at the East German Mission?" I nodded, and he laughed even harder than earlier. "Poor Leo," he said. He shook his head in amusement. "I don't think Leo is your man. Everybody in my business knows Leo. We think the Germans sent him because this is where he'd do the least damage."

Disappointed and irritated, I said, "He was a friend, and he's here."

"Leo's a penny-ante trade attaché—a glorified paper pusher. He's not much use to me—he certainly wouldn't be useful to the CIA." He patted my sleeve. "Keep in mind, this is my racket."

Stubbornly, I said, "It's worth looking into."

"Sure," he said, "sure. But if I were you, and you truly believed your theory, I'd try to find some of the others. Try immigrant organizations, the musicians' union, Holocaust scholars, reporters who cover the UN, reporters who cover the diplomatic corps in Washington, Hadassah, B'nai B'rith, hotels in the Catskills, hotels in Miami, retirement villages, the Workmen's Circle; put a classified ad in *Variety*, in the Local 802 paper, in any music publication you can find—there are a lot of Jewish survivors in America."

I smiled. "You'd do pretty good at my work."

He smiled back. "I'm in the information business."

I paid the check, and we went out to Sixth Avenue. The air had become moist and heavy, and while I fished out one of my business cards for him, we both began to leak sweat. Rydell studied my card diligently, as if he expected to find a cosmic secret on it. When he raised his head, he said sympathetically, "You have no idea where he is?"

"Lilli says he's in enemy territory. 'A missing person in enemy territory' is the way she puts it." I chuckled. "She says he's among the goyim."

"The goyim?"

"To Lilli, the enemy are always the goyim."

"You're worried for him, aren't you?"

"Uhuh." I flashed on Cesar Concepcion and Sacha. "I'm afraid they'll kill him if they think I know he's alive."

"No, no, Mr. Fitzgerald. If he's as valuable as you believe, they'd simply hide him better. If."

"You think I'm full of shit, don't you?"

He nodded ruefully. "You're extrapolating backwards. You don't *know* the Americans got to him in forty-five, you don't *know* he agreed to work for them, you don't *know* he stayed close to his friends; all you know is that right now he's living anonymously in New York, apparently a willing captive of the CIA."

"What's your theory?"

"I don't have enough information to construct one. Offhand I'd say the agency is temporarily using him for a low-level operation and once it's finished, he'll surface."

"No," I said emphatically. "He's been underground for nearly forty years. No, it's not low level. The stakes are high. I can smell it."

He shrugged and slipped my card in his breast pocket. "You're a man with a mission, Mr. Fitzgerald. Good luck." A drop of rain splashed on his suit, and he reached for my hand.

"Thanks for the help," I said.

"For a friend of Fiona's, anytime."

He started to withdraw his hand, but I held on to it.

"Just like that, huh?"

"Fiona is a friend of mine, and when she asks me to do a favor . . ." He glanced down at our clasped hands and nodded slowly. "Yes, Miss Shaw and I . . . did indeed once have a . . . relationship." He pulled his hand free. "Of course, we're just friends now."

"Of course."

He grinned, turned north, and bounced away.

As I watched him disappear among the pedestrians, I tried to imagine the chemistry between him and Fiona Shaw. Both her husbands had been tall, careless types, while Rydell was short and careful. He had the moves of a good mechanic; he put things down so he could retrieve them without looking for them. His mind worked the same way, which struck me as odd in a man who wore seersucker and white cotton socks.

The sky was so dark it was as if night were falling, but the rain refused to drop. Far to the west there was a pale wedge in the overcast, like a white necktie on a gray shirt. I needed to move, but I didn't know where to go. For a few minutes I stood under the heavy sky and tried to think of what I'd do and where I'd go if I were holding Max Weill. I replayed the scene I'd watched in apartment 6R, Weill and Holt and the Chinese girl, and tried to make sense of how they all fit together.

A thousand possibilities occurred to me, but no one made any more sense than any other. It certainly wasn't rational to believe that Max Weill was anywhere where I could find him; it was rational to believe he was far away, underground and invisible; a missing person in enemy territory.

A drop of rain fell on my shoulder; then another. As I moved to the curb to hail a taxi, thunder rolled across the sky. I glanced up. The sky was almost black, but the wedge in the west had grown bigger and whiter. I knew exactly what to do—Rydell's advice was on the money—but my feeling that time was running out kept pressing harder and harder. I didn't want to be the surgeon who performed the perfect operation while the patient died. I needed a shortcut, any shortcut.

The only one available was Leo Hirsch, so I swung south and loped through the drizzle to the mission.

33

Behind his antique desk, in his spacious office, Leo Hirsch looked like the last of a line of Prussian bankers rather than the mournful victim of Auschwitz I'd bearded at the UN. His face was composed, his hands rested quietly on his empty desk top and his light brown eyes stayed evenly focused on me.

"I must apologize for walking off so rudely," he said, "but what you told me stupefied me. Will you accept my apology?" I nodded. "Thank you. You are very kind. Please, tell me how I may assist you." He said the words as though he repeated them a thousand times a day, and maybe, in his line of work, he did.

"I'm looking for any other survivors from the orchestra—epecially if they're here in New York. But I'll take them anywhere."

"Wouldn't we all?" he said softly. He turned over his hands in a gesture of emptiness. "I know nobody. You must understand, we do not hold reunions. We are not the graduating class of an American high school."

"So Sacha was the only—"

He lifted a finger to stop me. "Not even him. When I saw the obituary notice, I went to the funeral. I hadn't seen him since the war. His was the fifth funeral. One in East Berlin, one in West Berlin, one in London, one in Washington, and Sacha."

"Just by reading the obituaries?"

He smiled faintly. "Does it strike you as ghoulish, Mr. Fitzgerald? Some of us who were there look for the people we knew; others religiously skip past that page in the newspaper. Just as some retain the number"—he stretched his arm so that his wrist extended past his shirt-sleeve—"others remove it. There is no reason to judge either group."

"You never ran into *anybody*?"

"Of course. But so what? You go to school somewhere for four years, or you serve in the army, and ten or fifteen or twenty years later, you run into a person. He is older now, and plump. His bones do not protrude through his skin. Fine clothes cover him instead of rags. He does not stink. His eyes are not those of a trapped animal. 'Hello, how are you?' 'I'm well, and you?' 'Also well.' 'We must have a drink, or a lunch.' 'Certainly, here is my card.' The drink is never drunk, the lunch is never eaten. Usually, as we meet, we must remind each other—woodwind, brass, strings. Usually, the names do not leap to the tongue." He drew a line across the desk top with his thumbnail. "What will we chat about— the jolly times playing Wagner and Beethoven? The night the French horn player went flat on the coda? The joyous hours of rehearsal to achieve the ultimate harmony? It was not a *summer* camp, Mr. Fitzgerald. The memories are not for noisy jokes over a stein of beer."

"Do you remember any names, and where they were from originally?"

He wrinkled his forehead. "I could try to make a list. It would not be easy."

"It would help."

"If it would help, I will try."

He opened a desk drawer and took out a small gold lighter. From his inside pocket he drew a slender cigar and lit it. He inhaled quietly, as if he were afraid someone might overhear. To change the mood, which was the same as in an undertaker's reception room, I said, "Do you still play?"

He chuckled. "Sundays. A few of us—some are even, believe it or not, from NATO countries—gather and play for a few hours. By us, I mean members of the diplomatic community. You must understand that I was never, truly, a professional. I was not"—he showed his teeth in a funereal smile —"fit for the orchestra. Fortunately, I had a protector—Max, of course."

"So it wasn't like losing a career?"

"No, not at all. Before the war, I was a student and a zealot. A good Marxist, but a bad German. After the war, I became a bureaucrat—what Westerners like to call a faceless bureaucrat. It is quiet work, but these days I am a quiet man. An ex-zealot. I did not play for years. Now, it is relaxation. I play, I buy records, I attend recitals, I no longer cower when I hear Mozart. I have become, shall we say, recivilized."

I enjoyed the joke, and I smiled. He joined me. "I would appreciate that list," I said.

"I understand; and naturally you would appreciate it even more if you received it quickly." I nodded. He looked past me for an instant. "Mr. Fitzgerald, I don't know Mrs. Weill, but—I'm certain she is a fine, fine woman—but—"

"You believe I'm wasting my time and her money?"

"Yes. I do."

"You may be right," I said, "but I promised her I'd look."

His tone hardened. "Mr. Fitzgerald, you hide behind the morality of a promise, but I believe that what pushes you onward is greed. As long as you go back to Lilli Weill and offer her even the most ephemeral of hints, she will pay you. It is not morality to steal from old ladies."

For a second I was so angry I was ready to tell him I'd seen Weill. Instead, I took my time about lighting a cigarette and pinching out the match and dropping it into the ashtray in front of him. "I see why you'd think that," I said finally. "But it's not the case."

"No? All right, Mr. Fitzgerald, I will take what you say at

face value. You are an honest detective with an honest—if impossible—mission. You have come to me for help. Weill is a friend, and I am honor bound to help you." He stood up, dismissing me. "I will prepare a list, and it will be here"—he glanced at his watch—"at noon tomorrow. Will that do?"

I tried to ease the tension. Smiling, I said, "Not tonight?"

"I am attending a concert. Otherwise, you would have it tonight. Noon, tomorrow. Will you call, or will you send a messenger?"

"I'll call."

Outside, I walked across the street and turned back to look at the mission. I should have felt content—I'd more or less gotten what I'd come for—but I felt frustrated. Something had happened in his office that had knotted up my muscles, and it wasn't simply anger. I started walking slowly to the corner and in my mind replayed the conversation. Nothing seemed out of place: he had been polite, sympathetic, intelligent, even humorous in a mordant way, and his accusation—from his point of view—was fair enough. I replayed it again, trying to catch undertones or overtones, listening for pauses, hints, inflections, watching for shadows across his face. It all fit, and because it fit, I felt more frustrated than ever. There had to be a wrong note, I felt it. But I couldn't hear the damn thing.

I was so busy brooding I crossed against the light. I heard, a horn, then a scream of brakes, then a cabdriver yelling:

"You dumb fucker! Get off the fuckin' street! Why don't you go where you can't do any fuckin' harm!"

He roared past me as I leaped on to the sidewalk. As I landed, I remembered Rydell's description of Hirsch, and I realized that was what didn't fit. Leo Hirsch was not Poor Leo. Leo Hirsch was not an incompetent. Leo Hirsch was not sent here because he wouldn't do any harm.

I ran to Madison Avenue, found a newsstand, and bought a *Times*. My hands were shaking as I scrambled through the pages to find the entertainment section. There were five concerts listed for the evening. I saw a phone booth across the street, ran into it, and called Azenberg. Before his secretary could do her routine, I said, "Tell him it's Fitzgerald and tell him it's an emergency."

He came on. "Emergency? What kind of emergency?"

"Listen," I said, "there are five concerts tonight in the city?"

"I know," he said, "I booked—"

"Norman, will you please listen." He was quiet. "Can you find out for me which one Leo Hirsch is going to—don't interrupt, Norman. I'm betting he's got a subscription. I need the seat location."

"The seat location? You don't ask much, do you?"

"How long will you need?"

"Call me in fifteen minutes."

I spent the next fourteen minutes in a bar on Madison, trying to concentrate on the chatter of the bartender, who was explaining why his daughter turned lesbian. The fourteen minutes took even longer than the last fourteen minutes of a school day when I was in the sixth grade.

Azenberg's secretary put me right through. "This is worth more than a lunch," he said. "This is definitely a dinner. Lutece, I think. Are you ready?"

I held my pen over my pad. "Go ahead."

"Carnegie Hall, dress circle."

"Carnegie Hall, dress circle."

"Third row, six and eight."

"Third row, six and eight," I repeated. "Are those on the aisle?"

He laughed. "You don't go to Carnegie often, do you? One and two are aisle seats. Oh, you were right—subscription. He's got a good show tonight—Youri Egorov. A great Russian pianist—one of mine, naturally. Okay?"

"Perfect," I said. "Lutece."

It only took me ten minutes to run over to Carnegie Hall, only another three minutes to scan the seating plan and count seven rows in the dress circle, and only another five minutes to find a digger and pay him seventy-five dollars for a balcony seat with an unobstructed view. The poor bastard couldn't understand why, when I gave him the money, I was laughing.

34

Carnegie Hall seats around twenty-eight hundred people, and that night, for Egorov, who was the hot ticket then, all the seats were filled.

I was up in the balcony, way over to the side. Though I couldn't see much of the stage, I had no trouble—using the binoculars I'd brought—seeing Leo Hirsch.

He was in seat eight of the third row. In seat six was Max Weill. Two rows behind them, in the aisle seat, was Andrew Holt. They'd arrived nearly as early as I had, which had given me plenty of time to memorize what their shoes looked like.

Before I'd taken my seat, I'd sought out the dress circle men's room; sure enough, it wasn't far from where they all sat. I'd found the stairway closest to it, and I knew I could run down the steps and beat them into the room. The only question was when one of them would need to piss.

The lights dimmed, the recital began, and I tried to lose myself in the music—he was a hell of a pianist—but it was hopeless. Whenever I leaned back, the Beretta I'd stuck in my waistband nudged my spine; and that made me lean forward and swing my binoculars around to check the dress circle.

Weill and Hirsch looked as if they'd been transported to heaven; Holt looked as if he'd just swallowed a cup of rancid oil.

When the crowd applauded the last number before the first intermission, I scrambled from my seat, ran down the stairway, and locked myself in the last stall of the dress circle men's room. After a half minute, I heard the taps of heels and murmur of voices, and I bent low to watch the shoes. The room filled up quickly, making me anxious, so I stood on the toilet seat and checked the faces.

Neither Weill nor Holt nor Hirsch was there.

The second part of the concert was more intense than the first part, and as wired as I was, I got so swept up in what Egorov was doing that I almost stayed in my seat to applaud when he was finished. By the time I reached the men's room, a couple of guys were already there, but the stalls were all empty, and I parked myself again. The room took longer than before to fill up, I guess because Egorov was taking a few curtain calls, and the waiting was giving me a headache.

Men pissed and flushed, pissed and flushed, and then it was down to a handful of stragglers. There'd been no sign of the shoes I was watching for, so I stood on the seat again. My eyes were coming level with the top of the booth door when Holt walked in.

I ducked and eased my feet to the floor. Another pair of shoes sounded on the tile and I bent double to look at them. The shoes belonged to Max Weill, and they headed over to a urinal. Holt's shoes headed for the stall next to mine. There was no sign of Hirsch.

The instant Holt shut his door, I flushed the toilet, opened my door, went to the urinal next to Weill, and fiddled with my zipper. He was just finishing, shaking himself dry so he wouldn't drip in his pants, and he didn't look my way.

175

I slid my right hand under my jacket, took out the Beretta, and brought it around so that the barrel was pointing straight into Weill's mouth. I touched my left forefinger to my lips. Weill shut his eyes, opened them slowly, shook his head, and smiled the saddest smile I'd ever seen.

From Holt's stall came a grunt, then another, the music of a constipated man trying to force a shit out. I pointed at the exit door, then at the stall, to let Weill know we'd be moving on Holt's next grunt. Weill nodded and waved at his crotch: his fly was still open, and his pecker, looking like an old wrinkled sausage, hung down his thigh. I nodded, and he zipped up.

No noise came from the stall, so we stood there, frozen, Weill with his hand on his zipper, me with the Beretta pointed at his mouth. He looked resigned more than frightened, breathing quietly and blinking normally, with no extra bubbles of sweat beading on his forehead or oozing down his neck. I was doing all the sweating—my shirt was pasted to my chest, and my armpits felt completely waterlogged.

Holt took a deep breath and Weill and I tensed. A half second later, Holt began to grunt. Weill moved toward the exit, with me right on his heels, and we went through the doorway just as Holt grunted one loud last time and then sighed in relief.

In the corridor, I pushed Weill toward the stairway, not letting him pause or turn his head. I did the same on the stairs, forcing him to trot down so fast he nearly fell. On the last step, I caught him by the arm and said, "We're going through the lobby, on to Fifty-seventh Street; then we make a left at the corner and go south on Seventh Avenue. Do you get that?" He nodded. I put the Beretta away and gave him a quick push.

He did exactly as I'd told him and we made it around the corner to the avenue in less than thirty seconds. There was an empty cab waiting for a light to change at the corner of Fifty-sixth, and I ran for it, dragging Weill behind me. I yanked open the door, shoved Weill on to the seat, climbed in beside him, and told the driver, "Make a left here, go over to Fifth, and head south to Forty-second and then east to Grand Central."

"It's quicker if I—" the driver started to say.

"Do it my way!" I said. "Now! You've got the light. Make your left."

The driver cursed me under his breath, started his meter, and swung east on Fifty-sixth. I lowered my head and looked through the rear window. There was no sign of Holt. Nor was there any sign of him during the ride to Grand Central. We got out in front of the station and I hustled Weill into a cab waiting there and told the driver to go to Sixth and Forty-sixth. There was no sign of Holt during that ride, either.

I led Weill to the plaza of an office building and pushed him into the shadows. From where I stood, I could see Sixth Avenue, east and west on Forty-sixth Street, and at the far end of the plaza, a short stretch of Forty-seventh. For fifteen minutes, I waited, my fingers wrapped around the butt of the Beretta, watching every passing car, every taxi, every walker.

I pulled Weill away from the wall and steered him down Forty-sixth Street. A few feet from the secondary entrance to the building with my temporary office, I abruptly turned him hard left into the gutter. "Stand still," I hissed. The block was empty except for a private sanitation truck down near Sixth. I pointed to the entrance. "Go!" He ran in, and I followed.

On my floor, when we were fifteen feet from my office, I pushed Weill to his knees and signaled him to wait. I went past my door, rapped on it sharply with my key, and listened; no sound. I put the key in the lock, sat on the hallway floor, turned the key, and pushed the door open two inches. No sound. I brought out the Beretta, counted to five, and kicked the door open.

The office was empty, and I was so relieved I could barely make it to my feet.

35

In the ugly light of my office Max Weill looked old. He sat behind my desk and simply breathed, each intake an effort, accompanied by a sigh and a rasp. He wasn't quite out of it, though, because the first thing he said was, "For months, I am telling Andrew to use suppositories. Now perhaps he will listen to me." He peered at me. "You are who, please?"

"Kevin Fitzgerald."

"Kevin Fitzgerald . . . a surprising choice. It has color, it has harmony. Who chooses it for you?"

"My mother," I said.

"Let me ask another way," he said mildly. "For whom do you work—you will notice that after all these years in America I have taught myself to say 'whom.' For whom do you work?"

"Lilli Weill."

The polite, worldly smile remained on his mouth, but his eyes turned inward, away from what he was seeing and hearing.

"This is not fair," he said. "I understand that people such as yourself must be merciless, this I understand, this is the way of the state. But this is not fair."

Quietly, I said, "I'm working for Lilli Weill."

With effort, he stood up. "You have harmed her?" he said.

"Answer me. I am promised she will not be harmed. Is it so important that I leave Kleinman and come to you that you must harm her? Is it so important?"

He came around from behind the desk and moved toward me. His beautiful hands were clenched into tight fists. He should have looked funny, but he didn't.

"I do not care for whom I work," he said. "The Central Intelligence Agency, the National Security Agency, to me it makes no difference, you are all the same, *sheis*. But I am told she will not be harmed. I am *told* this."

He was moving his fists in unison, like a baby beating on its mattress. "Why do you do this to her? Why? Is this trivial game you play so important that you must harm her? She is old and poor—why do you harm her? Why? Why?"

I caught his wrists and held him at arm's length. "I'm working only for Lilli Weill."

"Liar!" he shouted, and spat in my face.

"If you stop shouting and spitting, I'll set up a meeting. You'll see for yourself. She's not hurt."

He shook his head angrily. "No. I do not trust you."

"What's your choice?" I said.

He thought that over, bowed his head a couple of inches, and smiled his sad smile. "A nice point. May I sit?"

I let go of his wirsts, and he retreated behind the desk. I wiped my face, got the Daniels, poured us drinks in my jam jars, and sat opposite him.

"Tell me something," I said, "if you knew she was alive and you care so much, why didn't you go back to her—or at least get in touch with her?"

He swallowed the bourbon and waited for me to refill the glass. Finally, he said, "When we were arrested . . ." He stopped. "During the war . . ." He stopped again. He held his hands out and tensed and relaxed the fingers. "Once, I could . . ." He looked up at me. "I do not know you; I cannot talk about these things."

179

Nastiness sometimes works, so I tried it. "Well, she is a lot older and staler than the Chinese girl."

For a minute I thought he was going to attack me all over again. But he changed his mind and grinned. It was an eerie grin, that of somebody who's just heard a sick joke and relished it.

"In the beginning I want Lilli so much that when I think of her, I am hard," he said. "I think of her when I am playing a concert, and I am afraid I will poke the piano. When I practice and she comes into the room with a cup of coffee, the coffee grows cold while I take off her clothes and make love to her, there, on the piano bench, or on the floor, even on the piano—yes, we lower the lid, and there, on the instrument built by the brothers Steinway in 1899, we make love; and Lilli's worry is that she will not be able to remove the stains from the wood." He made a scrubbing motion and laughed.

"When she is young, she is impossibly beautiful. Impossibly, you understand. Her breasts are up, like so, and her nipples are a red so deep it is nearly burgundy, and it is only to breathe near them, through a dress, through a coat even, and they are hard like rasberry lollipops. Lilli's lollipops. Mornings I wake up and spend I do not know how long playing with them, for we both love this.

"Down her belly is a line of hair. It goes from just above her navel to her little forest, and this line of hair, when I feel it with my cheek or when I dip my tongue along it, I am going berserk with desire. I *am* desire." He looked at me. "Surely you understand desire, Mr. Fitzgerald.

"And then I am traveling, and still Lilli is beautiful, and when I am home, we still are making love. But now, when I am playing a concert, I do not get hard when I think of her, because I do not think of her.

"Why? Because waiting for me in my dressing room, or at the hotel, is a little cupcake. Sometimes she is sixteen, seventeen years old; sometimes she is forty and not more beautiful

180

than Lilli. No. But new. A blank sheet of paper on which Max Weill will write his signature.

"They are everywhere: Paris, London, Amsterdam, Venice, Rome, the city does not matter, the program does not matter. They do not care about the piano; to them Bach is the same as Mozart, and Mozart is the same as Chopin. But the pianist, ah!

"In each city I learn another lesson—in London I learn about silken ropes, in Stockholm I learn about cold water and straw, in Paris I learn about married women, in Amsterdam I learn about mothers and daughters. I am a willing student; I carry my lessons with me here, in my head, like scores of music. Always, I refine, always the search for the optimum technique.

"For then, I make them shriek with pleasure. Shriek so, that the hotel manager calls and whispers, Herr Weill, we acknowledge that the artist must have his recreation, but the other guests try to sleep, perhaps if the lady will bite the pillow . . . Yes, they shriek, and in each city they shriek longer and louder, and then I am very happy. I know at last that I do not need to be with Lilli to make a miracle, because it is I, Max Weill, who is the creator of this miracle.

"Ah, you say, what vanity. Has there ever been such vanity? Doesn't he understand that the women who would throw themselves at a pianist would also feign their pleasure? No! But doesn't he understand that it takes two people, two particular people, to make such a miracle? No! For me to understand this, for me to concede this, is not simply a wound to my vanity—it is a mortal wound.

"If it takes two particular people to make a miracle in bed, then how many does it take to make a miracle in the concert hall? If I grant that I must have Lilli to create a miracle in bed, then who must I have in the audience to create a miracle at the piano?

"No. The *who* cannot matter. If it is Lilli, I will make

a miracle, if it is a sixteen-year-old cupcake, I will make a miracle, and if it is the wife of the chief of police, I will make a miracle. At the piano the same. If it is the rich in their jewels, or the students of a music school, or the members of the electricians' union, I will make a miracle."

"Or the SS." I said.

"Yes. Or the SS. Nobody is immune, only the deaf." He glanced at his hands again and grimaced. "After the war, I am given certain choices. And I think, if I go back to Lilli, we will have a life; not the life we have before, but a life."

"Why not the life you had before?" I asked.

He brushed aside the question. "We will go to concerts and opera, we will watch the moving pictures, we will listen to the radio, we will talk, we will buy things, and Lilli will cook, and I will teach, and perhaps, if the opportunity presents itself, I will undress the young students and lose myself in their sweet young forests and Lilli and I will put on weight and begin to look like each other; and one day we will sit next to each other and turn the pages of a photo album, and our hearts will break.

"For some people, this life, it is enough, more than enough. But for me it is not enough.

"I am given certain choices—one is always given choices, even in Auschwitz there were choices—and I think to myself, I cannot be what I once was, do I then search for Lilli, who is probably gassed and burned to ashes, or do I say, the old life is over, Auschwitz is over, Max and Lilli is over, it is time now for the new life?"

He stared at me, waiting for what I didn't know, maybe some sign of forgiveness. I gave him nothing, neither okay nor not okay.

He went on. "So I ask these people who are offering me choices, will you give me money, and they say, yes, we give you money; and I ask, will you give me music, and they say, we give you music; and I ask, will you give me women, and they say—so quickly, they say, yes, we give you women, all the women you want, old ones, young ones, ones with hair from head to feet and ones with no hair at all; white, black, yellow, red; two at a time, three at a time; ones you can beat and ones who can beat you; ones with six toes and ones with no breasts; ones who used to be princesses and ones who used to be nuns; ones who will pretend to be mothers and ones who will pretend to be dogs. Whatever you want, we give you. And this they do. They drown me in women.

"There are people who live to eat. I am a person who lives to *shtupp*—a lovely word, *shtupp*. Much more lovely than fuck. Fuck—pfui; it is from the German, fuck. It is hard and cruel, it tells you nothing. I say to you, fuck, you think of what? Duck. Cluck. Buck. Muck. *Dreck*.

"But *shtupp* . . . You think of a woman with legs open, the pretty pink lips enlarged in hope and welcome, the little curly hairs becoming wet and matted as her nectar seeps out. *Shhhhhhtuppppppppp*." He laughed in delight.

"They say to me, Max, take it easy, you'll have a heart attack. And I say, so? What is better? A stroke? Cancer? Emphysema? Are these better? With a heart attack, if it is big, you die"—he snapped his fingers—"like so. If it is not so big, you run in the park with the other heart attack people.

"I am in love with lust. Lilli I love. It is not hard to love someone; it is not even so hard to keep loving someone. But love without lust is friendship. Friendship is good enough for dying together but not for living together. Here, Mr. Fitzgerald, a joke for you—give me liberty or give me lust."

He refilled our glasses and raised his to me. His eyes were alive with excitement, and he looked like a high school freshman who found a peephole in the wall of the girls' locker room. "Lust!" he sang.

I waited till he drank. "Did you recognize Lilli when she saw you on the street?"

He waggled his finger at me in reprimand for clouding his mood. "Not immediately," he said. "But after a moment, yes, I know it is she. I can say nothing; they are always afraid she will know I am alive, and I am always afraid they will harm her if she knows. I think, perhaps I will send her a little card, but I do not do this. One lunchtime I nearly take Andrew into the restaurant where she is working, to sit at her station and have a piece of cake and a cup of coffee. But this I do not do, either." He looked through the window at the blank wall. "How is she?"

"Fine," I said. "Lonesome but fine."

He turned back to me. "You are telling the truth? I will see her and speak with her?"

"Uhuh."

"She wants this?"

"Yes."

"I too," he said. "Yes, I think so."

A new expression came on to his face, a mixture of terror and despair.

"Will she hate me?" he said.

"Let's find out," I said, and picked up the phone.

I called Ronni Gibson, who, when she answered, said, "I've been trying to reach—"

"I need your help," I said. There was silence. "Are you there?"

"I'm here," she said. "Shocked but here. Go ahead."

"I'm going to give you two numbers. The first belongs to Lilli Weill. Call her and—"

"Is she the woman who—"

"Ronni, don't interrupt now, for Chrissake! Call Lilli Weill, tell her to go to a neighbor and once she's there call you with the number. When you've got it, call me." I read my number to her. "Don't mention my name on the phone—just say that her guest who ate all the latkes wants her to do this. Do you get all that?"

She repeated what I'd told her. "Is that all?"

"Later tonight," I said, "I want to bring a couple of people to your place and—"

"You found her husband!"

"Ronni, goddamit!"

"Sorry."

"As soon as I figure out exactly how we'll do it, I'll let you know."

"Okay," she said. "Call you right back."

I lit a cigarette. Halfway through it, the phone rang. Weill and I both jumped. "Yes?"

"The neighbor's number is 787–9970," Gibson said. "She's waiting for your call. When will I hear from you?"

"Fifteen minutes."

It was eleven forty. I poured Weill another drink, put the bottle away, and finished my cigarette. Weill picked up a paper clip, straightened it, and then tried to fold it back to its original shape.

At eleven forty-three I dialed. After one ring, Lilli Weill said, "Mr. Fitzgerald?"

"Yes. Now listen—"

"Who is this woman who calls me?"

"Lilli, be quiet and listen."

"I listen."

"This is what you do: take the one-oh-four bus up to Broadway and Ninety-sixth Street. Get off the bus and run across Broadway to the southbound side. There'll be a taxi with a woman in it, a black woman. Get in the taxi and do what she tells you."

"Mr. Fitzgerald, who is this woman?"

"Lilli, tell me what you're going to do."

"Bus to Ninety-six,' across Broadway, to taxi with black woman."

"Right. Move."

"Mr. Fitzgerald, will you tell me what—"

"Lilli, move!"

"All right. I move. But I am not happy."

I called Gibson, told her where to wait and how to recognize Lilli Weill. "Go west on Ninety-sixth," I said, "then north to a Hundred and tenth, then east to Fifth Avenue. Go down Fifth till you come to Mount Sinai Hospital at a Hundred and first. Take Lilli in, and just past the door you'll see a door to the left. It leads to a passage in the basement that goes through the hospital to the Madison Avenue entrance. Send Lilli that way. You come back out on Fifth and take a cab around to Madison and pick her up. A different cab from the one that got you to the hospital. Then take her to your apartment. I'll give you an hour. Wait."

"What?" she said.

"If you pass a liquor store on the way downtown, pick up a bottle of champagne."

At twelve forty-five Weill and I went outside. Except for two men walking arm in arm, Forty-sixth was empty. We went east to Sixth Avenue, north to the Hilton, found a cab, and rode up Broadway to 120th. During the ride, Weill put his head back on the seat, shut his eyes, and hummed to himself. I didn't know the piece, but it was packed with intricate intervals, the musical equivalent of a tongue-twisting rhyme.

We reached Gibson's building at five after one, and before I could ring her bell the magnetic buzzer crackled, which meant she'd been watching for us from her window.

At her door, I took out the Beretta and motioned Weill to stand to one side, flat against the wall. I tapped softly, and at my fourth tap I heard two locks being unbolted and a chain being unhooked. The door swung open ten inches.

Gibson stood there, her face and body so taut that her cheek muscles were twitching. She saw the pistol and reflexively covered her throat.

"Mr. Fitzgerald," a voice said from behind Gibson, and Lilli Weill appeared in the doorway.

Max Weill stepped away from the wall to where the light shone on him.

Lilli Weill saw him, and her face, which was beautiful but sixty-nine years old, became beautiful but twenty-five. Without a sound, she spread her arms wide, crossed the threshhold, and enwrapped him. As her hands crept up to stroke the back of his head, he pulled her into him and buried his mouth in the curve of her neck. I glanced over them at Gibson. She was straining not to cry, and I wanted to reach out, caress her, and say, it's okay, go ahead, it's okay; and I wanted her to do the same for me.

36

Max and Lilli Weill stayed in Gibson's bedroom till daybreak. The bedroom was a good way down the hall from the kitchen, where Gibson and I started out the night, so we didn't hear anything. Later, around three-thirty, when we moved to the living room, we heard an occasional whisper.

Gibson made some coffee, which I laced with the dregs of a Christmas bottle of vodka she had, and we sat sipping and smoking on her sofa. We wanted to talk, and if we'd known each other better, or if we'd been less controlled, we might have. We might have traded stories about romances and the ends of romances, and we might have laughed ironically at how foolish we'd been and how God forbid we should ever be foolish again. Hearing the whispering from the bedroom, I wanted to ask Gibson about her mother and father and maybe tell her about mine. I wanted to ask her about Melissa, what it was like to have a child, and was there more good than bad, and did she think about not having it, and try to explain why I'd never had the courage to have one. But we didn't talk.

When Lilli and Max emerged from the bedroom, they were holding each other. Not tight, not for support, easily, familiarly, like two kids about to cross a wide street. Lilli let go of Max's hand and came over to me. She pushed my hair back from my forehead and smiled. The warmth from her smile made me feel innocent again, which was inane.

"The remarkable Mr. Fitzgerald," she said. "Oh, the truly remarkable Mr. Fitzgerald."

She took the coffee cup from my hands, put it on an end table, and embraced me.

After a long minute, a minute during which I felt so many warring emotions that my eyes swam, I gently pushed her back. "Not now," I said. I looked over her head at Weill. "Max, what's your deal with Kleinman?"

He shrugged. "Many years ago he tells me that so long as I do not work for his 'competitors' I am free to go when I wish."

"How do you stand with Immigration?" I said.

"I do not exist," he said. "Not officially."

"What do you want to do?" I said.

He glanced at Lilli and then pulled her close to him. "I do not know," he said falteringly. "I am . . ." Looking down at the floor, he said to her, "Do you hate me?"

She shocked me by bursting into laughter.

"Oh, Max," she said, "you are so stupid. I am sixty-nine years old. Do you think I have time to hate you?" She laughed again. "I know everything terrible about you—I have always known it. Weaknesses are never a secret. My weakness is you. How can I hate my own weakness?"

She rested her head on his shoulder.

To me, he said, "Perhaps . . . it is time for me to speak to Kleinman. He is not an unreasonable man."

"Let's wait till he comes to us," I said. "It gives us a better bargaining position."

"Yes," Lilli said, "stay with me."

"You believe he will come to us," Weill asked.

"As sure as the rain falls down instead of up," I said.

"Tomorrow, we will go shopping," Lilli said. "We will go to Macy's and—"

"He can't stay with you," I said. She gave me a look that would have broken the heart of a statue. "They'll be watching you."

"With you, then?" Weill asked.

"Same problem," I said, and twisted my body to stare at Gibson.

For an instant she didn't get it. Then she did. "Shit," she said. "You really collect your IOUs, don't you, Fitzgerald?"

"I pay them too," I said, stung.

Gibson looked at Weill. "I hope you don't mind kids," she said.

Weill bowed. "I hope your child doesn't mind me."

Lilli let go of Weill and tried to hug Gibson, who stiffened and held back. "Get out of my face, woman," she told Lilli. "It's for him, the remarkable Mr. Fitzgerald."

Lilli drew back. "You are right. An embrace is not thanks enough. One day, I will give thanks enough."

After throwing some water on my face and combing my hair, I said good-bye to Weill and Gibson and took Lilli outside to put her in a taxi. Once I'd sent her home, I walked along Broadway to find a taxi for myself.

My head ached, my mouth tasted foul, my clothes stuck

to me, and I could barely see because of exhaustion. I felt as if somebody had stuck a suction pump in me and drained me till I was shriveled. The sunlight was blinding, and when it flashed off the oil patches in the roadway it threw grotesque images into the air, floating ghosts that danced jaggedly above the black tar. Once, I thought I saw a green and blue face rising from one patch. It was an ugly face, its cheeks gouged with scars and its eyes distended into serrated ovals. I tilted my head, and the face frowned, twisting and stretching its mouth so it looked like the gash a slaughterer cuts in a steer's throat.

To lose the face, I walked quickly to the crowded corner of 116th Street. As I waited for a cab, I glanced over my shoulder; the face was gone. But the afterimage of it stayed in my head, and I couldn't figure out why till I sat back in the cab and closed my eyes. Then I realized that the face looked the way I expected Richard Kleinman's face to look when I told him Max Weill wanted liberty instead of lust.

I opened my eyes and shook my head, hard, and the face disappeared. But five blocks later it returned. And this time it was joined by a second face, and both of them seemed to be hovering over the grave of Sacha Cherkhov.

37

I went to Grand Central, showered, shaved, checked in with Gibson, walked to my office, typed up another batch of notes and mailed them, went outside and checked Gibson again, and sat at my desk and stared through the window at the traffic on Sixth Avenue.

Waiting was 60 percent of my work, and I should have

been used to it, but that morning it was grinding me into a nice quiet frenzy. I couldn't understand why they were taking so long; I'd half expected to find them camped on the doorstep. It nagged at me, because I thought I had things nicely figured—they had nothing, I had Max, and they had nothing to make me give them Max.

The phone finally rang at ten to twelve. I dragged it close to me, leaned back in my chair, put my feet up, and picked up the receiver on the fourth ring. It felt wet and heavy.

"Kev?"

Fiona Shaw.

"Listen, can I call you back," I said. "I'm waiting for a call."

"Have you talked to Lilli today?"

"Last night," I said, and lowered my feet. "Why?"

"She's not home and she's not at work."

"She said she wanted to go shopping," I said, "Macy's."

"Was she okay when you talked to her?"

"Fine. How long ago did you try her?"

"Five minutes ago," she said. "Kev, the restaurant said she didn't call in sick—she just didn't show."

"Happens all the time," I said, not believing it.

"It's not like her, Kev. To not show without calling. That's not Lilli."

"Maybe it's her day off."

"She's off weekends," she said.

"Let me check around," I said easily. "She probably went to Macy's. As soon as I hear anything, I'll give you a call."

I tried the restaurant; she wasn't there, she hadn't called, it wasn't her day off. I tried her home; no answer. I tried her doorman; she'd come in at seven-fifteen and left at eleven-fifteen, the time she usually left for work; she'd come in alone, and she'd left alone. I tried Gibson; she hadn't heard from Lilli.

During all this, I told myself I was getting all cranked up for nothing, that Lilli Weill was a sixty-nine-year-old woman who'd just been through an emotional whirlwind and probably had gone someplace to think things out: Central Park, maybe, or a bench in the middle of Broadway, where lots of old women sat and gossiped, or maybe down to Macy's to buy Max a bathrobe or a pair of slippers, or maybe to Sloane's to buy a double bed. There were a thousand possibilities.

I warned myself not to do anything dumb or hasty, like jump from my chair, stick the Beretta in my pants, and get ready to chase over to Broadway and Eighty-first. I told myself all that while I was turning out the lights and closing the inner door.

I pushed the Beretta down an inch to lodge it comfortably in the small of my back and opened the outer door.

Holt put his hand on my chest and pushed me back in the room. Kleinman followed us in and shut the door.

38

Holt was wearing his sunglasses, and Kleinman was wearing his smile. Holt's hand was under his jacket, so I raised my hands very slightly, palms out, and stood still.

"Good morning, Mr. Fitzgerald," Kleinman said. "May we go inside?"

I unlocked the inner door, strolled to my desk chair, and sat in it. Kleinman took the visitor's chair. Holt pushed the door shut and leaned on it. His hand under his jacket hadn't moved.

Kleinman crossed his legs, hitched up his pants, and sniffed the air delicately. "Would you mind opening a window, Mr. Fitzgerald?" I swiveled around and pulled it open. "Thank you." He leaned forward and patted the desk top. "I'd appreciate it if you wouldn't record this conversation. Legally, I could undoubtedly confiscate any such recording, but I'd rather avoid the trouble . . ." I nodded. "Good." He leaned back. "Now, I think we agree that we're both reasonable men, adults, not children, and that difficult situations are best dealt with in an adult manner. You do agree, of course?"

"Of course," I said.

"I was certain you would." He shook his head and made a regretful noise. "I must confess that I consider our present situation—predicament, if you will—my responsibility. I should have impressed on you more forcefully the urgency of my position. I apologize for that. However, what's done is done. We're not past the point of no return, and I'm sure matters can be resolved to everyone's satisfaction. Don't you agree?"

"I hope so."

"Now I believe it would be in our mutual interest to negotiate an exchange of sorts. Correct?"

I didn't say anything, I didn't nod, and I didn't blink.

From the door, Holt said, "He asked you a question."

"Andrew, please . . ." Kleinman said, like a father admonishing his son for waking him from his evening nap. "Mr. Fitzgerald . . . ?"

I tilted my chair back and put my feet up and tried to tell myself I was in a great bargaining position. I had my notes, I had my tapes, and I had Max Weill. I tried to tell myself that it was business, that all I needed to do was make the best deal possible and nobody would get crunched too badly. I tried to tell myself that Kleinman had no leverage, his only chip being a sixty-nine-year-old waitress who was of no use to anyone, not him, not her husband, not me.

"You mentioned an exchange?" I said. "What for what?"

"Don't be ingenuous, Mr. Fitzgerald," Kleinman said affably. "Lilli Weill for Max Weill."

"I don't follow you," I said. "Are you *holding* Mrs. Weill?"

Kleinman waggled his forefinger at me. "Mrs. Weill consented to be our guest."

"How do I know that?"

Holt smirked, and I was so tense I popped out of my chair. His Browning appeared in his hand.

"Go ahead," I said. "There are eight tenants on this floor."

"Andrew," Kleinman said, "please. I realize we're all a bit on edge, but please."

Holt put the Browning away. I sat down.

"Rest assured, Mr. Fitzgerald, Mrs. Weill is staying with us." He smiled cheerily. "She's quite well."

"What if I'm not in a position to deliver Max Weill?" I said.

Kleinman frowned and buffed his thumbnail on the sleeve of his jacket. When it appeared shiny enough to him, he said, "You haven't turned him over to . . . anyone, have you, Mr. Fitzgerald?"

"I didn't say that. What about this: all my notes and tapes for Lilli Weill."

"Naturally, we'd like to have your records, Mr. Fitzgerald, but they're secondary. No, I'm afraid that what I want is Max Weill."

"What if he doesn't want you?"

"Ah," he said with a muted sigh. "Yes, that was always a possibility. I'm afraid I'd have to negotiate that directly with him."

"He's authorized me to represent him," I said. "I have carte blanche."

194

Kleinman shook his head. "Unacceptable. After an exchange, I might be persuaded to let you be a party to my negotiations with Mr. Weill."

Each of us leaned back in our chairs. "I don't see how we can do business."

Holt moved forward a step. "Don't forget, asshole, she's an old lady. Old people . . . shit, terrible things happen to them."

"You mean the way they did to Cherkhov?" I said.

Kleinman quickly said, "Mr. Cherkhov took his own life. It's a matter of record."

I looked past him, at Holt. "What happened? I can't believe he sent you there to waste him. Nah. I bet he sent you over there to find out what Sacha knew, and you just couldn't believe he didn't know anything—and so you got pissed off and gave something away." Holt's hand twitched under his jacket. "What'd you do then—stick the barrel into his ear and make him eat his pills? Clever." I turned to Kleinman. "You should fire him; he makes bad mistakes."

With a fierce glance at Holt, Kleinman said, "Mr. Holt never encountered Mr. Cherkhov."

"He encountered Cesar Concepcion," I said. "I was present at that encounter." Kleinman looked puzzled. "One-two-six Hester. He kept pigeons."

Kleinman sighed. "The boy fell to his death in an unfortunate accident. Again, a matter of record."

"Maybe the homicide people will see it differently," I said. "Even if they don't, it wouldn't make your lives any easier."

Kleinman smoothed his pants and pinched the crease. "Mr. Fitzgerald, I surmise that you're whistling in the wind. We came to you in good faith and in order to save time and trouble. We would prefer not to embark on a prolonged search. But we are prepared to make such a search."

"Hah!"

He ignored it. "While we make such a search, Mrs. Weill

195

would remain our guest." He glanced over his shoulder to smile paternally at Holt. "She would be the special responsibility of Mr. Holt, in whom I have every confidence. Of course, he's never played host to a frail, elderly woman—have you, Andrew?"

"If she's a waitress, how frail can she be?" Holt said. "Waiting on tables, that's pretty tough work. I bet she can take it."

I could feel the vise around my balls getting tighter, and I didn't know what to do about it. Most negotiations are easy, because there's always a way to chop the prizes into pieces. You shave a little off the top, you trim a little off the bottom, the other side does the same, and you're home. I didn't have that luxury. I could have stalled a while longer, but it wouldn't have changed anything, just delayed it.

"Tonight?" I said.

Kleinman breathed in satisfaction. "Certainly."

"I choose the time and the place?"

"Of course, Mr. Fitzgerald. When and where?"

"I'll tell you at ten o'clock," I said. "That's when you call me at home."

"Ten," he said, "at your home."

"You'll put Lilli Weill on the line so I can make sure she's okay." I looked up at Holt. "If she's not, I'll find you." He laughed, and it made me want to shoot both his eyes out. I said to Kleinman, "Once I know she's okay, we'll fix when and where."

"That sounds acceptable," Kleinman said. He stood up and shook the wrinkles from his pants.

Holt finally took his hand from under his jacket. Kleinman joined him at the door.

"Ten o'clock," I said.

Kleinman nodded, then said matter-of-factly, "Mr. Fitzgerald, please don't be tempted to . . . ask for any assistance.

From anyone. Let's look at this as a simple exchange between principals. We don't want to clutter matters with any outsiders." He raised his hand in an informal salute. "We do look forward to seeing you later. Don't we, Andrew?"

"Fuckin' ay," Holt said. He opened the door for Kleinman, waited till he went through it, gave me the finger, and followed the boss out.

39

By nine o'clock all my muscles were so tight I couldn't stand without feeling pain in twenty different parts. I'd spent the rest of the day inventing hopeless schemes and imagining superhuman miracles and generally carrying on like a rabbit gnawing through its jaw, which is what rabbits do when they having nothing solid to chew.

I called Fiona Shaw. "Can I call you back?" she said.

"I'm not at a number where I can be reached."

"Shit. Okay, let me get rid of this call," she said, put me on hold, and came back with: "Did you find Lilli?"

"I don't know where she is, but I know how to get hold of her."

"What do you mean?" she said.

"I found Max Weill, and—"

"Where is he?"

"He's safe, but—"

"Where?"

"Fiona, will you shut up for one goddamn minute," I shouted. "He's with a friend of mine. The trouble is that the people who had him have got Lilli."

"Oh, no," she said. "Oh, God, no."

"Oh, yes," I said. "I'm going to have to give them Max for Lilli. We're—"

"You can't do that," she said.

"There's no choice."

"Kev, there must be some—"

"Fiona, I'm telling you there's no goddamn fucking choice."

She was quiet for half a minute. "When are you going to make the swap?"

"Tonight."

"What time?"

"Around two, I guess."

"Where?"

"I'm not sure yet," I said. "I want it safe."

"Do you want to do it in my apartment?" she said. "I can drop off a set of keys for you." She laughed bitterly. "You should have taken them when I offered them."

I ignored it. "It's got to be outside. An alley, or a parking lot. I know a lot downtown that might be okay."

"Where?"

"On Third Avenue."

"An open lot, you say? Is that safe, Kev? I don't want anything to happen to Lilli. I feel funny about an open lot."

"There's no fence around it, so you can drive on to Third Avenue or Ninth Street or Tenth Street or Stuyvesant Street."

"Do you want me to drive for you?"

"No," I said, though I was touched by the offer. "I want to keep the risks to a minimum."

"Will you call me afterward to tell me how it went?" she asked.

"Still looking for your story—should I take notes?"

"You're a prick, you know that."

"Sorry," I said. "Force of habit."

"I'll wait till I hear from you."

The harder call came next. I dialed Gibson's number and asked for Weill. When he got on the line, I didn't bother easing into it:

"They've got Lilli, and the deal is you for her."

He chuckled softly. "It is not a surprise, is it, Mr. Fitzgerald?"

"How do you feel about it?"

"Does it matter how I feel about it?" he said. "If I say to you, I will not return to them, does it matter?" I had no answer to that.

"For Lilli, you will give me to them—not so, Mr. Fitzgerald? You will not let harm come to Lilli only to protect me—not so?" Again he chuckled. "But you are correct to do this. They will not harm me."

"Kleinman said he's willing to talk about letting you off the hook," I said, praying I sounded sincere.

"Then we will talk," he said. "What time shall I expect you?"

"Around midnight."

"Oh, Mr. Fitzgerald, come a little earlier. Mrs. Gibson will make us coffee, we can have a glass of schnapps, we can all three talk. Come a little earlier."

I locked the office, took the car from the garage, drove uptown, and found a vacant meter on Second Avenue, around the corner from my building. As I locked the car, I noticed an old woman sitting on a pile of newspapers in the doorway of an antiques shop. She was methodically emptying a large white shopping bag that was lettered Dry Dock Savings Bank. On her head she wore a dirty khaki cloth that was knotted at its corners. She had on a torn print dress that was held to her body by a wide red plastic belt. Over her shoulders hung an army greatcoat; one of its sleeves was falling out of the armpit. Spotted all over the front of the coat, like a résumé of her gastric system, were smudges of blood and vomit.

Her toes were black and green and protruded through the holes in her blue sneakers. Lovingly, she unwrapped a slice of gray rye bread, trimmed the crust with a plastic knife, and wrapped that to put in her shopping bag. She began to bite into the bread when she saw me watching her. Instantly, she stuffed the slice of bread down her dress and pressed both palms to her chest. She opened her mouth wide, and I stepped backward, expecting her to yell.

But no yell came from her; no sound at all. It was like seeing a pantomime of somebody screaming. I didn't know what to do, whether to offer her money, or ask her if she needed help, or call the cops to lug her to the nearest hospital. I moved toward the doorway. Her mouth still gaping in her silent scream, she scrambled to her gangrenous feet, grabbed her shopping bag, and half limped, half ran down the avenue.

I was still thinking about her at ten o'clock when the phone rang.

40

Lilli Weill sounded fine.

"I am playing rummy with Mr. Holt," she said. "He is not a nice player. When he loses, he makes a mean face and bangs the table. To this moment, he owes me thirty-one dollars and eighty cents."

"Have they done anything to you?" I said.

"What can they do?" she said. "I am an old lady. I am not a dangerous person." She dropped her voice. "Once, Mr. Holt calls me a name—a horrible name—but that is because when he knocks with two points, I pick up his deuce of hearts and say, gin. He also calls me a senile old fart. How is a fart senile, do you know?"

"Did they tell you what's going on?" I asked.

"What is to tell?" she said. "They take me because they want Max. It is not so complicated."

"Right," I answered, and tried to think of something else to say.

"Hello. Hello. Are you there, Mr. Fitzgerald?"

"I'm here."

"What does Max say?" she asked.

"He says okay."

She was quiet for a while. "Will they hurt him?" she finally said.

"No," I said. "He's no good to them if he's hurt."

"Of course," she said. "I didn't think." She paused. "Mr. Fitzgerald . . ."

"I'm here."

"Will I see him again?"

I'd believed I was ready for the question, but I couldn't have been, because before I could answer, she asked a second time, "Will I see him again?"

"I don't know."

"I would like to see him again."

"Yes, I understand. They won't make it easy."

"But is it possible?"

"I'll do what I can."

"Yes, this I realize, Mr. Fitzgerald. But is it possible?"

"Lilli, I don't know."

She slid into a whisper. "I love Max," she said. "Do you think he loves me?"

"Yes," I said. "For sure."

"For sure?"

"For sure."

"And you will do what you can?" she said.

"You know that," I said. "Let me talk to Kleinman."

When Kleinman picked up the phone, I told him, "A couple of things. At the exchange, let them embrace."

"I have no problem with that," he said.

"Within twenty-four hours of the exchange, you, Weill, and I sit down to talk about what he wants to do—whether he wants to go on working for you."

"No problem," he said. "And your records, Mr. Fitzgerald?"

"You get delivery at the conversation about Weill's future."

"I'd rather have them tonight," he said offhandedly.

"Don't be an asshole," I said. "Have you got a pencil?"

"I'm ready," he said.

"There's a parking lot on the east side of Third Avenue that runs from Ninth to Tenth Street. That's where I bring Weill, and that's where you bring Lilli. Don't arrive before two. I'll be there already. When I see a car pull into the lot, I'll blink my lights. When you see the lights blink, drive to the back wall of the lot, all the way so your bumper is touching the wall, and kill your engine. When your engine stops, I'll blink my lights again. Are you with me so far?"

"Yes," he said.

"Count to twenty, and then the three of you, Holt, Lilli, and you, leave the car. I don't want anybody else in that car, not on the back seat, not in the trunk; and I don't want any backup cars. All three of you get out on the passenger side. You stand with your hands flat on the trunk. Send Holt out with Lilli. I'll be coming out with Weill.

"I want Lilli to be walking by herself—I don't want Holt

touching her and I want to see his hands empty. If he's touching her, or if his hands are out of sight, or if there's anything in his hands, even a goddamn candy bar, I turn around with Weill and go back to my car. Get that?"

"Yes."

"When the four of us meet, he looks Weill over, and I look Lilli over. That's when the two of them get to embrace.

"Then: Weill, Holt, and I wait till Lilli goes back to my car. When she's in and on the floor, I go back to it and start the engine. When I start the engine, and not before, Holt takes Weill to your car.

"Once I've pulled off the lot and onto the street, and not before, the three of you get in your car. Clear?"

"Yes, I have it," he said.

"If you don't do it exactly that way, or if she's bruised, I'll kill you both."

"I'll see you at two, Mr. Fitzgerald."

41

It was close in the car, and each time I lit a cigarette, Max Weill opened his window another couple of inches. We were parked slantwise at the south end of the lot so that I could drive away in any direction. We'd been there since twelve-thirty, and in forty minutes I'd smoked five cigarettes and Weill had taken five gulps from the fifth of cognac on the seat between us.

We kept ourselves diverted by watching the hookers parade up and down Third Avenue. Weill would chuckle whenever he spotted one he calculated was under sixteen and spat out the window whenever he spotted one with broad shoulders and a square jaw.

"Transvestite," he muttered when a six-footer in a miniskirt minced by. "Once I am drunk and make a mistake. Very beautiful and small. A mouth so soft on me, it is like being sucked by an angel. A smooth belly." He laughed. "And balls as big as grapefruits."

Occasionally, a hooker would manage to flag down a customer; she'd climb in his car, and the car would drift into a dim corner of the lot. Most of the girls were black, but all the customers were white, and their registration plates showed they came from the outer boroughs or New Jersey.

No other cars pulled on to the lot, and no cars parked at the meters along the avenue.

Weill sucked at the cognac again and watched a tiny hooker in shorts pace back and forth under the streetlight.

"In Auschwitz," he said, "they have many whores. The SS officers like Jewish girls. The whores tell me that their work is not so bad. Not so good as in the orchestra, but not so bad. Often, they are permitted to go to Canada—Canada is the place in the camp where we buy things, it is our black market. I too go often to Canada."

A Ninth Street crosstown bus stopped at the corner, and a middle-aged man climbed off. Weill waited while the man eyed the hooker. The man moved on.

"One day Sacha Cherkhov needs a truss—he suffers with a hernia—and I find for him a truss. That night, he plays like a man inspired. You see, music is from the scrotum." He hummed a snatch of melody. "He is a good violinist, Sacha. When Mengele comes to hear us, Sacha plays the Brahms concerto. Brilliant. The best Brahms I ever hear."

The middle-aged man had returned to stand near the corner. The little hooker saw him and sauntered in his direction.

"At first I am luckier than Sacha. Those who can carry their instruments walk alongside the prisoners on the way to the chambers. Who can carry a piano? But the SS does not like exceptions. They bring me one day an accordion, and so I, as well, walk alongside the prisoners." He swallowed another drink. "The musicians and the *capos*."

The middle-aged bus passenger and the hooker were deep into a negotiation.

"Every night we play, and Sundays more, two, three times. The SS sit and beat time, boom, boom, boom, boom, and if they are feeling benevolent, if they are feeling like spreading culture, they allow to the concert one hundred prisoners, and they, too, are encouraged to beat time, boom, boom, boom, boom.

"One Sunday we play the Beethoven Third, and the second violinist, who has an ulcer and dysentery, goes wrong. Far wrong. We are halted. 'Who does this?' the SS man asks me—I am conducting today, the conductor is dying of typhus. 'I do not see,' I say.

"But a flautist, a German who is proud to play for other Germans, so proud he grows six inches when the SS marches into the room, he points his flute at the second violinist and says, 'He does this.' That evening the second violinist goes to Block Eleven."

The little hooker had her arm twined around the bus passenger's and was guiding him north, toward a bunch of quickie hotels on Twelfth Street.

"I am walking with the prisoners one day, playing the accordion, and on the line is my schoolmate Fritz. The best storyteller of Vienna. A raconteur who can make a mortician smile. I try to look away, but Fritz sees me. He gives a little wave, like so, like a child waving to a bird in the sky, and he walks into the gas chamber.

"His back is very thin, and I think, Is my back so thin?

Will somebody watch my back when I go into that room? Is somebody watching my back at this moment?"

The bus rider's back was pudgy under his poplin jacket, but the hooker's back, nearly naked in the halter top she wore, was bony; and even in the shadowed light from the streetlamps her scars were visible.

"One Sunday there is an upheaval. A cellist goes berserk, he strangles an interpreter—a dispute, would you believe it, about the meaning of a word. The interpreters are prisoners, but they are like the *capos*, very close to the SS.

"For this act, the SS wants ten musicians." He laughed mordantly. "Had it been one of their own, they would demand the entire orchestra. Ten is not so many, they tell me. Which ten, I ask. You choose, Max, they tell me."

He drew from the cognac again and watched the traffic light go from green to red four times.

"So I choose." He waited for me to say something, but I kept my mouth shut and my face still.

"At first," he said, "I choose musicians I do not like, musicians who play badly. Next, I choose *people* I do not like, the Germans in the orchestra, a Pole, a Belgian who lies. Next, I choose those who joke with the SS. Next, I choose those who are fat—they must be traitors, or how would they become fat? Then, those who are thin—after all, they will die soon, anyway. Then, those who are old, those who are ill, those who are grieving for lost families.

"All through the night I choose. At last I have ten names." He held up both hands and spread the fingers wide. "Ten. A brave man would give them a blank sheet of paper. I think of this. But I say to myself, Max, if you do not choose, someone else will choose, and he will choose worse." He shook his head mockingly. "Not an original excuse."

The hooker had her arm around the bus passenger's waist and her head on his shoulder. From a distance, they looked like a slightly mismatched romantic couple.

"I cross out the tenth name, and in its place I write, Max Weill. But this is not brave. This is fake brave. The SS does not like volunteers, they will not permit me to choose myself, and this I know. It is a gesture, the gesture of the fake brave. I give them my list.

"The next night they come to the barracks and take me away. They transport me to Bergen-Belsen, and there, later, I am liberated. Free."

"And the nine?" I said.

"I do not know," he said. "Probably they are gassed. At one time after the war I begin to search for their names; I have no stomach to continue. I do not know."

"Was Sacha on the list?" I asked.

"Sacha?" he said incredulously. "No, not Sacha. How could he be on such a list? He is here."

"Was Leo Hirsch on the list?"

He hesitated. "At first." He hummed a snatch of melody again. "Do you have children, Mr. Fitzgerald?"

"No."

"I, too, have no children. Lilli wanted them, but I am an ambitious man. Leo had children, young children, useless for work at the camp. They used to take the young children to the infirmary and carefully and methodically and experimentally break their bones. Many, many times. To test certain medical theories about bones. And about pain. Afterward, they would carry them to the ovens and toss them in. That is, the ones who could not walk. But some could walk—perhaps I should say, hobble. Leo's son could hobble, so they put him in the line to the chambers. He was holding the hand of a stranger. We, of course, doing our duty, were accompanying this line, playing. Leo was playing the clarinet. As the stranger and Leo's son came to the door of the chamber, the boy looked over his shoulder, at his father, the woodwind player, and said, 'Papa, it's dark, it's so dark, and I was being so good.' And Leo kept playing.

"When it came time to make the list, I remembered this, and I write Leo's name."

"And?" I said.

"And I also remember that he has saved my life once."

After a silence, I said, "How did you end up with Kleinman?"

"At the end of the war, I am interrogated by the OSS. Very polite gentlemen. German looking, but American. They ask me about my friends in the camp. After some weeks of asking, they tell me Lilli is dead, they tell me they know my career is kaput, they tell me they would like to explore—this is the word they employ, explore—my unique gift for friendship. For some weeks, we 'explore.' They offer me work. I think it over; I accept."

"I don't get it," I said. "Why didn't you just pick up your career where you left off?"

He reached for the Courvoisier, and some cognac sloshed on to his lap. I hadn't noticed how drunk he'd gotten.

"My career was kaput."

"Did you think because you'd played for the SS you'd have trouble getting jobs?" I said.

"No," he said curtly.

"Well, I just don't—"

"Mr. Fitzgerald, you are a fool. In Bergen-Belsen, I am talking to a Frenchman, and I am explaining to him how I come to leave Auschwitz. He listens with much sympathy. Big tears roll down his cheeks. I am moved that one human being can understand another human being's weakness so well. We embrace, and we weep.

"That night, he comes to me, he and four others. Three hold me still while the Frenchman and a Hungarian break first my arms, then my wrists, and then, one by one, joint by joint, all the bones in my hand. As they are about to kill me for my 'collaboration,' I am saved by the guards' night check." He put his fingertips on the dashboard. "Bergen-Belsen, you understand, is not such an ideal place for orthopedic surgery."

"Okay," I said. "You couldn't go back to playing. Okay. But why—"

He struck the dashboard with the edge of his hand. "Mr. Fitzgerald, in the world are people who are very strong and very philosophical; there are painters who are blinded and can no longer paint and dancers who are crippled and can no longer dance. They go on, they accept, they invent a new life. I am not so strong and not so philosophical. A part of me is taken away, and in me there is an empty space. I do not believe anything will fill this space, so I do not try to fill it. You must understand, Max Weill is a man who plays piano. I no longer can play piano; I am no longer Max Weill. How can I go back? There is no going back. The people who loved me, the people who admired me, loved and admired Max Weill the piano player. Who is dead.

"I accept the offer of the OSS." He smiled. "SS—OSS, it is a difference of only one letter. Later, the OSS becomes the CIA, and I am adopted by Richard Kleinman. Of German descent.

"Kleinman is not so bad. He likes music; he eats quietly. Holt is like a corporal in the SS. Kleinman and I have a simple understanding. I will help him; he will give me what I want. It is not so difficult. We live here, we live there, and I talk to my old friends. Mostly, the talk is worthless. Later, the talk is more valuable—as my old friends achieve positions and prestige. And finally, the talk is very valuable indeed, particularly with my old friend Leo Hirsch."

"Valuable, how?"

"All over America, in California, in Massachusetts, are businessmen. They make marvelous instruments—computers and other such toys. The East wants to buy these toys, so they

209

find go-betweens—Swiss traders, Lichtenstein brokers, Mona-can financiers—and these go-betweens buy these toys. It is not against American law to sell a wonderful machine to a Swiss businessman. The Swiss businessman then resells it to the East. Now this is a complicated affair, with complicated routes and complicated records. But the East is not interested in buying the same wonderful machine from a Swiss and a Monagesque and a Belgian. So there must be a place, a person, who to make sure there is no duplication sees the records of all these transactions."

"Leo Hirsch," I said.

"Leo Hirsch," he repeated. "It all goes through him, the discreet, pleasant trade attaché. This means that Leo knows precisely what wonderful machines the East is secretly buying from these patriotic businessmen in California and Mas-sachusetts. And if Leo tells me—which he does—and I tell Kleinman—which I do—the United States can monitor these sales. You see, Mr. Fitzgerald, what somebody buys not only tells you what he lacks, it tells you what he has."

"Very neat," I said, meaning it. "I'm surprised at Leo."

For a long moment he stared at the street. "I do not be-lieve you are a nice man, Mr. Fitzgerald, but you still carry a little morality, no. You still believe there is good and evil, right and wrong; you believe such things, no?"

"Sometimes."

He held up his forefingers and twisted them together. "During the war, I am this close to Leo. Watch—I move one finger, the other must move. I know everything about him—who he loves, who he hates, who he betrays; what makes him laugh, what makes him weep, what makes him swell in pride, what makes him cringe in shame. He trusts me. He is like a child."

"Or like an audience."

"Astute, Mr. Fitzgerald, astute. Yes, like an audience. Be-fore I play, I say to myself, I love this audience, I worship this

210

audience, I will please this audience, and if this audience resists me, I will twist it this way and that, until it hears what I want it to hear. Leo is easy. Like me, he no longer is burdened by beliefs. It is not so hard to convince him that I am still his friend and that nothing we do, nothing we talk about, is more important than our friendship. What are a few pieces of paper? What is East and West? What is capitalism and communism? If he talks to me, he will make me happy, and I will make him happy—money in Swiss bank accounts, safe passage for anyone left in his family, a new identity if he ever wants it—and nothing is more important than that friends make each other happy."

"And he bought it?"

Weill smiled. "In installments. Mr. Fitzgerald, I offer Leo love and riches—how can he not accept? After all, he and I believe in nothing else."

"He never tried to back out?"

"Of course. He is afraid. But I assuage him. Lately . . ."

"Lately?"

"Lately, he is terrified. I don't know why. Perhaps there is purge in Berlin; perhaps he loves me less. If he grows more terrified, he will stop." He laughed harshly. "The end of my second career."

"Do you always meet at recitals?"

"No, no. At first, we meet like real people—we eat a meal, we drink a cup of coffee and a schnapps, we go to the zoo—Leo is mad about pandas—we try to learn the intricacies of baseball." He smiled to himself. "Leo is very German; once he understands the game, he cheers only for the Yankees—the dynastic team. We are friends; fraudulent, but real. Does this make sense to you? Why should it? It makes no sense to me. But then, at the suggestion of Kleinman, we meet at recitals, and nowhere else. For me, it is perfect. Holt detests it. Leo acquiesces."

"I thought he liked music," I said.

211

"Oh, he does. But he likes me, and he tells me I am deserting him. I am cheapening our friendship, I am turning it into a squalid business arrangement. Let us meet in Central Park, let us have dinner. Friends do not sit like conspirators in a concert hall, there is no privacy. Naturally, Kleinman will not permit this, and Leo becomes more resentful—and more terrified."

"Does Kleinman know Leo is terrified?"

"Of course not. This would be the end of me. Kleinman does not worry about Leo. He worries only about me. Where did I take a stroll? Did I see anybody I know? Did anybody stop to stare at my face? Did I make any phone calls? Did I post a letter? He asks me; he asks Holt. This is why he no longer allows me to give lessons. He is afraid I will defect to the enemy. The enemy are his competitors—the National Security Agency, the Defense Intelligence, even another section of the Central Intelligence Agency. He does not tell me this—he tells me he is concerned that an assassin will reach me. I learn this from Leo—that all these agencies would be delighted to learn of my existence and employ me."

"Didn't you ever want to stop?"

"Richard Kleinman is a persuasive man—he would have made himself rich in real estate. He makes promises, he paints pretty pictures. I will live in a penthouse, I will have the finest surgeons, I will own two pianos, I will have complete freedom—except the freedom to be visible. And what need have I to be visible? I will have so much freedom, I will become an American citizen. I believe him. We believe what we need to believe.

"So much do I believe him that some days I drag Andrew to the courthouse in Foley Square and we sit in the back when the judge is swearing in new citizens. 'I pledge allegiance to the flag—' it is ridiculous, is it not?"

He glanced out the window at a high-rise apartment building across the street. Only a few windows were lit, but to a drunken mind their pattern could have resembled a flag. "For me," he said, "America is paradise. Not to you, you are born here, to you it is a just a rich country. You do not see paradise. But I see it. I am not happy that Kleinman does not keep this promise."

"Why didn't you leave him?" I said. "If that was important to you."

"I tell you a story—listen to this. Max Weill is now sounding like an old yid in the Garden Cafeteria on East Broadway." He thought that over. "A drunken old yid. There is once a village called Chelm, not a real place but a magic place, the village in the East that stands for all the other villages. One day, the elders of Chelm hire a man to sit at the village gate and wait for the coming of the Messiah.

"He sits and he sits and he sits, and he grows tired, and he goes to the elders and says, I sit and I wait, and I sit and I wait, and nobody comes, and the pay is very low. And the elders answer him, You're right, the pay is low. But consider this: the work is steady."

The little hooker and the middle-aged bus rider had disappeared into one of the hotels.

Weill reached over to pat my hand. As he did, a long dark car made a U-turn on Third Avenue and drove onto the sidewalk fronting the parking lot. I pushed Weill's head below the dashboard, fumbled for the switch, and blinked my lights. The lights of the long dark car blinked in reply, and the car rolled quietly forward along the gravel until the front of its hood was three inches from the back wall of the lot.

42

The driver of the long dark car cut his motor.

I jacked a bullet into the chamber of the Beretta, put the pistol back in its holster, blinked my lights, and began my count. I counted the way I did in the fifth grade—one, one thousand, two, one thousand, three, one thousand . . .

At seventeen, I unlocked the door on Weill's side of the car. At nineteen, I bent down and opened my door.

"Don't move till I come for you," I whispered to him.

At twenty, I slid out of the car on to the gravel. Moving sideways, like a crab, I scuttled around the back of the car and along the passenger side to the front door. Slowly, I inched it open. "Wait," I said.

At the long dark car, Kleinman stood at its rear. He was bent slightly, his hands stretched flat in a wide V on the trunk.

The front passenger door opened and Holt wriggled out. He held his hands chest high, away from his body. He looked like an after-dinner speaker trying to quiet the applause of the crowd. Keeping his back to the car, he sidestepped along till he could reach the handle of the rear door.

He lifted his left hand above his head and opened the door with his right hand. Once it swung wide, he took three deliberate paces forward. On his third step, Lilli Weill put her feet on the ground, gripped the door handle, and pulled herself out of the car.

"Now," I said to Weill, and moved out of his way. "Stay down till I tell you to stand." Breathing laboriously, he crawled out of the car to the ground. "Stay behind me," I said.

I raised my hands so Holt could see them and stood up. Behind me, I heard Weill inhale deeply and rise. To let them know I was about to move, I kicked the ground twice. Holt nodded his understanding of the signal.

In measured twelve-inch strides, I started to walk to a clear space in the center of the lot. Weill followed close behind me, reaching forward every couple of steps to touch me in the back, an inch or two above the butt of the Beretta.

As soon as Kleinman saw the direction we were heading, he rapped on the trunk. Lilli began to walk toward the clear space. Holt trailed her by around two feet. She moved slowly, so I shortened my stride, and Weill bumped me. "Sorry," he said.

From twenty feet away, Lilli seemed healthy enough, but I couldn't be sure because the light falling on the parking lot was such an odd greenish color that one instant her face looked gray, another instant yellow, another nearly black.

Suddenly, a blue and white police cruiser, its dome light flashing, raced west on Ninth, braked at the corner of Third, and skidded on to the avenue.

I stopped in mid-step and lowered my foot as daintily as if I were walking along a thin pane of glass. Lilli stopped, too, and Holt put his hand on her shoulder.

The police car roared north on Third; at Eleventh Street, its siren began to whine. None of us moved till we saw it turn east on Fourteenth.

We began walking again, and by then I could hear their footfalls—Lilli's quick and syncopated, the waitress darting from table to table; Holt's steady and pounding, the executioner mounting the steps of the scaffold.

When we came within six feet of each other, we stopped. I reached behind me to bring Weill to my side. He took my hand and joined me, and didn't let go once he was next to me.

Lilli saw him and blew him a kiss.

Holt and I nodded to one another.

"Don't move," I told Weill, and started toward Lilli.

At the same instant, Holt started toward Weill.

We each took two steps. The sound came then.

The sound was like the pop of a light bulb, only without the splintering of glass. A timid little pop.

The bottom of Holt's face flew away. A piece of his jaw bounced off a van, and another piece glided through the air and skittered under a car. His blood sprayed out in separate streams and one of the streams splashed onto Lilli's hair and shoulders. Holt looked shocked, insulted; he couldn't believe that *he* was hit, that *he* was hurt, that *he* was about to join his victims.

As I threw Weill to the ground, there was another pop. I kicked Weill to keep him moving, rolled over, got the Beretta out, and rolled over again.

Holt had dropped to one knee and was holding his Browning straight out in front of him. Blood bubbled from his half face on to his coat sleeve. He swung the Browning in a languorous hundred-degree arc.

There was another pop, and again I rolled over, trapping my leg under the rear wheel of a car. I tried to pull it free too fast, and I had to bite my lip to keep from crying out when I felt a ligament tear.

Lilli was still standing. "Get down!" I shouted. "Lilli! Get down!"

But she was too frozen to hear me or to move. I began to drag myself over to her, but before I could advance three feet, Weill sprang up and ran toward her.

"Max!" I yelled, but not quick enough. There was another pop, and he pitched over as though he'd run into a trip wire.

216

He clutched his ankle with both hands. He made no sound.

Again, I dragged myself toward Lilli.

Bright lights spiked me to the ground. An engine revved up, and from across Third Avenue a car tore toward the lot.

As if he were taking practice on a range, Holt began to fire his Browning at the car. His first shot took out its left headlight, and the car veered two feet. His second took out the right headlight and it veered again. His third shattered the windshield, and it veered a third time, mounting the sidewalk and barely avoiding the prefab booth at the front of the lot.

By then, I was firing as well, and the car changed course one more time. And its left fender, with its headlight dangling in crystals, rammed into Lilli Weill. Her body crumpled as though it were made of felt; she careered sideways, then backward, and at last tilted forward and fell face down on the gravel.

Before the car stopped, a large black man wrenched open the passenger door, leaped out, and ran toward Weill. In his hand was a sawed-off shotgun. I locked my elbows and aimed the Beretta at his chest. Before I could squeeze the trigger, Holt fired twice.

The black man broke stride, took one more step, dropped the shotgun, and put both hands on his belly. He held his fingers laced there, like a satisfied dinner guest fondling his meal. But as he pressed, blood began to seep around his palms. He pulled his hands away and stared at them. A pain hit him, and he clasped his hands back on his belly. His body jerked, and he stared in shock at his pants. The stink of his shit was overwhelming, but he couldn't grasp why *he* was shitting. He didn't understand that a shot into the guts opened the sphincter the way a hanging opened the trap door under the victim. He reached back to feel his pants, but before his hand got there, Holt shot him straight through the right eye.

Holt turned to me and swung the Browning around. I sighted along the barrel of the Baretta and tensed my finger. He keeled forward, his forehead bouncing twice on the ground before it lodged.

I twisted about to go to Lilli. Weill was already on his way, crawling through the blood, dragging his destroyed ankle behind him. I sat up so I could see into the car, and at that second the driver reversed it, spun it into a tight turn, and aimed for the Ninth Street end of the lot.

Weill was nearly at Lilli's side when the brakes screeched, the car lurched, and the driver pointed something out his window.

"No!" I screamed. "No! No!"

My third no was so loud I almost didn't hear the discreet little pop.

The car—the maroon car—skidded across the lot, turned on Ninth, and vanished west.

By the time I reached the Weills, Max had collapsed on Lilli's back.

In the right side of his neck was a hole about the size of a nickel. In the left side was a hole the size of a half dollar. Blood leaked out it.

I forced my hands underneath him and felt along Lilli's back till I found her neck, then traced the contour of her neck till I came to the vein in her throat. I shut my eyes and held my breath. For the first ten seconds, I wasn't sure, but after the second ten I let myself breathe and shouted, "Kleinman, call an ambulance!"

He didn't answer me.

"Kleinman!" I called out, and twisted my head so I could see him. He and the long dark car were gone.

I pulled loose, stood on my good leg, and hopped over to

my car. I drove it to within six inches of the Weills, crawled out, and rolled Max off Lilli on to the gravel. "Sorry," I said. Then I lowered the front passenger seat, picked Lilli up, and slid her on to the seat so her feet were at the back of the car.

I checked Max one last time, then drove east on Stuyvesant and turned north on First Avenue, toward Bellevue.

Every block, I glanced at Lilli. She wasn't moving. At Twenty-first Street, I noticed that her head had flopped over, and I reached down to shift it. A rivulet of blood dribbled from the corner of her mouth toward her chin. I pushed down the gas pedal and began to press the horn in fierce blasts. The few cars on the avenue cut sharply out of my way, and I had the right lane clear straight to the hospital.

When I braked to make the turn into the driveway, a savage pain flashed up my leg. It was so harsh a pain it nearly made me stop trying to figure out who had set me up.

43

They had heard my horn, and when I pulled into the Bellevue ambulance entrance they were waiting. Before I could roll down my window to explain anything, three of them eased Lilli on to a stretcher and, loping alongside it, sped it through the swinging doors, past the adult emergency service, straight into the emergency ward.

I moved the car out of the way and hobbled in. A guard stepped up to block me, but when he saw the blood on my clothes, he backed off and waved me through.

The cart holding Lilli was surrounded by half a dozen

people. Others were wheeling equipment over, an EKG machine, an oxygen bag, IV units. Somebody was cutting away her clothes; somebody else was inserting a catheter.

A tall, black-haired nurse was talking brusquely into a wall phone: "I don't know yet, but I want a trauma team, I'll tell you that." She spotted me. "What are you doing in here? Did you register at the desk?"

"I brought her in," I said.

A tiny plain-faced woman with restless eyes whipped her head around; her plastic tag identified her as a neurology resident. "What happened to her?" she asked.

"She was struck by a car moving around thirty-five miles an hour," I said. "The car hit her here." I held my right hand above my kidney and my left at mid-thigh. "It hit her once, and she fell, face down, on hard gravel."

The neurology resident wrote it down as I spoke it. "Did her head strike the gravel?" I nodded. "Who is she, do you know?"

"Lilli Weill. Sixty-nine years old."

The resident frowned.

"Temperature nine-five-seven," someone shouted.

"Pressure eighty-five-fifty," someone else shouted.

The resident tapped her pen on her pad. "Has she ever had a stroke or any other neurological condition? A cardiac condition?"

"I don't know."

"Is she allergic to any antibiotic?"

"I don't know."

The resident tightened her lips and looked at me as though I were pissing on her floor. "Is she diabetic?"

"I don't know."

"Does she have any chronic con—"

"Listen," I said, loud enough so that a couple of the people around Lilli glanced my way, "I don't know her medical history, I don't know her personal physician, I don't know her Blue Cross number or her Medicaid number or her social security number.

"Her name is Lilli Weill, she lives at two-two-one West Eighty-first Street, she's sixty-nine years old, and she spent the war in Maedenek. That's a concentration camp in Poland. I don't know what they did to her there, and I don't know what diseases she got. Dysentery. She had dysentery."

The resident had moved back a foot. Quietly, as to a hysteric, she said, "Has she regained consciousness since the impact?"

"Not that I noticed," I said.

She went back to writing.

"Pulse falling," someone said.

"Urine's bloody," someone else said.

"Shit," someone replied. "Get sugar, blood urea nitrogen, SGOT, and LDH."

"Pyelogram, too?"

"Yeah."

"Goddamn," a small Indian said, "I don't know what's a clot and what isn't. Wipe away some of this blood."

"The skin's broken over here," a nurse said. "Wait. This looks like paint."

"She was hit by a car," I said.

"Tetanus and supertet," the Indian said.

"The blood in her hair isn't hers," I said to the Indian.

He stared at me.

"The blood in her hair isn't hers."

He rolled his eyes upward and hissed, making it plain that he had enough to contend with and didn't need any extra from me.

The neurology resident leaned over Lilli and said to the Indian, "Can I run a few tests before you anesthetize?"

"In prep," he answered.

221

"But that's not—"

"In prep," he said, and he meant it. "Let's roll."

"She's not really stable," someone said.

"She's stable enough for me," the Indian said. "I don't want to lose her. Let's roll."

They wheeled her away, and I took a few steps after the cart until a nurse blocked my path.

Lilli lay dead still, her eyes shut, her mouth open. They didn't bother covering her till they reached the door, so she was naked, IV tubes attached to her like tentacles, the catheter slithering between her legs.

A heavyset bald man, with a tag reading Head Nurse, came over to me. "Did you register?" he asked kindly.

"No," I said. "Are they going to start right away?"

He glanced at the door through which they'd wheeled her. "Oh, yeah. This time of night, they got plenty of ORs." He put his arm around my waist. "Come on, let's get you registered."

He helped me out to the adult emergency service, but I stopped him before he could take me to the desk.

"It's okay," I said. "It's just a torn ligament." He looked at the blood on my clothes. "It's not mine," I said. "It's hers. Or Max's."

"We can bind the leg," he said. I shook my head. "Okay, but stay off it."

He started away, and I caught his arm. "Listen," I said, "is there a place I can wait?"

"It could take them all night," he said. "You never know what you'll find in a hit-and-run."

"Doesn't matter," I said. I looked around the room, filled with the sick and the wounded. "Is there someplace else?" I found some cash in my jacket pocket and peeled off a twenty.

He shook his head at the bill, thought for a second, and helped me to an empty examining room. After he left, I sat down on a white iron chair. I felt dizzy and out of control. I kept seeing the parking lot in front of me, with the headlights coming across the avenue and the blood spewing from Holt's face onto Lilli's hair. The sound of Holt's Browning echoed in my ears, and so did the sound of the silenced pistol that had cut down Max Weill. The only sound missing was a scream: Holt had not screamed, and neither had Max when the shell penetrated his neck, nor Lilli when the maroon car knocked her into the air.

The door of the examining room opened, and the head nurse poked his head in. "There's someone here to see you."

"The police?"

"No, a woman," he said.

I looked at my watch; it had cracked and stopped when I'd fallen. "What time is it?"

"Four-forty," he said.

The neurology resident appeared in the doorway.

"Is she out of surgery yet?" I asked.

She shook her head.

"What did they find?"

The neurology resident said, "Fractured pelvis, five fractured ribs, fractured neck—we think she sustained that when she fell—and some internal damage."

"What?"

"Kidney. Spleen. Internal hemorrhaging."

"What about her head?" I said.

"Well," she said carefully, "that's more difficult to determine." I stared at her eyes till they wavered. "Concussion. Fractured skull."

"Is she in coma?" I said.

"Well, coma is a technical term," the resident said, "and I don't feel comfortable—"

"When do you expect her to wake up?"

"She's still under the anesthetic—they haven't finished

their stitching and basting." She attempted a smile, but it got stuck halfway there.

"When do you expect her to wake up?"

She swallowed. "We can't give you a precise prediction on that."

"A day, a week, a month, a year? When?"

Without meaning to, she took a half step backward. "I'm telling you, at the moment there's no responsible way to make a precise prediction."

I expected her to look away, but I underestimated her. She was around thirty-three, five-five or so but built low to the ground, so she appeared shorter. She had dark shiny hair, cut straight and close to her head, so that she looked more like a light-jawed man than a woman. Under her eyes were large dark circles; her eyebrows met in little hillocks of fur above the bridge of her nose. The eyes, which she had trouble keeping still, were round and pale gray, like the eyes of a predatory nocturnal rodent.

Without warning, she reached out and patted me clumsily on the shoulder. "She's getting the best care," she said.

"Richie's an ace," the head nurse said.

"And Jeff is, too," the resident said. "And Ko."

I didn't have anything to say, so I took her hand from my shoulder and touched her fingers. I saw she wore a wedding ring. I smiled at her, and she smiled in return, which made her eyes bigger and bluer, and not at all predatory.

The two of them helped me out to the waiting room. Standing at the registration desk was Ronni Gibson. When she saw me, she ran over and took my hands. The skin on her face was tight, as though she'd wet it and stretched it before gluing it to her bones.

After the resident and the nurse left, Gibson said, "I heard it on the radio. A shooting in a parking lot."

"How did you know that had anything to do with me?" I said neutrally.

"Max told me where you were going—" She stopped and looked around. "Where is he?"

"Dead."

Her fingernails pierced my palm, and I snatched my hands away. "What about Lilli?"

"They're operating now," I said.

"But she's alive."

"Not by much." I rested against the wall for a second. "Can we go outside?"

She nodded and supported me as we left the hospital. When we reached the sidewalk, I gripped her by the elbow joint, where the nerves bunch. Gripped her hard.

"Kev, that—"

"Did you tell anybody where I was going? Did you?"

"Are you out of your mind? Let go of me. You're hurting me."

"Did you?" I squeezed harder.

"Goddamn!" she cried, and tried to pull loose. "Goddamn, Kevin, let go of my goddamn arm. Shit!"

"Did you?"

"No, goddamit!"

I let go, and she scrambled away from me. "Shit, what the fuck is the matter with you, man?"

I was about to tell her but there was no point. Like Sacha Cherkhov, like Cesar Concepcion, she was just somebody who'd fallen into my cesspool, and it was useless for me to complain that she smelled of shit.

The car was where I'd left it, with a tag on the windshield telling me I shouldn't have left it there. She watched me stumble to the door and almost fall when I tugged it open.

"Are you planning to drive?" she said sarcastically.

"I have to go home and change, and I have to make a stop."

"A stop?" she said, unbelieving. "It's after five in the morning."

"I promised somebody I'd let her know what happened," I said. "She's waiting up to hear from me."

For a long minute she just stood there and looked at me. Then, quietly and accusingly, she said, "You've got a woman friend who's waiting up for you at five in the morning—is that right?"

"Right."

"Jesus fucking Christ. Get in the goddamn car," she said. "I'll drive you to *your* house. You can—"

"Nobody's asking you to—"

"Get in the goddamn car!"

At the Thirty-fourth Street light, she turned my way and said, "How come she wasn't at Bellevue?"

"I don't know," I said. "Maybe she wasn't listening to the radio."

"Ain't it lucky for you I was?" she said. "Or who'd drive you home so you could change your goddamn clothes to go and see her?"

"It's not that simple," I said.

But she had set her face and was driving as though she were delivering a contaminated object to the quarantine section. Maybe she was.

44

A shade over an hour later, at six-fifteen, I rang Fiona Shaw's bell. After a longish time her voice said over the intercom, "Who is it?"

"Kev."

"Oh my God," she said. She buzzed me in without saying anything more.

When I got off the elevator, she was standing in front of her door. She wore a floor-length pink robe, and her hair was tied back with a flaming red ribbon. Her face was clean of makeup, and there were muddy fatigue blotches under her eyes.

"I was waiting for you to call," she said when I reached her. "How did it go?"

"I'll tell you inside."

She nodded, kissed me on the cheek, and led us in. While I waited on the couch she went to the kitchen to fetch ice for a drink. I'd been in her apartment many times, but that night everything looked new to me. On the walls were framed front pages of newspapers—whenever a story of hers appeared on page 1, she put it on display. There were also framed prize certificates—from the Newspaper Guild, from the police department, from various universities. Over the fake fireplace hung a poster; in it an old-time newspaperman, hat on head, press card in hatband, was saying into an old-time phone, "Hello, sweetheart, get me rewrite."

On the coffee table on which I rested my leg were a set of photographs: Fiona by herself, Fiona with her brother and sister, Fiona with her mother and father, and one of her father alone, squinting into the sun as he lounged on a beach. He looked hung over and anxious to sneak indoors.

She handed me a drink and sat next to me. "What happened?"

"The unexpected," I said.

"But you're all right?"

"Wasted," I said. "I feel as if I've been left in kitty litter for a week."

She touched my knee gently. "I'm sorry. Do you want to stretch out—I can put a cushion under your leg."

"I'd rather go to bed."

She grimaced. "To bed?"

"Just to sleep, I mean. To sleep for hours, with somebody warm and loving close beside me."

"I wish I could, but I have to get up and go to work."

"When?" I said.

"Not long. An hour, hour and a half."

"Well, let's lie down for an hour," I said.

She reached up and tightened her red ribbon. "I'm not really sleepy right now, Kev."

I hauled myself upright and turned toward the bedroom. "Right this minute, I can't think of a single thing I want more than a bed." I smiled. "Even by myself."

"Wait," she said.

I looked at her. "You've changed your mind—you're coming with me."

"The bedroom's a mess, Kev."

"Who cares?" I said.

"Wait."

"What is it, Fiona?"

"Kev, I'm surprised at you—you know how insecure I am about a mess, and the bedroom is a terrible mess. I'd be ashamed to have you look at it—you don't want me to hang my head in shame, do you?"

"I'll keep my eyes closed," I said, "and feel my way to the bed."

"No, Kev."

I took a step toward the bedroom and she bounded over from the couch. "Kev."

"Okay," I said. "No rest for the weary tonight."

The tension left her body, and she reached for my hand. Before she could touch it, I said, "Fiona, why don't you tell whoever's in there to come out. Then we can all relax."

She jerked back. The bedroom door opened, and Jeff

Rydell walked into the living room. He had on a different seersucker suit; his shirt was buttoned, his necktie pulled tight.

"Hi," I said. "I thought you told me you two were just friends these days."

He looked at the tips of his shoes and coughed.

"Hey," I said, "it's fine, it's none of my business. But if you don't lie, you don't get caught. Fiona, relax, it's fine." Nobody moved. "Can we sit down?" I said. "My leg hurts like a bitch."

I went back to the couch. After glancing at each other, they sat in two armless easy chairs. When I'd taken another sip of my drink, I said, "You haven't asked me about the Weills."

"Oh, my God," Fiona said. "I was so worried about you I completely forgot. Tell me."

"Well, it got kind of messy, but I'm straightening it out."

"But you made the exchange?" she asked.

"Sort of," I said. "I can't tell you any more—I'm waiting to hear. Can I have another drink?" She didn't seem to hear me, so I limped over and refilled my glass.

When I sat down, she said, "When will you know?"

I glanced at my watch. "Pretty soon." I yawned noisily. "Say, Fiona, how did you say your father died?"

She switched her gaze from Rydell to me. "What?"

"Gas, wasn't it. That's not so quick. Do you know how long it took?"

"What?"

"For your father to die?" I said.

"Kev, please."

"Well, do you?"

"Kev, stop it."

"I can't," I said. "It's late; I get morbid when it's late. What did he do—your father, I mean?"

"Kev, I told you; he wrote for TV."

"Right, right. He wrote the jokes, didn't he?"

"Yes," she said.

"How come he killed himself?" I said.

"Kev, what is this?"

"How come he killed himself?"

"He was unhappy."

"Why was he unhappy?" I said.

"Mr. Fitzgerald," Rydell said, "this is not the—"

"Why was he unhappy?"

"He was having trouble working."

"You mean he couldn't write jokes, or he couldn't get a job writing jokes?"

"Mr. Fitzgerald—"

"Which?"

"Kev, what difference does it make? He's dead."

"Right, right. He's dead. Like Sacha Cherkhov. Head in the oven. Over and out. Fiona, tell me something. Was he blacklisted?"

"Kev, it's so long ago and so—"

"Was he blacklisted?"

"What goddamn difference does it—"

I raised my voice and drowned her out, "When did they get to you, Fiona?"

"What?"

"When did they get to you?"

"What are you talking about, Kev?"

I didn't look at Rydell. "I'm talking about *them*, whoever the fuck they are. When did they get to you?"

"Kev—"

By then I was on my feet, the pain in my leg obliterated by my fury.

"Who are you working for, Kleinman asked me, and me, the remarkable Mr. Fitzgerald, said, Lilli Weill. But I was working for you all along, wasn't I Fiona?"

"Kev—"

"But who are you working for?"

"Kev—"

"What did he tell you, Fiona?" I leaned over her, forcing her deeper into the chair, shouting into her bent neck. Rydell made a move to rise. "Don't!" I said, and he sank back down.

"What did he tell you, Fiona? That you'd never work again? No. He'd never show the stick—he'd hold out the carrot: an endless supply of good tips and great sources, story after story after story, leading to—well, who knows where that could lead? For someone like you."

She lifted her face. She must have had some makeup on that I hadn't noticed, because rivulets of mascara crawled from the corners of her eyes. "Kev, you don't understand."

"I understand," I said. "It's not that hard." I knelt next to her. "You worked and you worked and you worked, onward and upward, better and better." I waved at the framed stories on the walls. "Raises, promotions, prizes. One day, a nice man casually wandered into your life. Bright, amusing, sexy— and a storehouse of good tips. A hot lover and a hot source.

"He was so *interested* in you, he just loved hearing about your life. And one day, or maybe one night, you told the nice man who wandered casually into your life about your friend, this sweet little Jewish old lady with her funny obsession about her dead husband, Max Weill.

"And your nice man grinned and said casually, why don't you give her a hand, it would be a friendly gesture, a daughterly gesture—and it sounds like it might make a great story. And you replied, you're right, I'll help little Lilli Weill with her funny obsession.

"And so you came to me to ask a favor. Kev, you said, in my bed, can you do me a favor."

"Kev," she said, not bothering to hide the anguish, "don't go on."

"And naturally you kept him up to date on how I was

doing—after all, he was so nice and so casually curious. Not pushy; never pushy. When he offered to help, he was very tentative—wasn't he? What'd he do—offer to make a few calls to his European contacts?"

She didn't mean to nod, and she didn't nod much, maybe a half inch, but it was enough for Rydell to start up from his chair. I turned to face him and he eased back.

"Rydell, what did you do before you got in the tip-sheet business?" She looked straight at him. "Was it CIA? DIA? NSA?"

Ignoring her stare, he kept his eyes on me. Nothing showed in his face.

"Jeff . . . ?" she said. During the silence, her mouth slowly twisted in hurt. "You shit," she said to him. "You shit."

"You see?" I said, "I do understand. You were doing a little old lady a favor—and getting a handle on a great story—and at so low a price: a white lie or two to the funny old lady, a doubt or two in the middle of the night, and a quick lying fuck with a tired detective."

"Kev, that's not true."

"Right. It wasn't a quick fuck. A slow fuck."

"Kev, you know how I feel about you."

"Do I?" I said.

She looked hard into my eyes. "You know how I feel," she said.

"No," I said quietly, "I don't know how you feel."

She glanced at Rydell, then down, then straight at me. "Kev, I love you."

I breathed deep before saying, "Is that how you feel?"

"I want to love you. You won't let it happen, but I want it. You know that."

"How do I know that?"

Again she glanced at Rydell.

"Kev . . . Kev, you were with me the other night. We were with each other. You know that. You know that."

She seized my hand in both of hers.

"I don't know it," I said, and ached as I said it.

"Kev, you're lying. You were with me. Kev, don't make it worse. It's bad enough, don't make it worse."

"I'm sorry," I said. "I know you were under pressure." She nodded gratefully. "I know you've paid a price."

"Yes, I have."

She turned her head to face Rydell, and I grabbed her chin and twisted her back to face me.

"When did you tell him about the parking lot?" She tried to move but I held her rigid. "When did you tell him?"

"Kev, I swear—"

"When did you tell him?"

Without letting go of her chin, I hit her across the nose with the edge of my free hand. Rydell came at me from his chair, so I kept my hand moving in its arc and caught him flush in the windpipe. He gagged and sat down on the floor.

"When did you tell him?" Blood ran from her nostrils into her mouth and onto my hand. "Fiona, it's your face. If you don't care for it enough to save it, I don't give a shit." I raised my hand.

"Right after you called me. Ten minutes after."

I released her chin and stepped back. Rydell pulled himself upright; his breath rasped as though a fish bone were stuck in his throat.

"Mr. Fitz—"

"Lilli Weill is at Bellevue and she might die tonight, or she might die tomorrow, or she might die next week. Or she might live and be a vegetable."

Both of them were leaning forward like two sprinters waiting for the starter's pistol.

"Max Weill is dead." She let out a tiny shrill cry, like a bird stunned by a pellet. "So is a man named Andrew Holt. So is a big black man whose name I don't know."

After it sank in, she said hollowly, "What happened?"

"I just told you what happened," I said.

Rydell asked, "You're certain Max Weill is dead?"

"Dead certain," I said. "He was shot close up, from a car. Through here." I touched my neck, chilling it with my fingertip. "There was a silencer on the piece, so . . . pop, like a cork leaving a bottle. Very quick. No pain." Before she could begin to weep, I hissed: "Rydell, what color car do you drive?"

His mouth froze, and his hand moved toward his belt. Then his hand froze, too.

"You didn't bring it," I said. "What would you need a gun for here?"

He let his hand fall to his side.

"A maroon car, right?" I said. "With mud on the registration plate. And two broken headlights, a broken windshield, and Lilli Weill's blood on the left fender."

Fiona's hand went to her eyes. Rydell twitched in her direction, but he didn't touch her.

"Did he forget to tell you that part, Fiona?" I said. "I guess even nice men have their little secrets. He drove the car. He had the pistol with the silencer. Lilli and Max. Double play."

In a pinched voice, she said, "Jeff . . . Jeff, is that true?"

Without taking his eyes off me, he answered, "Fiona, this isn't the time."

She screamed, "Is it true?"

He said nothing, and after a painful minute I broke the silence:

"He drove the car, and he fired the shots. Because that's what he was paid to do. He was hired to kill Max Weill."

Her head drooped on to her chest.

"Leo Hirsch hired him. Poor Leo. Poor Leo was terrified of being blown, and he knew Max could do it, so he went looking for an exterminator, and what better exterminator than an ex-spook."

234

With effort, she lifted her head to look at him.

"I'm sorry, Fiona," he said, sounding like a party guest who's just flicked ashes on the carpet.

"What did he tell you?" I asked her.

"He told me—" She swallowed for air. "He told me it might not be safe for me to go down there, so he would go and take notes for me." She paused to glance at his closed face. "He was worried for me, he told me. He told me he thought you saw him and maybe recognized him, and so he got out of there before they came with Lilli."

"And you believed him?"

"Yes, I believed him—goddamn you, I believed you!"

"Nice of him to drop by in person to tell you everything. Considerate. I'll bet he called and said, listen, Fiona, I know how much you care for Lilli, and if you're going to sit up all night worrying, at least let me sit up with you. Something like that, no?"

She nodded.

"And you believed that, too. Did he make any calls after he got here?"

Puzzled, she looked at him. "A few."

"Right. The police, the hospitals, the morgue, maybe. But nobody could tell him anything because Max Weill doesn't exist. The only way he could find out what happened to Max Weill was to wait till I told you—and you told him. Welcome to the suckers' club."

Without warning, she dove at him. He flicked his arm up and caught her in the gut with his elbow. She collapsed, sucking frantically for breath. I went over, helped her into the chair, and stepped close to him:

"If Lilli Weill dies, I'll find you and kill you."

He shrugged, and I wanted to kill him then.

Shaw got enough breath to stammer, "Kev, if Lilli dies, you're not—" Her eyes flickered in fright.

"No," I said. "I'm not going to kill you. You were just an instrument, like a piano." She exhaled noisily. "But if Lilli survives, I'm going to tell her about you." She nodded in resignation. "And I'm going to tell the Associated Press."

Her head jerked up. "What?"

"I'm going to tell the AP."

"Tell them what?"

"That you were dumb enough to let an ex-spook use you to set up a murder."

"You can't prove that," she said.

"Don't be an idiot," I said. "I don't need to prove anything. All I have to do is draw the dots for them; they'll make the connections."

She glanced at Rydell, who gave her no comfort.

"Kev, that would ruin me."

"Not at all," I said. "You could find another line of work. Maybe you could cover for Lilli—how are you at waiting tables?"

Her face went through a montage of changes—doubt, disbelief, shock, horror. She stood up and came to me. "Kev, this won't help anybody. It won't help us." I laughed meanly. She touched my hand. "Kev, I love you. Why won't you believe that? You said I was only an instrument. I didn't do anything bad. I didn't, Kev. All I wanted was—"

"A great story."

"There's nothing wrong with that, goddamnit!" she shouted.

"Fiona, how much do you love me?"

"As much as I've loved anyone. More."

"That much?"

"Yes, that much."

"Will you still love me when you find another line of work?"

She rocked backward, then moved even closer. "Kev, I'm not evil. Please, give us a chance."

"Will you still love—"

She seized both my wrists. "Don't destroy us, Kev."

I shrugged and pulled loose. As I stepped away, she stretched out her hands. Her fingertips were white, and for an instant I wanted to stroke them to restore her circulation. But I kept on shifting toward the door.

"Kev . . ."

As I opened the door, I heard her mumble something, and then I heard a glass break. I tried to hop into the hallway and pull the door shut behind me, but I landed on my hurt leg and slipped.

Rydell flew at me, the broken glass cocked in his raised right hand. When he got within striking distance, he jabbed the glass toward my eyes. I rammed my head forward and down, smashing the top of my skull into his balls. He screamed and collapsed on my back.

I heaved as hard as I could, and he rolled over twice, his hand reaching automatically for his groin. Then he rolled over again, down past the head of the staircase. I scrambled after him. He was wedged about midway on the flight of steps.

As I came close, he swung the glass, slashing my shirt just above my belt. I tried to dodge sideways, but there wasn't enough room, and his next thrust ripped through my pants leg into my thigh. I reached for his arm as it swung around again, missed, and jumped two steps so I could land on his foot. He toppled forward, and I grabbed his head in both hands. The spiky glass was arching toward my belly. I took a deep breath and twisted hard and fast until I broke his neck.

When I let him fall back, he slumped down like a tired drunk, except that his head and shoulders didn't go together right, like a puppet without a puppeteer's hand in it.

Fiona was at the top of the stairs. She had both her hands in her bloodstained mouth.

"If you get rid of the glass," I said, "you can tell them he fell down the stairs. Otherwise, they'll think you pushed him."

Like a squirrel, she ran down the stairs, snatched up the broken glass, and scurried back.

"Don't forget the slivers in the hallway," I said. Immediately, she went to her knees to search for shards.

I stepped over Rydell, found a piece of glass, and tossed it up toward her. I heard it fall on the landing, but I didn't see her scoop it up because by then I was at the bottom of the flight and on my way out.

45

Four hours later I was sitting in a luncheonette across from Bellevue and reading the *Times* and *News* so I wouldn't think about the naked, desperate look on Fiona Shaw's face when she'd told me she loved me.

The *Times* never did know what to make of multiple killings, so it buried the story in its metropolitan news section—3 FOUND SLAIN ON LOWER EAST SIDE, a headline that let its readers know that the victims weren't important or even respectable and that their deaths wouldn't affect the stock market or spoil any openings at the Whitney Museum.

The *News* knew all about multiple killings—3 GUNNED DOWN IN CRIME WAR, a headline that promised its readers juicy tidbits about kingpins of the underworld. The readers weren't cheated. Although the paper said the bodies were unidentified, "a reliable source close to the investigation said the killings were obviously the work of a team of professional hit men." Drugs were at the bottom of the whole business, the reliable source said—a vendetta by members of the Genovese family against members of the Costello family.

The *News* had a picture on page 1 of three bodies covered with cloths. I was turning the page upside down to figure out who was who when a shadow fell across the paper.

"May I join you?" Richard Kleinman said.

He was in a faultless linen suit, a straw panama, and gray-tinted glasses. For a change, he wasn't smiling. He slid on to the banquette opposite me and ordered a Sanka. After the waitress brought it, he glanced at the headline in the *News* and said, "I'm sorry about Mrs. Weill. Is she going to be all right?"

"I don't know," I said. "I'm going over there in a minute to find out. Want to come along?"

He removed his glasses and held them at arm's length. "The tint is wrong," he said. "Too deep." He put them back on. "Perhaps we could arrange a pension—it could be done through you, if you wish." I didn't answer him.

We drank our coffee for a while. "It's been a hard morning," he said. "I was over there." He pointed through the plate glass to the medical examiner's office, just north of Bellevue. "They wanted me to identify Mr. Holt."

"Did they ask you to identify Max Weill?"

"They asked. I told them I didn't recognize him," he said. "The lies one tells for questionable causes."

I lit a cigarette and blew the smoke over his shoulder. "Now that he's dead, somebody should give him his name back."

His smile returned. "Are you thinking of doing that, Mr. Fitzgerald?"

"Who knows?"

He decided to let it pass. "Mr. Fitzgerald, do you recall our speaking about your records in this matter?"

"Uhuh."

He leaned forward. "I thought perhaps we might come to some agreement . . . the fee, naturally, would be considerable . . . say, in the high five figures. That's not including any pension for Mrs. Weill."

"If she lives."

"If she doesn't," he said sorrowfully, "her pension would go to you—there are no other survivors, I believe. That likewise would be in the high five figures."

"Uhuh."

"Oh, by the way," he said, "I owe you an apology, Mr. Fitzgerald—you were indeed working for Mrs. Weill. Or at least so you believed."

"So I believed."

He picked up my matchbook and studied an offer to buy one hundred first-edition foreign stamps. When he'd had enough of that, he said "How do you feel about what I've offered?"

"I'll think about it."

"Until when, Mr. Fitzgerald?"

"Who knows?"

He leaned even closer. "I hardly need to mention that holding on to records in a matter as sensitive as this . . . well, there are hazards . . ."

"Not for me," I said.

He wasn't slow. "I'm to assume you've taken precautions." He sighed. "Yes, I suppose I should have anticipated that. That, of course, would raise the fee, would it not?"

"Both fees."

"Oh, dear," he said primly, "I do hope this won't turn out to be very expensive." An ambulance passed outside, and he waited till it turned into the hospital. "Would you say impossibly expensive, Mr. Fitzgerald?"

"Nothing's impossible."

"Let me ask you bluntly," he said. "Do you believe we can reach a satisfactory agreement about your records?"

"Sure," I said.

"Sure?" He tried to hide his joy, but he looked like a man who'd bent down to wipe dog shit from his shoe and found a hundred-dollar bill stuck to his instep.

I grinned hugely. "What the fuck, Kleinman, it's all over. We can make a deal." I patted his arm. "Let's talk outside."

We stood on the sidewalk, our heads angled together like two cranes. A thin line of sweat was forming on his neck. "Well, Mr. Fitzgerald, what would you like?"

I wrinkled my forehead and moved my lips like a fifth-grader calculating the worth of his Yankee cards. "Well . . ."

Quickly, he said, "Don't forget, this is all tax-free."

"Right, right, tax-free." I counted along my fingers. "Sacha Cherkhov, Cesar Concepcion, and Max Weill."

"Ah, wouldn't we all?" he said. "I mean, what would you like realistically?"

"Oh, realistically," I said. "Okay. Sacha Cherkhov, Cesar Concepcion; and Max Weill."

He tried a different smile; lots of irony in this one.

"Mr. Fitzgerald, not even I can raise the dead."

"Too bad," I said. "That's my deal."

After a long moment, a white spot the size of a dime appeared on each of his cheeks. He opened his mouth to say something, closed it, opened it again, bit it shut, spun on his heel, and walked north on First Avenue.

I watched him till his furious back rounded the corner, and then I ran across the street to the entrance to Bellevue.

46

Five weeks later, Lilli Weill left Bellevue and went home.

Nine weeks after that, she invited me to dinner. She served me chopped liver, chicken soup with matzoh balls, roast duck and boiled flanken, hot potato salad and cold stringbeans, and two bottles of Veuve Clicquot champagne.

As a gift, I'd brought a cassette recorder and a copy of Sacha Cherkhov's tape of Max Weill—Caruso and Davis had lived up to their word. After dinner, we sat on her sofa, drank champagne, and listened to the tape over and over. Once in a while, she took my hand; once in a while, I took hers.

Two days after that, on a golden breezy afternoon in October, Lilli Weill went for a walk in Central Park, found a pool of shade under a tree near Seventy-seventh Street, and lay down and died.

Fiona Shaw came to the funeral, but we didn't speak, and we didn't look at each other.